Also by Kieran Scott:

She's So Dead to Us
He's So Not Worth It
This Is So Not Happening
Only Everything
Complete Nothing

WHAT WAITS IN THE WOODS

KIERAN SCOTT

Point

No part of this publication may be reproduced, stored in a retrieval
system, or transmitted in any form or by any means, electronic,
mechanical, photocopying, recording, or otherwise, without written
permission of the publisher. For information regarding permission,
write to Scholastic Inc., Attention: Permissions Department, 557
Broadway, New York, NY 10012.

Library of Congress Cataloging-in-Publication Data

Scott, Kieran, 1974– author.
What waits in the woods / Kieran Scott. — First edition.
pages cm
Summary: A hiking trip in the woods in upstate New York is out
of the comfort zone for sixteen-year-old city girl Callie Valasquez,
but she wants to bond with her new friends Lissa and Penelope,
not to mention her new boyfriend, Jeremy—however, nothing could
have prepared her for the true human darkness that waits for
her in the woods.
ISBN 978-0-545-69111-6 (jacketed hardcover) 1. Hiking—New York
(State)—Juvenile fiction. 2. Murder—Juvenile fiction. 3. Mental
illness—Juvenile fiction. 4. Jealousy—Juvenile fiction. 5. Trust—
Juvenile fiction. 6. Friendship—Juvenile fiction. 7. New York
(State)—Juvenile fiction. [1. Mystery and detective stories.
2. Hiking—Fiction. 3. Murder—Fiction. 4. Mental illness—Fiction.
5. Jealousy—Fiction. 6. Trust—Fiction. 7. Friendship—Fiction. 8. New
York (State)—Fiction.] I. Title.
PZ7.S42643Wh 2015
813.6—dc23
2014021728

10 9 8 7 6 5 4 3 2 1   15 16 17 18 19 20

Printed in the U.S.A.   23
First edition, April 2015
Book design by Christopher Stengel

For my mom, who imparted
a love of scary stories

RECOVERY JOURNAL

ENTRY 1

There's no question things could have gone differently out there in those woods. One zipper more tightly zipped, one foot more carefully placed on a rotting wood plank, and I might not be here today. I might be roaming free instead of sitting locked up in this hole, sucking my every meal through a straw, staring at a padded wall.

There might not have been so much bloodshed. Or there might have been even more *death. There's no telling how everything might have turned on a chance.*

What could never have been different was the why. That is the only nonvariable. And yet, that is Doctor Pea Brain's favorite ask Every. Single. Time he walks into my tiny square cell.

"Have you thought about why?"

"Any more insights as to why?"

"I can't help you unless you tell me why."

Well, here's the thing, Doc. If you're so entirely brain-dead that you can't figure it out for yourself, then I can't help you. Because the why is obvious, you potato-headed, Afrin-snorting idiot. The why is all there is.

What I can tell you is this: They deserved to die. Every last one of them. And if you can't see that . . . well, then no one can help you.

ONE

Callie Valasquez wasn't ready to die.

Not here. Not now. Not like this. Not standing in the middle of the pitch-black forest clutching a roll of toilet paper. No. That just seemed wrong. She was only sixteen.

But it was going to happen. Especially if that thing—that snorting, breathing, hulking thing—managed to pick up her scent.

Callie stood perfectly still. She tried as hard as she could to keep her breath shallow, but the terror gripping her heart kept making her want to suck in air, to cough. Her knees quaked and her stomach twisted itself into horrible, ever-tightening knots.

Why had she used that strawberry shampoo this morning? The sugary scent wafted from her thick, dark, meticulously straightened hair. Or could the thing out there smell her coconut body wash? Or maybe the chemical odor of the olive-green nail polish she'd applied to her toes in the kitchen after breakfast, thinking it was oh so hiking-appropriate? Callie looked down at her bare, throbbing toes in her new Teva flip-flops.

Maybe it was her feet. They'd been pretty rank when she'd peeled off her sweaty socks and carefully applied first aid cream and Band-Aids to her lovely new blisters. Oh, God. Could it smell her feet?

Another snort. This one even closer than the last. She could feel the thing's presence just behind her like a pulsating warmth. It was so large it radiated heat. She imagined a huge brown bear with a snout as wide as her father's hand. A wild boar, awful fangs glinting in the moonlight. A mountain lion, crouched low and taut, primed for the kill. Her instincts told her to run, but her fear kept her frozen. That and some vague notion from a movie she'd once seen as a kid that the best policy in this situation was not to draw attention. Bears couldn't see you unless you moved. Or was that dinosaurs?

What was she even doing here? Was being part of the popular crowd in the tiny upstate town of Mission Hills, New York, really so important to her that she had to risk her life? Just because she had some insane need to prove that she was no longer the nerd she'd been back in Chicago, now she was going to die?

The moment Lissa Barton and Penelope Grange had noticed her in the cafeteria that second week of school, when Callie had been the shy new girl, she'd latched on to them like a life raft in a storm. And that moment had led directly to this one.

Callie had never been camping in her life. Had never felt the *need* to go camping. But this was apparently what people did for fun in upstate New York—at least, what her new friends did for fun—so here she was, having loads and loads of fun.

When her boyfriend, Jeremy Higgins—yes, Callie had a boyfriend now, another upside to being newly popular—had picked her up this morning, she'd been so nervous she started up a kind of mantra—*four nights, four nights, four nights.* That was all she had to get through.

Yet here she was, evening one, about to get eaten alive.

She vaguely wondered if the thing would maul her friends after it was done with her.

"Hey, Callie!" Jeremy shouted from their campsite, which was probably forty yards from where she was standing. "Are you okay out there?"

There was a surprised snort and, suddenly, the thing took off into the woods. Callie whipped around in the direction of snapping twigs and crunching leaves, but saw nothing. Just some low, weak branches crushed in the underbrush nearby. She heaved a breath, bent at the waist, and pressed her hand to her heart.

"You're okay," she whispered to herself, tears squeezing from her eyes. "You're okay, you're okay, you're okay."

She was going to live. *Four nights.* By Sunday, she'd be back in her dad's car and they'd be driving to the airport to pick up her mom after her summer in São Paulo. Then, next week, she and her mom would go to New York City for a back-to-school shopping trip. Callie was going to live to see her mother again. To finish writing at least one of the ten short stories she'd started since June. To read the rest of the *Black Inferno* series and finish painting her new bedroom now that she'd finally settled on that pretty aqua after three misguided attempts in the purple family. Everything was going to be fine.

Except.

Callie stood up straight and turned around. She had no clue which direction she was facing. She'd lost her bearings when she'd whirled to spot whatever it was that had crept up on her. Was the camp in front of her, behind her? Where was the skinny, muddy trail she'd taken to get here?

A low mewl escaped her lips. Callie brought her hands to her head, the soft triple ply of Penelope's toilet paper soaking up her sweat. She thought about shouting out for help, but she didn't want to look like an idiot. Lissa and Penelope had already spent half the day teasing her for not breaking in her hiking boots, for packing her makeup bag and a change of earrings, and for forgetting to bring her water bottle, which she knew for a fact was sitting on the kitchen counter where she'd thought she wouldn't miss it on her way out the door.

She didn't want them to think they needed to babysit her every time she had to use the bathroom, too. If that was what you could even call what she'd just done—squatting next to a tree. Ew.

If only she'd had her phone. She could text Jeremy and he would come find her without alerting Lissa and Pen to her total lameness. But she'd left it in the pocket of her hoodie, which was tossed uselessly on a blanket by the fire.

"Callie," she muttered to herself. "Think. You're a straight-A student. You survived getting lost on the Chicago L by yourself when you were ten years old. You can figure out which direction to walk to get back to camp."

It was funny, really. Until now, she'd always thought of herself as a survivor. Her parents had been letting her walk home from school with her friends in Chicago since she was eight. At twelve, she'd flown to Brazil, alone, to visit her grandmother, and hadn't freaked out or cried once.

With her friends back in Chicago, she was the leader—the one who could navigate the map at Six Flags, order the exact right number of pizzas for a party of fifteen people, *and* figure out the tip. She hadn't even crumbled when her parents had told her that her dad had gotten the job at Cornell Law and they were moving to New York, leaving behind the friends she'd had her entire life and the only neighborhood she'd ever called home.

But it seemed upstate New York survival skills were entirely different from Outer Loop Chicago survival skills.

Callie looked up. It was past eight o'clock on an August night. The sky was deep ink blue beyond the tangled canopy of branches and leaves, and every last tree trunk looked black in the darkness. Black and exactly the same.

Okay. Forget pride. Pride was stupid. It was time to shout for her friends.

She opened her mouth just as a hand came down on her shoulder.

TWO

Callie didn't shout. She screamed.

"Hey! It's just me."

Jeremy trained his flashlight on his face, the bright white light illuminating the dark flop of hair over his concerned brown eyes. Gleaming green dots peppered his chest and disoriented Callie momentarily, until she realized that his Milky Way galaxy T-shirt was of the glow-in-the-dark variety.

Callie felt a rush of warm relief. The fact that Jeremy was at least a foot taller than her, with his runner's legs and his broad shoulders, was suddenly very comforting. Nothing fazed Jeremy. He was smart, practical, reliable, funny, and—thank God—*here*.

Callie reached over and hugged him as tight as she could.

"There's something out here," she said into the soft cotton of his shirt. The little rubbery stars were cool against her skin. "Some kind of animal."

"Really? Where?"

Totally casual. Like she was about to point out some rare variety of plant. It seemed that growing up surrounded by mountains had inured her friends to what Callie saw as obvious dangers.

Jeremy shone his light around them in a circle and Callie gripped his free hand. She held her breath, dreading the thought of feral eyes glittering in the dark.

"Don't. I don't want to know. Let's just get back to camp."

"Hey." Jeremy trained the light at her shoulder to better see her without blinding her. "Seriously, are you okay?"

She tried to imagine how she looked to him right then. Her white T-shirt streaked with dirt and sticking to her skin. Sweat saturating her hair and probably making it frizz, even after she'd worked so hard to get it perfect that morning. Her mascara was waterproof, but she wasn't sure if it was perspiration, stress, and exhaustion–proof.

When Jeremy had asked to come on this trip with her and her friends, she had jumped at the chance, not wanting to be away from him for five whole days. But now she wondered if it was a bad idea. Between her camping cluelessness and her total inability to groom, he wasn't going to be seeing her at her best.

"I'm fine," she said. "Just do me a favor and don't look at me. At least not until I've washed my face and braided my hair."

"Why?" Jeremy tilted his head. "You're beautiful. You're always beautiful."

He hadn't even blinked. It was so cool, how he stated it like that—like her beauty was an accepted fact. Callie knew she had her moments—those days when her nearly black eyes shone and her light brown skin was blemish-free—days when she didn't mind being an unremarkable five foot five and when she inspected her curves in the mirror, she saw a bit of her beautiful, soft-yet-strong mother looking back at her. But that wasn't "always." It was once in a while.

Even so, she was glad Jeremy didn't see it that way.

"And you're crazy," she joked. "But thank you." She tugged at his hand. "Come on. Let's get back to camp."

"I'm serious!" he said, falling into step with her. "Even in chem lab, when you're wearing those foggy goggles and they're pinching your cheeks next to your nose, you're, like, the hottest girl in school."

Callie laughed and leaned into him. She had almost forgotten about the nameless animal by now.

"I'm glad you're here," she said.

He kissed the top of her head. "Me too."

They had only taken a few steps when they heard Lissa's voice.

"I told you, no!" she whisper-shouted. "Zach, I don't care. It doesn't matter. You can't come up here."

Jeremy raised his eyebrows and Callie almost laughed, realizing that Lissa was on the phone.

Nothing like stumbling on to a lover's quarrel. Zach Carle was Lissa's über-popular linebacker boyfriend. Callie glanced around, but couldn't figure out which direction Lissa's voice was coming from.

"So what if Jeremy Higgins weaseled his way on to this trip?" Lissa went on. "*I* wanted it to be girls only so I'm not going to be responsible for bringing another guy. Just because Callie is clingy, doesn't mean I am."

Callie felt like she'd just been punched in the gut. Was that what Lissa really thought of her? She glanced at Jeremy to see his jaw drop.

Lissa was still talking. "Look, it's five days. If you can't handle life without me for five days, then I don't know what to tell you."

Jeremy snorted a laugh, then slapped his hand over his mouth.

"Wait, shh," Lissa said. There was a pause, then: "I have to go."

She stepped out of the trees, so impossibly close by that Callie almost yelped in surprise. How could she not have seen her friend when she was standing ten feet away? These woods were the greatest camouflage ever.

Lissa's long blond hair was pulled back into a ponytail and she still wore the brown cargo shorts and white ribbed tank top she'd had on all day, only now she had a blue Mission Hills High basketball hoodie zipped halfway over it.

"Stalk me much?" Lissa asked, her blue eyes flashing.

Callie flinched. "We were just on our way back. Is everything okay?" she asked, gesturing at Lissa's phone.

Lissa looked down at the cell in her hand as if she'd forgotten it was there. "Zach," she said, then scoffed. "For a football jock, he's seriously needy. But whatever. He'll live."

She shut the phone off and shoved it into her sweatshirt pocket. No apologies or acknowledgment that she'd said anything wrong, even though it was clear Callie and Jeremy had overheard her. Jeremy rolled his eyes; he'd known Lissa since they were little kids and never seemed rattled by her. But Callie's stomach felt tight. She knew Lissa could be callous, but Callie hated any sort of conflict or tension, even if it was unspoken.

As Lissa turned to walk back toward camp, Callie saw a flash of something white near Lissa's heel.

"Hey, Lis. You dropped something."

Lissa stopped and Callie bent to pick it up, but then recoiled.

It was a wad of torn white gauze, soaked with blood.

"What is that? Is that yours?" Callie asked, standing up again so quickly she almost tripped backward, but instead found Jeremy's steadying hand.

Lissa crouched over the scrap. "Nope. It was probably dropped by some other camper. Just leave it."

"Like we were really going to risk the hepatitis?" Jeremy asked.

"Nice one, Science Boy," Lissa said archly. Then she walked off, her ponytail swinging jauntily behind her.

"That is so gross," Callie said, hugging herself as she edged around the wad of gauze. "I hope whoever used that wasn't seriously hurt."

"Don't worry about it," Jeremy said. "It's probably been there forever."

"Yeah. I'm sure you're right."

But she shivered nonetheless, because Jeremy hadn't noticed the most important detail—which he probably should have, since he had taken a special elective in criminology last semester.

The blood had shimmered in the beam of his flashlight, wet and sticky. There was no way it had been there forever.

That blood was still fresh.

THREE

"Ever so slowly the girl approached the basement door," Jeremy intoned, lowering his voice to a chilling octave. The fire's flames made shadows dance across his face as he crept around the circle of stones where the girls sat. "All she could hear was the incessant sound. Tap . . . tap . . . tap . . . tap . . ."

Callie huddled against Lissa's side, her eyes wide with fear as she gripped her friend's sweatshirt sleeve. Penelope clung to Lissa's other side. Lissa, of course, was totally calm. She followed Jeremy's progress with a smirk.

"Her hand shook as she reached for the brass handle. Tap . . . tap . . . tap . . . tap . . ." He crossed behind them so that it felt as if the rumble of his voice was tingling down Callie's neck. "She held her breath, her tongue dry. Tap . . . tap . . . tap . . . tap . . . And just as her fingertips grazed the cold, rusted knob . . . *the beast came flying out of the cabinet and sunk its teeth into her neck!*"

Jeremy flung his arms around them from behind. Callie's heart jumped, and she and Penelope screamed, the dissonant sound echoing across the placid waters of Mercer Pond and through the mountains.

"Oh my God!" Penelope shouted, covering her pretty, heart-shaped face with her hands. "You are so evil!"

Jeremy laughed, standing up straight. Penelope gave his bare calf a whack as he strode by. "Hey! Ow! Nice claws."

Penelope glanced at her fingernails, which were ragged and bitten to the quick, then curled her hands into fists like she was trying to hide them. In Callie's opinion, Pen's nails were about the only imperfect part of her. By the flickering of the firelight, the girl looked like a delicate doll, her latte-colored skin flawless, her high cheekbones regal, her lips plump. Her light brown hair was woven into a side braid that looked like something out of *Teen Vogue* and made Callie almost green with envy. Pen was, hands down, the prettiest girl at Mission Hills High, but she acted as if she didn't know it. She was the dainty to Lissa's coarseness, the saccharine to Lissa's snark, the meek to Lissa's powerful. Every guy wanted to date her and every girl wanted to be her. When they weren't busy wanting to date or be Lissa Barton. It really just depended which type one preferred—the alpha girl, or the sweet sophisticate.

"We never should have let you come on this trip," Penelope said to Jeremy, shaking her head. The tiny diamond studs she always wore sparkled against her earlobes. She bent her skinny legs and hugged them to her, the dozens of colorful handwoven bracelets on her right wrist bunching up around the cuff of her sweatshirt sleeve.

Callie's heart skipped a nervous beat as she remembered what Lissa had said on the phone. Did Pen feel the same? But then Penelope smiled at her across the fire and she knew that Pen was just messing with him. Penelope and Jeremy had known each other for years—their families were old friends who belonged to the same country club and sometimes vacationed together—so she knew that Pen thought of Jeremy as a pseudo brother.

"Way to go, dude," Lissa said to Jeremy, reaching for the bag of marshmallows. "You scarred them for life."

"*You* weren't scared?" Callie gasped.

"No. Please. That's a classic. I've heard it, like, a dozen times." Lissa pierced a marshmallow with a stick. "But I give Science Boy points for entertainment value, because the look on your face right now is hilarious."

Callie gave Lissa a tiny shove, which made Lissa laugh. She lifted her thick blond hair over her shoulder as she leaned in to hold the marshmallow to the flames, looking completely comfortable. Her tanned skin shone in the firelight, her muscular calves tapering into thick, marled socks and perfectly broken-in hiking boots. Girl could have been starring in her own ad for granola bars. Or vitamin drinks. Or maybe recycling. Anything healthy and American.

Lissa's marshmallow caught and she retracted the skewer, blowing out the flame in one burst of air. Every movement Lissa made was confident and sure. No fidgeting, no blushing, no second-guessing. This, the outdoors, was Lissa's world. Everyone else was just visiting.

Lissa handed the skewer to Callie, then made another one for herself.

"Thanks," Callie said, rejoining Jeremy on the blanket they'd been sharing before he'd gotten up to terrify them. Her pulse was just now beginning to slow to a normal rate. Jeremy had pulled on a gray Mission Hills High track sweatshirt, so well-worn there were holes frayed into the seams along the collar and cuffs. He reached out to pull her to him, his adorable grin practically glowing by the light of the fire.

"Okay, never do that again," Callie said, leaning into his side.

"Do what?" he asked, kissing her temple.

"Scare me half to death," Callie said. "Promise?"

He smiled and put his arm around her. "I promise."

Penelope sighed and ran her slim hands over her braid.

"Your hair looks so nice like that, Pen," Callie said. "You should braid it more often."

Penelope's tanned skin darkened. "Please. Lissa says it makes my head look too small for my body."

"What?" Callie snorted in disbelief. "No way. You look like a ballerina or a model."

"You think?" Penelope's green eyes darted to Lissa, who tilted her head, considering.

"Yeah, it's actually not bad," she told Penelope. "Maybe you've grown into your head."

Jeremy laughed and Penelope rolled her eyes but smiled. "Okay, maybe I will wear it back more often."

Callie nibbled on her marshmallow, trying not to feel slighted. When she'd told Pen she looked nice, Penelope had shot her down, but as soon as Lissa had chimed in, Penelope agreed. As always, Lissa's word was gold.

"So listen." Lissa casually blew out another marshmallow fire. "We should probably tell Callie about the Skinner."

"The what now?" Callie asked.

Penelope and Jeremy exchanged an uncomfortable look and Jeremy squirmed.

"I don't think that's strictly necessary," he said.

"What? What's the Skinner?" Callie asked, sucking glue-like melted marshmallow from her thumb.

"You mean *who's* the Skinner," Penelope corrected with a shudder. She zipped her sweatshirt all the way to her angular chin. Suddenly her thin frame looked even smaller, like she could easily fold up inside her hoodie and disappear.

"Okay, *who's* the Skinner?" Callie asked, trying to sound nonchalant even though her chest felt tight.

"Back in the early eighties, there were these three kids who came up here for a day hike," Lissa began, leaning forward. "They were supposed to be back at the parking lot before nightfall, but they never showed up. Their parents were there waiting to meet them, but the sun went down and nothing. Then an hour passed, another hour, another hour. Finally the parents decided to call the rangers."

Callie swallowed hard. Her palms were starting to grow slick. "And?"

"The rangers searched all the trails. Every last one. They found what they thought were the kids' footprints and followed them up the mountainside, toward where we are now. Mercer Pond," Lissa said.

Callie's shoulders instinctively coiled toward her ears. She glanced around at the other three fire pits dotting the dirt nearby, none of them occupied. They somehow looked ominous in the dark, the charred rocks like broken fangs jutting up from the ground.

"And?"

"And they just disappeared," Lissa said.

"The kids?" Callie asked.

"Their footprints," Jeremy chimed in. He pulled his fingers inside his sweatshirt sleeves. "Their trail just stopped. There was no sign they'd tried to make a camp, no trail leading off in another direction. Nothing."

"Not even a sign of a struggle," Penelope said quietly, staring into the fire. Her index finger was hooked through her bracelets.

"They were just gone? Were they ever found?" Callie asked, breathless with fear.

Lissa's gaze flicked to Jeremy's face. She looked at Penelope, too, but Penelope was studying the dancing flames.

"Three days later, one of the kids came stumbling into the backyard of one of the rangers," Lissa said. "He was naked."

Callie gripped her knees with her damp palms. "What?"

"And covered in blood," Jeremy added. "Like smeared across his face and chest."

"Why was he naked? Whose blood was it?" Callie demanded, her pulse thrumming loudly in her ears.

"No one knew. Not for a whole year," Jeremy said, poking a twig into the crackling fire. "The kid went mute. He wouldn't talk to anyone. Not his parents, not the cops, not his therapist. He didn't say anything for months."

"So what happened when he finally talked?" Callie asked. "What did he say? Where were his friends?"

"His friends were skinned alive," Penelope said tonelessly.

Callie grabbed Jeremy's leg, her fingernails digging into his shorts. *"What?"*

"This psycho, they called him 'the Skinner,' used this huge hunting knife to skin the other kids right in front of the guy," Lissa said with a glint in her eye, almost as if she was enjoying the story. "When the surviving hiker finally told the cops he had these details . . . I don't even want to say it . . . but he watched his friends die some pretty gruesome deaths, and the whole time the Skinner kept telling him he was next."

A wave of nausea crashed over Callie and suddenly the smoke from the fire seemed to thicken. She went light-headed and pressed the heel of one hand against her forehead. The sugar from the marshmallows formed a hard rock in the middle of her gut.

"I think I'm gonna be sick."

Jeremy reached over and wrapped both arms around her, drawing her close to him. She relished the clean scent of his clothes and his warmth.

"It's okay," he said. "It was a long time ago."

"How did he get away?" Callie asked.

"He managed to get hold of another knife when the guy's back was turned and stabbed him right in the spine," Lissa said, jabbing the air with her fist. "He said the guy was still alive and screaming when he ran off."

"Sometimes when we're out here, people swear you can still hear the Skinner howling," Penelope said, glancing across the stagnant pond. Another breeze rustled the leaves. Branches creaked. Callie looked from Penelope to Lissa to Jeremy. A smile twitched the corners of Lissa's lips, but otherwise no one moved. Suddenly Callie's chest inflated with relief.

"Very funny, you guys. You had me until the howling part." Callie laughed. "How long did you rehearse that one?"

"What?" Jeremy asked, his eyes wide and innocent.

"The Skinner? Really? Did you really think I was going to fall for that?" Callie casually reached past Lissa for the bag of marshmallows, but Lissa caught her wrist tight in her grip. Callie's heart slammed inside her chest.

"It's not a joke. It was a real thing," Lissa said, looking her directly in the eye. She released Callie's hand and sat back. "They never found the guy. I just thought you should know."

Callie felt a flash of anger and vaulted to her feet.

"What is the matter with you people?" she shouted, backing away from the fire.

"Callie, it's okay," Penelope said.

"Okay? Are you kidding me? Why did you bring me up here? You couldn't have told me this story *before* we hiked a whole day away from town? I don't want to be out here with some psycho murderer!"

"God, Callie, chill," Lissa said, piercing another marshmallow with her stick. "Even if the Skinner could survive a knife wound like that, it's not like he's still out here somewhere. He'd be, like, our grandparents' age."

Callie hugged herself. Somehow that assertion didn't make her feel any better. She glanced around. Suddenly the landscape seemed to close in on her, every shadow concealing an awful threat.

Someone could be out there right now, watching them. She felt as if she could hear them breathing. At any moment the person, the thing, whatever it was, could pounce. And just like that, they'd all be gone. Vanished.

FOUR

Callie couldn't sleep.

It was no surprise, really, considering the Skinner story. Plus, by the time Callie had gotten around to laying out her sleeping bag earlier that evening, Lissa and Penelope had already claimed their spots against opposite walls of the tent, which left Callie in the middle. At first, she had thought this might be a good thing—that she'd feel safer when warmly ensconced between her two friends. But three sleepless hours into the night, she understood why the more experienced campers had chosen the ends.

Penelope was a restless sleeper. Every five seconds she took a new position, which meant that every five seconds a new part of Callie's body was jabbed. A foot to the ankle, a knee to the side, an elbow to the neck. Meanwhile, Lissa had passed out on her side facing Callie, and whenever Callie rolled over to try to get comfortable, she was greeted with Lissa's wide-open mouth. It was so wide open, in fact, that for the last ten minutes Callie had been counting her friend's teeth by the dim light of the headlamp she'd turned on after the others had fallen asleep.

Suddenly, Lissa snorted and rolled onto her back. With a sigh, Callie did the same, readjusting the balled-up sweatshirt she was using as a pillow. Unfortunately, she found herself half lying atop Penelope's crooked knee. Callie shimmied around on her back until she found a semi-comfortable position, and closed her eyes.

"You can sleep," she whispered to herself. "People do this all the time. Just . . . sleep."

A twig cracked outside the tent. Callie sat up straight, gasping for breath. She looked at Penelope, then at Lissa, but both lay still. How was that possible? How could they be sleeping so deeply in the middle of the wilderness? It wasn't natural. For a few long seconds Callie sat and listened, but there were no other strange noises. Her heart was still pounding so hard she couldn't imagine ever relaxing, let alone dozing off.

She thought for a moment about digging out her journal, but the last thing she wanted was for Lissa or Pen to wake up and catch her writing. They'd probably think it was dorky—or worse, demand to see what she'd written. That would be a nightmare, especially considering all she had was the first two pages of ten different stories.

Callie had been trying forever to put down on paper one of the many tales that always seemed to crowd her head, but after a few hundred words she always, *always* got stuck. When school had ended that year she had made a vow to herself that she would complete at least one fifteen- to thirty-page story this summer. Just one. And she'd tried. She really had. But now school was starting in a week and a half and she hadn't even managed to get halfway through any of them.

Epic creative fail.

So instead of reaching for her journal, Callie pulled from her backpack the book she was reading. It was a heavy, hardcover copy of *The Black Inferno #3: Jensen's Revenge*, which she'd bought at the bookstore downtown earlier that week. Callie knew she'd get mocked if she was caught doing this, too, but at least the journal would remain secret.

Tingling with anticipation, Callie opened to her marked spot, the first page of chapter two, and started to read.

The world was dark as pitch. Jensen took a breath, then another, waiting for his eyes to adjust. Waiting for an outline to appear. A shadow. Anything that could indicate where he was, what sort of peril he was in. But waiting didn't help. There was nothing. Nothing but a low, distant rumbling that seemed to grow more insistent with each, broken, breath . . .

Yeah, this wasn't going to make her feel any less freaked.

A rapid scratching at the vinyl tent made Callie flinch. Some-one . . . some *thing* was scraping away at the door. Was it an animal trying to claw its way in with its tiny, sharp nails? Or was it just a branch being worried by the breeze? Or was it . . . could it be . . . a knife?

The Skinner.

Callie craned her neck, afraid to move any other muscle, and stared, half expecting to see the outline of some Gollum-like psycho on the other side of the flimsy wall. Then, suddenly, the scratching simply stopped.

Total silence aside from the croaking of the frogs around the pond and the strange, constant ticking of the cicadas in the trees. Callie shoved the book back into her pack.

It's okay. Everything's okay. This time on Sunday you'll be safe in your bed at home. On Monday morning, Dad will make chocolate-chip pancakes and we'll go to pick up Mom.

Callie imagined herself and her dad at the airport, and her mom coming down the escalator, running toward her, throwing her arms around her. She saw them gabbing into the night, sharing the stories of their trips, laughing over the Skinner and the forgotten water bottle. She imagined the shops they would visit in New York City, the food they would eat, the hotel room they'd stay in. Maybe they'd even spot a celebrity at Barneys. Walk past the perfume counter just as a supermodel was spritzed with a tester of the latest fragrance . . .

"Hey, Evelina," Callie would say to her mom. *"That scent is totally you."*

It was working. It was actually working. Callie felt herself begin to melt off into the imaginary world she'd concocted. Slowly, her eyelids began to close . . .

A thud sent her eyes open wide. Callie sat up again, gasping for breath. Right outside the tent, a shadow rose up from the ground. A distorted hump that curled and straightened and stretched before her eyes, until she was looking at the perfect outline of a man. A man with something long and ominous clutched in one hand.

FIVE

"Callie?" the man whispered.

Her breath caught in her throat. *"Jeremy?"*

The headlamp slipped down over her face, landing with a thump against her collarbone.

"Ow."

She was so relieved she couldn't move.

"Sorry. Did I wake you up?"

No, but you scared me half to death, Callie thought. "What're you doing?" she whispered.

"Come out," Jeremy said. "Let's go for a walk under the stars."

Still trembling from the scare, Callie carefully got on all fours and quietly unzipped just enough of the door so that she could peek out. There Jeremy stood in shorts, boots, and his track team sweatshirt, his flashlight trained at the ground. His plaid blanket was folded over his arm and an excited, daring sort of smile lit his handsome face. Dirt covered his knees and Callie realized he must have tripped outside her tent. That was the thud, and the reason for his shadow seeming to grow out of the ground. She felt so silly now. Clearly it was a flashlight in his hand and not a knife. Why did her friends have to tell her that stupid story?

"Hey," he said. "Are you in?"

Callie hesitated. It was the middle of the night in the woods. There were living, breathing animals out there, just waiting for a couple of idiot kids to wander into their clutches.

And the Skinner. There was also the Skinner.

"I don't know, Jeremy . . ."

"Come on. We'll stay out in the open by the lake, away from the woods," he suggested, interpreting her hesitation perfectly. "You have to see these stars, Cal. It's amazing."

He offered his hand. She blew out a sigh, told herself to stop being such a wuss, and took it. Once outside, she shoved her feet into her flip-flops, which she'd left on the ground, and immediately began to shiver. It was cold—welcome to the mountains in August—and there was no denying that she was scared. Jeremy put his arm around her.

From the corner of her eye, she saw something move—a huge mass swinging from a nearby tree—and she flinched. But it was just the nylon bag full of their food, which Lissa had tied up to keep the bears from getting at it.

Bears. Yay. So not what she wanted to think about right now.

"You okay?" Jeremy asked.

Callie exhaled. If she didn't have a heart attack before this trip was over, it would be a miracle.

"I'm fine," she muttered at a whisper. "Should we tell them we're going?"

"Nah. Don't wake them. We won't even be out of sight of the tents."

Callie zipped up the tent door and felt along the length of the braid she'd worked into her hair before bed. It felt like it was mostly intact. Then she quickly smoothed her sweatshirt down, wiped under her eyes for excess mascara, and pressed her lips together to bring some color into them, all before turning around again.

"Ready," she said with a smile. She pulled her headlamp off over her head and flicked it on, holding it like a flashlight.

"Look up."

Jeremy touched beneath her chin with one finger and nudged her gaze skyward. The view took Callie's breath away. Stars. There seemed to be more stars than sky.

"Okay. This was a good idea."

"Sweet. Go me," Jeremy said, rising up on his toes adorably.

Their footsteps crunched on pebbles and twigs as they strolled toward the lake. Callie leaned her cheek into the side of his arm. In the trees around them the cicadas' hum was punctuated by the chirp of crickets. Off in the distance, an owl hooted, and Callie felt the sound inside her chest, comforting somehow. Maybe there wasn't a blood-lusting psychopath waiting fifty yards away. Maybe they were only surrounded by peaceful, happy little animals, like the cast of some old Disney cartoon.

A girl could dream.

"Let's lay the blanket out over there," Callie said, pointing to a large, flat outcropping of rock near the water's edge.

Jeremy whipped the blanket out and let it flutter to the ground, then held out a hand.

"After you."

"Why, thank you, sir," Callie joked.

She sat down, laying her headlamp aside, and the coldness of the rock seeped through the blanket and her clothes. It was amazing how swiftly and completely the temperature dropped after the sun went down. Jeremy sat right next to her, and she instantly felt warmer. They smiled shyly, sharing a little thrill over being alone together in the dark. When Jeremy leaned in to kiss her, her heart did the happy dance it executed every time their lips touched. Then Jeremy pulled back and gazed at her.

"How great is this?" he said quietly, his breath warm on her lips.

"Pretty darn great," she replied.

Then they both lay down flat on the rock, side by side.

"Whoa," Callie said.

"I second that whoa," Jeremy replied.

Every inch of Callie's vision was filled with stars. A million tiny pinpricks of light, everywhere. It was like they were lying under a dome sprinkled with glowing sand.

Callie turned her head and found Jeremy staring at her. She was so surprised her pulse skipped.

"Why are you looking at me? You should be looking at that!" she said, gesturing at the sky.

"Nah. You're way more interesting."

Callie blushed deeply. "You're gonna give me an ego."

Jeremy pushed himself up on his elbow. "You deserve to have an ego. You're smart, you're sweet, you're creative, you're loyal—"

"Loyal?" she laughed. "Like a dog?"

"No. I just mean it was cool of you to come on this trip with your friends. I know it's not easy for you."

Callie looked down at her hands, which were folded across her chest. The pink polish on her nails was chipping and black dirt made crescent moons under a few of them. She curled up her hands so Jeremy couldn't see.

"Just because I got a little lost on my pee break—"

"No, I just mean you're out of your comfort zone for five whole days. Not everyone would do that for their friends," he said with a shrug. He reached for her arm, tugged her hand out, and traced a circle in her palm with his fingertip. It tickled in the best possible way and she forgot about how hideous her fingers were. "I know you're hoping to bond with them or whatever, and I just wanted you to know . . . a) I think it's going well and b) if it doesn't . . . I've got your back."

Callie's chest expanded. "Thanks, Jeremy."

He smiled. "Anytime."

She lifted herself up onto one elbow as well, the better to face him. His long bangs had fallen sideways, making his face seem more open. Even in the dim light she could see the tiny gold and green flecks in his brown eyes. Jeremy had spent most of his summer volunteering at the half-day summer camp run by their town, playing hot potato with a bunch of first graders and patiently helping them learn to dog-paddle at the town pool. She'd visited him once on one of the pool days and he was having so much fun he looked like a big kid himself.

There was something so uninhibited about him. She admired that. And she loved how much he cared about people—his family, his friends, those kids in his camp group. He unapologetically cared, when most guys her age pretended not to care about anything.

He cared about her.

"Can I ask you something?" she ventured.

"Shoot," he said.

"Why did you kiss me that day on the bus?" she asked.

Jeremy laughed. "Um, victory high?"

Callie laughed, too. It had happened back in February, on the way back from an Academic Decathlon meet, where Callie had helped Mission Hills High beat Woodside for the first time in ten years. She and Jeremy were sitting side by side in the back of the bus—she hadn't given it too much thought when he'd sat down beside her, even though she had always found him cute. The team and their fans—mostly parents and siblings—had been shouting their way through the Mission Hills fight song when Jeremy had suddenly pulled her to him and kissed her. Luckily their moms had both been looking the other way, engaged in some deep conversation about the PTA and funding for the sciences, because that would have been super awkward. But a few of their teammates spotted them and cheered. Callie and Jeremy had been together ever since.

"So that was it? I answered that question about the theory of relativity and you couldn't resist me?" she joked.

Jeremy looked down at the slab of rock that peeked out from beneath the blanket. The rock was striated from years of weather erosion, shot through with all shades of gray and blue and black. Beautiful.

"Actually, I wanted to kiss you the first time I saw you."

"Really?" Her breath caught. "When was that?"

"Your first day at Mission Hills. You were wearing that black sweater and those big sparkly earrings that come all the way to your shoulders. You walked into calc and smiled at Mr. Finster—who no one ever smiles at, by the way—and that was it. It just took me a month and an adrenaline rush to get up the guts."

"Wow," Callie said, tingling from head to toe. "I had no idea."

Jeremy finally looked her in the eye. "Why did you kiss me back?"

"Honestly? I'd never met a mathlete science genius who also held the school record in shot put. I think my need to find a successful, testosterone-y mate kicked in."

"Ha ha. You're hilarious, you know that?" Jeremy said, pushing her shoulder. Callie inched closer to him and smiled.

"I just liked you, Jeremy. That's why I kissed you back. And," she added, feeling brave, "I like you more every day."

She leaned toward him, but just when their lips were about to touch, Jeremy pulled back and averted his eyes. "Cal, there's something I have to tell you—"

Callie's heart thunked with foreboding. She was on the verge of asking what was wrong when, out of the corner of her eye, she saw something move. A shadow the height of a tall man, but stooped, like someone trying to make himself smaller. There was the tiniest flash—some kind of reflector catching the light off her headlamp. Callie gasped and scrambled back on her hands and knees.

"What?" Jeremy sat up, alarmed. "What is it?"

"I saw someone. In the trees," she said, trying to catch her breath and failing miserably. Her skull felt weightless, like she'd just been dropped from an airplane at ten thousand feet. "There's someone out there."

Jeremy stood up and trained his flashlight on the tree line. "I don't see anything."

Callie sat up and brushed silt off her hands. "There was something there, I swear."

The flashlight beam moved back and forth across the trees as Jeremy searched. Callie stared hard at the spot where she'd seen the shadow, but the more she stared, the more her vision blurred. She'd see something move, but in the next second realize it was a trick of the eye. But still, she was certain they were not alone.

"Well. Whatever it was, it's gone now," Jeremy said. He had this tone in his voice like he was humoring her. "So as I was saying . . ."

As he started to sit down again, Callie reached for her headlamp and got up.

"I'm going back to the tent."

Maybe she was new to this, and maybe because of that she was a tad more skittish than her friends, but that didn't mean she was seeing things. Or that she was making stuff up. Or that she was crazy.

Which, exactly, did Jeremy think it was?

"Okay," he said, reaching for her. "Let's go."

She let him put his arm around her, and they made their way back to the camp. It was slow going, however, because Callie kept looking over her shoulder, scanning the trees.

There was someone out there. She knew what she had seen.

RECOVERY JOURNAL

ENTRY 2

I will not apologize for my keen sense of observation. It was clear, at the end of that night, that the girl had no backbone, no right to be in my woods. She was worse than a novice. She was a dissenter. The way she hugged herself away from that fire, the desperate, furtive looks she cast at her friends. She didn't want to be there, didn't care about the beauty around her. The majesty. The danger. What she wanted was to be close to that boy. She wanted him to take care of her. It was obvious by the way she kept retreating to his side, huddling under his arm.

That girl needed to be taught a lesson. Or two. Or three.

A lesson in survival. A lesson in inner strength. A lesson in knowing your place.

SIX

"Okay, kiddies. Time to turn off our phones," Lissa said, walking backward up the trail.

It was midmorning, and Callie was exhausted from a night of broken sleep, her eyes itchy and dry. Meanwhile, her boots were turning on her again, gnawing away on her pinkie toes as if the Band-Aids she'd painstakingly applied that morning weren't even there. Every step brought a twinge of pain. And just to make matters worse, she'd offered to carry Lissa's backpack today—the heaviest of the four—which was filled with not only Lissa's stuff, but all their food and supplies, the compass and map. After yesterday and all the teasing, she wanted to show her friends that she was tough, that she could handle anything, that they could trust her.

Now she was regretting her hubris, big time.

"I'm sorry, what?" she asked, the weight of her phone in her front pocket suddenly conspicuous.

"Lissa's right," Jeremy said. "We should shut them down and preserve the batteries, just in case." He pulled his phone out of the pocket of his cargo shorts. "It's not like we're going to be able to charge them out here."

"Just in case of what?" Callie asked timidly.

Lissa rolled her big blue eyes. She was always rolling her eyes. "In case we actually need them later. No one *needs* to look at TMZ every five minutes, right, Pen?" she said, holding out her hand as if to take Penelope's phone.

Penelope looked up from her screen, which she'd been scrolling over since breakfast. She pressed the device to her chest as if it were her precious firstborn. "No way."

"Yeah. What if my dad tries to call me?" Callie asked. She'd never been away from both her parents for this long, which was hard enough, but to be cut off entirely?

"So text him and tell him we're going radio silent," Lissa said, shrugging. "It's no big deal. I do it all the time when I'm out here. By midday today we'll probably be out of range anyway."

Great. It would have been nice if someone had told her *that*. Reluctantly, Callie dug out her phone, texted her dad, and turned it off. She handed it to Lissa, and Jeremy quickly did the same. Lissa shoved both phones into the monster pack on Callie's back, then reached for Penelope's.

"Oh no. I'll turn it off, but you're not taking it away from me," Penelope said, holding the phone above her head.

"You're such a freak about your phone," Lissa grumbled, but she backed off. It was one of the very few times Callie had ever seen her accept defeat.

Lissa looked down at her own phone and laughed. "Zach has texted me fifty-two times since last night. Could that guy be any more possessive?"

"I think it's nice that you have someone who cares about you," Penelope said.

Lissa pressed her thumb down on the off button without replying to Zach's messages. "Yeah, but there's such a thing as caring too much," she said. "I think this time apart will be good for him."

"Whatever you say." Penelope sighed, snapping her phone into a hard plastic box that looked like an eyeglass case before shoving it into her deepest pocket.

"What's that for?" Callie asked.

"It's an indestructible case," Penelope said proudly. "Waterproof, weight resistant up to two hundred pounds. Nothing's getting past that sucker. We could all fall into a ravine right now and my phone would survive."

"A ravine?" Callie whispered.

"She's just being dramatic," Jeremy said, kneading Callie's shoulders from behind.

"No. She's not," Lissa said over her shoulder. "Anything can happen out here, Callie. You'd better make sure you're prepared."

Jeremy stopped walking, so Callie did, too. The straps on the unwieldy bag cut into her shoulders, and there was an ill-placed bar across the bottom that kept knocking against her butt with every step. She was going to have a butt bruise when this was over. An actual bruised butt.

"Was that really necessary?" Jeremy snapped at Lissa. "I swear it's like you're *trying* to freak her out."

"Don't get all flustered, Science Boy," Lissa said. "I just want her to be ready."

Then she continued up the trail, her thick blond ponytail swinging behind her. The girl wasn't even speed-walking, just keeping her normal pace, but within two seconds she'd disappeared around a bend and was gone.

Jeremy put his hands on his hips, his chest heaving under the *Star Trek* emblem on his black T-shirt. "I know she didn't exactly want me to come with you guys, but does she have to mock my very existence?"

Before Callie or Penelope could answer, he shook his head and took off after Lissa.

"Well." Penelope paused and tore a little white bloom off a low-hanging branch. "This could be a very long trip."

"Seriously," Callie replied.

It's already been long enough for me, she added silently. *Just three more nights. One down, three to go.*

She couldn't wait to get to the airport and see her mom. Even though she understood why her mother had to go to São Paulo for the summer, she didn't have to like it. Callie's Uncle Marco—her mom's brother—was a widower with three little kids who had broken his leg in a motorcycle accident, so Callie's mother had volunteered to help out for a couple of months. It was nice of her. Selfless. But Callie and her mom were like best friends. Even with Skype calls and emails, not seeing her for eight straight weeks was a serious challenge.

"Well. At least it's a beautiful day."

Penelope tucked the white bloom behind Callie's ear and smiled. As much as she would never admit it, Callie relished the rare moments she got alone with Penelope. Lissa's constant presence could be a tad intense. She always had a plan to exact or a "helpful" suggestion to make or an outright snide criticism to share. When it was just Pen, Callie could breathe.

"Yeah. As long as you're a big fan of humidity and burning sun."

Penelope laughed. "Exactly."

They started walking again, much slower than the others, and Callie enjoyed the change in pace—the bar hit her butt much less frequently and more softly now. Penelope and Lissa were both on the varsity basketball team—the only sophomores to make the squad—and they both participated in other sports as well. But while athleticism seemed to be a way of life for Lissa, for Pen it was more of a pastime.

As they came around the bend, Penelope reached down and tugged a set of earbuds out of her pocket, placing only one in her right ear—the ear farther from Callie—so she could listen to music and still talk.

"Is that attached to your phone?" Callie asked.

Pen shook her head. "I brought my iPod, too. Don't tell Lissa."

Callie smiled, surprised that Penelope would ever share something with her that she hadn't with her BFF. "Your secret's safe with me."

They walked a few more steps, Callie considering what she wanted to say very carefully. She wanted to be a good friend to Penelope, but she also didn't want to step on anyone's toes. Especially not Lissa's.

"You know, Pen, you don't always have to take Lissa's word on everything," she said finally.

Penelope flinched. It was so small it was almost imperceptible. "What do you mean?"

"Like, the thing with your hair last night," Callie said slowly. Today, Penelope's hair was hanging in soft waves around her shoulders. "Did you really never wear it in a braid just because she said it made your head look too small?"

Penelope laughed in a self-deprecating way and looked at her toes. "I know. It's stupid, I know. She just . . . it's hard to disagree with Lissa," she said, looking Callie in the eye in an almost pleading way. "And honestly? She's usually right."

Callie laughed, thinking back to how Lissa had told her to break in her hiking boots for two weeks before the trip, that she should make sure to pack light, that she needed to triple check everything before she left the house.

Right. Right. Aaaand (water bottle) right.

"You got me there."

Callie could vaguely hear wailing guitar music coming from the second earbud. Surprising, considering all Lissa and Penelope ever listened to was top forty and hip-hop.

"Are you a closet hard-rock fan?" Callie asked.

Penelope blushed, a pretty pink color lightening her skin. "A little obsession I picked up last summer." She stared off into the distance as they crested a hill, and Lissa and Jeremy came into view down below. They were walking and—if their gestures were any indication—arguing. Great. "I know it sounds weird, but I find it calming for some reason."

"Yeah, that's not a sensation I equate with hard rock, but whatever floats your boat," Callie said with a laugh. They started downhill and Callie had to lean backward to keep the backpack from toppling her over. "You know, I didn't think you and Lissa had any secrets. From each other, I mean."

"Everyone has secrets," Penelope said quietly.

Something about the way she said it made the back of Callie's neck tingle. She was about to ask what she meant when Penelope suddenly brightened.

"For example, Lissa does *not* know that I used to have a huge crush on her brother," she said with a proud smile. "Or that I still have my entire My Little Pony collection hidden in the back of my closet." They both laughed. "I also never told her why I asked you to sit with us at lunch that day."

"Really? Why not?" Callie asked. "I mean . . . why did you?"

It had been a big moment for Callie—the new girl who knew no one—to get asked to sit at the table of the coolest girls in the sophomore class. She'd gone a whole week sitting by herself at a rickety corner table, unable to get up the guts to randomly sit with strangers. When Penelope called her over, she'd been missing her friends from home so much—missing math team practice and after-school pizza runs and rom-com marathons and just *conversation*—she'd been seriously considering spending all her savings on a ticket back to Chicago.

"You really don't know?" Penelope asked, her green eyes wide.

Callie shook her head and shrugged, which was next to impossible with the bag weighing down her shoulders.

"Do you remember that day at basketball practice when Coach Fox went ballistic on me?"

"Yeah." Callie was on the JV team, but she and a few of the other girls had practiced with varsity that day to make up for a handful of members who were out with the flu.

"Well, afterward Lissa was all 'Let's go lift weights! It'll make you feel better! Work out your aggression!' But you . . . you were so nice to me. You came over and asked if I was okay and got me a tissue and then you listened to me whine. And you didn't even know me. I thought that was so cool of you."

"Anyone else would have done the same," Callie said.

Penelope smirked. "You'd think that, but no one did."

Which was true, Callie realized. The rest of the girls on the team had given Penelope a wide berth. "Which is so weird. I mean, because you're always so nice to them. To everyone."

Penelope shrugged. "A lot of people can't deal with other people's feelings. It's like it's too messy or something."

Callie smiled, taking this as a compliment. "Well, messy doesn't scare me."

Pen grinned. "Good. Me neither."

They stopped walking as they heard Lissa's voice rise. She and Jeremy were still arguing. A line of concern appeared between Pen's eyebrows.

"What's with those two?" Callie asked.

"I don't know. They're being such freaks today," Penelope replied, then smiled sidelong at Callie. "At least we're normal," she joked.

"Go us."

They'd taken a few more steps when Pen's hand shot out to stop Callie. "What *is* that?" she hissed.

Penelope's alarmed tone set the tiny hairs on Callie's arms on end before she had even turned to look. She swallowed hard and braced herself, imagining some big hairy bug clinging to a branch or a rabid furry animal crouched beneath the brush ready to pounce and tear their throats out. Imagining, as hard as she tried not to, the Skinner and his blood-dripping knife.

"What?" Her voice was a terrified squeak.

"That!"

Penelope pointed into the woods along the right side of the trail. Tangled around a branch on a half-rotted, hollowed-out tree trunk was a scrap of pink fabric, torn and stained with mud. Callie didn't really feel the need to investigate further. In fact, she wanted to turn and run. But Penelope dragged her forward, clinging to her arm as their steps shuffled across the packed dirt.

The scrap of fabric was bigger than she'd thought, and decorated with small white flowers, like something a little girl might wear. It stretched out on the other side of the trunk, the delicate weave snagged and ragged. Callie's throat went dry. Beneath the smears of mud was something darker—a wide, deep, set-in stain. Dark. Red. Crusty.

Blood.

How had Lissa and Jeremy missed this? Were they so caught up in their fight that they'd blown right by it?

"Oh my God, Callie. What *is* that?" Penelope whispered tersely.

"I don't know," Callie said.

That was when she saw the hair.

SEVEN

Lissa and Jeremy raced back up the hill at the sound of Callie's scream. By the time they got there, Callie and Pen were huddled on the far side of the trail, clutching each other. Callie's face was pressed against Penelope's shoulder, her nose mushed flat.

"I knew it. I knew I saw someone in the woods last night," Callie rambled. "And that bloody gauze? There's someone out here and they're on a killing spree."

"You saw someone?" Penelope demanded. "Who? Where?"

But Callie didn't get a chance to answer.

"Are you guys okay?" Lissa demanded, heaving for breath. "What's going on?"

"There's a body!" Callie blurted, her finger shaking as she pointed. "A dead body!"

Lissa and Jeremy exchanged an alarmed look. They both inched toward the trunk, then stopped, staring down at the corpse. Then, horribly, Jeremy reached over to grab something.

"What're you doing?" Penelope screeched.

Jeremy stood up, lifting a bundle of white cloth. Penelope's fingernails dug into Callie's arms. Callie felt like she was about to faint—until she finally focused and saw what Jeremy was holding. A very old, very muddy, very broken baby doll. Its dark hair stuck out in all directions and its ceramic face was cracked on the side, causing one eye to yawn open so wide, the whole white ball was exposed.

Lissa burst out laughing.

"It's not funny!" Callie blurted.

A smile tugged at the corners of Penelope's lips. "Well. It's a little funny."

Penelope and Jeremy doubled over laughing and before long, Callie felt herself relax, too. She laughed, forcing out her fear and paranoia with each gasp for air, replacing it with cool, sweet relief. Bending at the waist, she used the opportunity to shift the weight off the small of her back temporarily.

"Hey. Don't you have a doll just like that?" Penelope asked Lissa. "It used to be in a carriage in your room when we were little."

Lissa narrowed her eyes. "Oh, yeah! Melinda." She laughed and took the doll from Jeremy. "My mom still has it in the hall closet. She's saving it for when she has grandkids. Zach went in there for a towel one time and thought it was a real baby. He screamed like a little girl." Lissa snorted, tossing the doll back into the underbrush.

Callie was still laughing when she looked up at Penelope. But her friend's entire expression had changed. She looked freaked.

"What is that doll doing all the way out here?" Pen asked. "I mean, I know it's not a real dead body or anything, but . . . what's that red stuff all over it?"

Lissa crouched over the doll again to check it out. "My guess is cranberry juice?" she offered. "Maybe some kid forgot it on a camping trip. Or decided she was too old for it and left it behind. Who knows?"

Penelope shuddered, still looking creeped out. Not that Callie could blame her. She was glad Lissa had dropped the ugly, staring thing out of view. But she'd take a mangled doll over a mangled body any day.

Callie thought of her journal. Maybe she could get a new story out of this. Something about the beloved childhood toy left behind . . . lost innocence . . . the uncertainty of growing up.

But no. *No.* She had to finish at least one story before she'd allow herself to start a new one.

Callie started to stand up straight again and realized she couldn't. Her back would not unbend. She grabbed Jeremy's arm and squeezed, letting out a very unappealing grunt of pain.

"Are you okay?" Jeremy asked.

Callie glanced over at Lissa, hating to admit what she was about to admit. "Not exactly. I don't think I can stand."

"All right, that's it. I'm taking the heavy pack." Jeremy slipped the bag off Callie's shoulders, then ripped his own bag off and dropped it at Lissa's feet. Callie let out a relieved groan and straightened her spine. She felt something crack near the center of her back and hoped it was nothing important.

"Aw! Look at you! So chivalrous!" Lissa teased, crossing her toned arms over her chest. "You know you can't be knighted, right? You're an American citizen."

"Just give hers back to her," Jeremy said, annoyed. "It's the lightest, isn't it?"

Callie rolled her shoulders. "No. It's okay. I can—"

"Cal, it was an impressive effort, but give it up," Lissa interrupted, slipping Callie's red backpack onto the ground. "And actually, I think Penelope's bag weighs less. What the heck do you have in here?"

Before Callie could stop her, Lissa had yanked open the zipper on her backpack.

"You have *got* to be kidding me," she blurted, and pulled out Callie's copy of *Jensen's Revenge.*

"You brought a *book*?" Penelope asked.

Callie's cheeks flushed hot. What had made her think she could keep that thing hidden from them for five straight days? But even in her humiliation, she was glad when Lissa dropped the bag again without pawing through it further. If she'd found and read any of Callie's journal, Callie might have actually died.

"Not just a book." Lissa flipped through the pristine pages. "A five hundred and forty-six page hardcover with topics for discussion in the back. Did you think we were going to sit around and read this together by the fire? Have some deep debate about"— here she paused to read from the discussion page—"Jensen's motivation when sparing the life of the evil troll king?" She looked up at Callie. "Seriously?"

Callie felt her blush deepen.

"Back off, Lissa. We all know Callie likes to read," Jeremy said, adjusting the straps on the backpack so that it sat higher on his shoulders. Something Callie sort of wished she'd known she could do, as it might have prevented her from having a permanently deformed rear end.

"This thing weighs, like, ten pounds!" Lissa laughed as she tossed it back in Callie's bag.

"It just came out on Tuesday!" Callie protested. She bent to yank the ties at the top of the pack as tight as she could get them before anyone could spot her leather journal. They could never see what was in there. Never. "I've been waiting to find out what happens for an entire year."

"You couldn't wait four more days?" Lissa suggested, raising an eyebrow.

"Or put it on a tablet maybe?" Penelope offered.

Callie itched to explain, but she knew they'd never understand.

To her there was nothing more satisfying than being in the bookstore the day the latest book in a series was released, picking it up off the shelf, reading the first page, bringing it to the counter, being one of the first people to buy it, then scurrying off to a corner to devour chapter one. She loved the feeling of a big, heavy book in her hands. She loved marking the pages with the flap of the jacket to see how far she'd read. That was who she was. She was not a tablet girl.

And besides, she didn't mock Penelope because she was obsessed with weaving bracelets or try to take Lissa down a peg because she was constantly talking about the tattoo she was going to get the second she turned eighteen. Sometimes she wondered why it was still socially acceptable to pick on brainy pursuits. But she wasn't going to start a fight about it with Lissa and Penelope. Especially not right now, when her survival literally depended on them.

"Even if I had a tablet, I couldn't keep it charged out here anyway."

Callie shouldered her own backpack, which felt much lighter than it had the day before, and tromped down the hill. After a couple of minutes, Jeremy fell into step at her side.

"Just ignore them," he said. "The idea of reading for fun doesn't compute in their tiny little brains."

He handed her a water bottle and she gratefully took a swig, wiping sweat from her brow as Lissa and Penelope caught up to them. She realized her hair was starting to frizz even more from the humidity, her natural curls winning out over the expert straightening she'd done yesterday.

Callie grimaced, half wishing she could look in a mirror and half grateful she couldn't. She was just going to have to accept the fact that she would be one huge frizz bomb for the entire trip.

If Jeremy didn't like her that way, well, then he wasn't worth it.

At least, that's what her mom would say.

Mom.

Three more nights. Three more nights.

Then home. Showers. Air conditioning. Shopping in New York City.

"I can't wait to get to soccer practice on Monday," Lissa said, brushing a fly off her arm. All the fall sports had practices the week before school started. "We're so going to the championships this year, right, Pen?"

"Yeah," Penelope said, sounding distracted. "I guess."

"Oh, come on. Don't start," Lissa said.

"What?" Callie asked, looking back and forth between them.

"Penelope wants to quit the soccer team," Lissa said, rolling her eyes as her feet stomped heavily downhill. "You *can't* quit, Pen. Only losers quit."

Penelope flinched. Callie knew she should say something to defend Pen or defuse the situation. But she couldn't seem to find her voice. Sometimes the very idea of standing up to Lissa was too scary, or too exhausting, or both.

"Check it out," Penelope said suddenly, holding up a hand to shield her eyes. "There's a bridge down there."

"Yeah? Where?" Lissa asked, turning.

Topic officially changed.

"Why do you sound surprised?" Callie asked. "Haven't you hiked this trail before?"

"Not this one." Lissa reached for her own bottle. "But Zach has. He told me it's got some really cool scenery, and won't be too challenging for the newbie," she joked, giving Callie a smirk.

Callie's battered toes curled inside her boots. "Wait a second. Do you guys even know where you're going?"

"Of course we do," Lissa replied. She gestured toward a blue metal square nailed to a nearby tree. "We're following the trail markers."

"And we have the compass and the map in case we get lost," Penelope put in. Then, clearly seeing how the blood rushed out of Callie's face, she quickly added, "Which will *not* happen."

Lissa unclipped a heavy silver compass from the pack Jeremy was now carrying. "See? The trail we're on heads north-northwest so as long as the arrow points that way, we're cool."

Callie looked down at the unfamiliar letters and markings. The red arrow wavered between the N and the W. Penelope and Lissa started down the hill again, but Callie hung back, needing a moment to breathe. Jeremy stayed with her.

"I wish I'd known we were on a new trail. Why doesn't anyone feel the need to tell me anything?" Callie asked as she clipped the compass back onto Jeremy's bag.

"Sorry. I should've told you," Jeremy said softly. "I think they just figure you're, like, along for the ride, but it's true, you should know what's going on. I'll keep you better informed from here on out." Jeremy reached over and tucked Penelope's flower tighter behind Callie's ear, letting his fingers linger for a second.

"Thank you." Callie looked down at her feet, which were throbbing. When this trip was over, she was going to soak them in the tub for at least an hour. They deserved it. "I guess we should catch up."

At the foot of the hill, the trail widened into a clearing, where Penelope and Lissa had paused to wait for them. Up ahead was the bridge—a long structure made of wood planks, with rope holds on either side. Beneath it, a body of water that was too big to be a stream, but too small to be a river, burbled over rocks and dipped down hills. The drop from bridge to water wasn't that far, maybe eight feet, but the idea of walking over those planks made Callie's stomach flop over.

"We're supposed to cross?" Callie asked, not bothering to hide her nervousness.

Lissa gave one of the ropes a good tug and tested the first board with her boot, rocking her foot from toe to heel.

"Yep. There's a blue marker on the other side." Penelope pointed confidently.

"Come on, Callie," Lissa said, her blue eyes glittering. "What's the worst that could happen?"

EIGHT

"I'll lead the way," Jeremy offered.

"And the chivalry continues," Lissa teased. Callie wished Lissa would give her boyfriend a break for once. She watched as Lissa stepped back from the bridge, giving a bow and gesturing with her arm for Jeremy to move forward.

Jeremy shook his head in annoyance, but he stepped on the nearest plank. It creaked under his weight and he suddenly turned around, flinching as he looked back at the trail. His hands grasped the rope holds. Callie felt a surge of fear.

"Did you guys hear that?" he gasped.

"What?" Callie's gaze darted to the trees, which tapered to wild underbrush and flowers near the edge of the water. Dozens of tiny white butterflies flitted around the tangled growth and a few bees zigzagged nearby, but otherwise the world was still.

Jeremy's alarmed brown eyes scanned the woods. Nothing moved. The air was so stagnant that nary a leaf twitched.

"I thought I heard a laugh," he said.

Callie whacked him hard on the shoulder. "Jeremy! Stop trying to freak me out."

"I'm not!" He looked at Callie and his face softened. Callie knew he could tell that her insides were now twisted into a million knots. "Sorry. I'm sure it was nothing."

"I hope so," Penelope muttered, hugging herself.

"Can we just get across the bridge already?" Lissa snapped, hands on her hips.

Jeremy nodded. "Sorry. Yeah. Let's go."

He edged tentatively forward and the bridge dipped and swayed. Callie's heart pounded inside her throat as she watched him. Each step let out another ominous crack, so loud that Callie was actually surprised when the bridge didn't collapse. Jeremy curled his fingers around the two rope holds tightly, bending forward from the weight of the huge pack on his back.

"Are you guys coming?" he called without looking back at them.

"Maybe we'll just wait to see if you make it across," Lissa joked.

"*Lissa*," Penelope said, nudging her friend. Callie was glad Penelope had spoken up—she was too anxious to talk right now.

"It'll be steadier if you're all on it with me," Jeremy shot back. "The combined weight will minimize the motion."

Callie looked at Pen and Lissa. When it came to matters of physics, Jeremy was the person to trust. He'd taken senior AP physics as a sophomore and had won more state science fairs than anyone in the history of their town.

"Okay, geek. We're coming," Lissa called out. Then she looked at Penelope and Callie. "You guys go. I'll bring up the rear."

Penelope went first, stepping lightly and with a sureness that awed Callie. She tried to mimic Pen's grace when she grabbed the two ropes and placed her foot down on the boards, but the bridge bucked and swayed and she realized that grace was not an option. She was just going to have to hold her breath and get through it.

Pressing her lips tightly together, Callie followed behind Penelope. After a minute she realized that if she matched her footfalls to Pen's, the bouncing wasn't as much of a problem because the boards weren't coming up to meet her feet in Penelope's wake. With each step, she felt a bit surer and she held her head high, actually taking in the beauty of the water as it gurgled downhill and around a bend up ahead.

Then the bridge gave a particularly stomach-dropping lurch and she found herself staring down at her yellow laces, trying to blur out the water rushing beneath them. A big, ugly dragonfly flitted up from the water and stared her right in the face. Callie had to bite down on her lip to keep from yelping. The dragonfly glared beadily at her, turned sideways, then darted away.

"Not bad, rookie," Lissa said from behind her. "Keep it up and I may just forgive you for bringing that book with you."

Callie managed a laugh. She was just about to toss back a retort when Jeremy let out a shout.

No, Callie thought in horror.

The boards under Callie's feet lifted and threw her sideways. The world swooped before her as she clung to the ropes, seeing nothing but trees and jagged rocks and foaming water. There was a loud splash and then Penelope screamed.

NINE

Callie didn't realize she'd closed her eyes until they wrenched open and the sunlight blinded her.

"Go!" Lissa shouted behind her. "Go!"

"What?" Callie gasped, clinging to the rope holds for dear life.

"They fell in! Pen and Jeremy are *in the water*!" Lissa shoved her from behind. "Go!"

Panic rose up in Callie's throat as she pulled herself shakily to her feet and started to run, catching glimpses of Jeremy's wet hair, of Penelope's outstretched hand in the water down below.

Are they going to drown? Please don't let them drown.

Callie and Lissa reached the last plank in seconds and Lissa threw her bag on the ground, then skidded down the steep slope bordering the river. Callie saw that Jeremy was being dragged downstream, Penelope right behind him.

"Try to grab on to something!" Callie shouted, her voice hoarse with fear.

"Like what?" Penelope cried back, getting water in her mouth. She reached for Jeremy, but his fingers were just out of her grasp.

Thinking fast, Callie grabbed a long fallen branch off the ground and tossed it to Lissa.

"It's too deep to stand!" Jeremy shouted, bobbing up and down in the foamy water. Callie's throat closed. She could see from here how his eyes were wide with fear. Behind him, Penelope's soaked face was a mask of terror.

"Swim toward me!" Lissa directed, her voice loud but firm. In front of her was a wide, slick, rocky area flattened by the current. She inched carefully toward the water with Callie's branch, her feet slipping and sliding over the algae-covered stones. Callie looked on, grateful that Lissa seemed to know what she was doing.

Penelope turned and started to swim upstream awkwardly, her pack still on her back. Jeremy tried to do the same, but the much heavier backpack weighed him down and he was unable to straighten his arms thanks to the bag's straps.

Callie's head spun. *Jeremy was going to drown.* He was going to drown all because *she* couldn't handle one day with the heavy pack.

"No! Not against the current!" Lissa cried as Callie picked her way down the incline. "Perpendicular! Swim toward the bank."

The dry dirt and rocks collapsed beneath Callie's feet and she slid on her heels toward the riverbank, catching herself on a branch before she went sprawling. She nicked her chin on the sharp edge of a rock but barely felt the pain. This was no time for whining. She shoved herself up and ran to Lissa's side. Penelope had clawed her way out of the current and was now on hands and knees in the shallow water, her hair matted over her face as she sputtered and coughed. Jeremy was still slowly cutting across the water.

"Here! Grab this!" Lissa crouched and held out the torn tree limb to Jeremy.

He reached for the end of the branch. His fingertips just barely grazed it before he was pulled farther away. Lissa jumped up and Callie ran with her down the bank, getting ahead of Jeremy.

"Try again!" Callie shouted, her voice cracking.

Lissa held out the branch, but it wasn't long enough. Jeremy was being swirled away, into the center of the water, which was wider here than at any other point Callie could see. If he got away from them, if he went around the bend, there would be no more shallow spots from which to help him. Up ahead, it was nothing but steep drop-offs from the trees to the water. What if there were bigger rapids up ahead? What if there was a waterfall?

Callie's pulse pounded in her ears. She felt like she was about to burst into tears, but she gritted her teeth, refusing to crumble. She was not about to let her boyfriend die because she was a weakling. She shed her backpack, whirled on Lissa, and grabbed the branch from her friend's hands.

"I've got this."

Lissa looked surprised but also somehow impressed. Callie took a deep breath and waded into the frigid water, the intense cold shocking her for a second. The water swirled through the eyelets in her boots and drowned her socks and toes. *It doesn't matter. Keep going*, she told herself. Her feet felt like blocks of ice but she ignored the discomfort, reaching out the branch until she could feel the strain in her shoulder muscles. Her eyes locked on to Jeremy's. He looked so scared, which was such an unfamiliar sight. But she knew she had to stay calm, even though every fiber of her being trembled with terror.

"Grab it!" she shouted.

Jeremy made one big lurch forward and his fingers closed around the branch. The sudden addition of his weight nearly knocked Callie over, but she held her balance and then leaned back, dragging him toward her, toward shallow water. Slowly, she began to step back, pulling Jeremy with her until his feet finally found the bed of the river. Callie fell over from the lack of resistance and her lungs seemed to freeze as the cold water rushed over her torso and head. She shoved herself up again, gasping for air, her hair clinging to her neck and face.

"Callie! Are you all right?" Jeremy sputtered.

"Fine. I'm fine," she lied. She was cold, she was soaked, she was scared, and she was quickly coming down from her adrenaline rush. But Jeremy was alive. That was all that mattered.

He staggered over and threw his soaked arms around her. They clung to each other, shivering.

"Are *you* okay?" Callie asked, placing her hands on his wet cheeks.

He nodded. "Thanks to you."

Then he kissed her, and for that one moment, the world—the rushing, terrifying water behind them, Penelope and Lissa standing nearby—fell away. All Callie felt was the warmth of Jeremy's embrace. It was the sweetest kiss they'd ever shared. Everything was going to be okay.

Then Lissa clapped her hands and whistled sarcastically. "That was *so* awesome, Science Boy!" she crowed. "Can you do it again?"

Callie's fingers curled into fists and she felt an almost frightening fury rise up in her. Really? Lissa was seriously going to pick on Jeremy right now? He'd almost just *died*.

Jeremy clenched his teeth, but he didn't respond to Lissa's taunts. He only locked his arm around Callie as they trudged to dry land and collapsed on the rocky shoreline. A dripping wet and wan-looking Penelope loped over, dropping her waterlogged backpack on the ground. Jeremy extricated himself from the big pack, then pulled the front of his T-shirt away from his body, making a sucking sound, and wrung out the hem over the rocks.

"What even happened?" Penelope asked, shivering and glancing up at Jeremy. "One second we were fine and the next second we were going over."

"I'm so sorry, Pen," Jeremy said, water dripping from his nose, his chin, his earlobes. "I saw something in the woods and lost my balance." He looked toward the far bank. "I saw someone."

Callie swallowed hard.

"Not this again," Lissa groaned, throwing up her hands.

"No! I'm serious! It was like this big flash of white. Like someone in a white T-shirt," he said, shoving his hair back from his face. He looked different with his bangs off his forehead—older somehow. "I'm sorry I didn't listen to you last night, Cal," he added. "Maybe you did see someone. Maybe someone is—"

Just then, a shrill shriek split the air. Everyone froze.

"What *was* that?" Penelope gasped.

There was a rustle in the trees. Callie's heart hit her throat. Suddenly a huge white bird took flight, its long neck stretched, its wingspan at least five feet wide. It swooped over the stream and up above the trees behind them, disappearing from sight.

Callie and Jeremy looked at each other. "Oh," Jeremy said, sounding sheepish.

"Great." Lissa laughed. "So you drowned our cell phones for a crane."

"What?" Callie blurted, turning around.

"Oh my God!" Penelope cried, her eyes widening. "You were carrying the supply bag!"

Lissa reached into the side pocket of the bag and pinched her cell phone between her thumb and forefinger. Water sluiced off its face as she drew it out. Callie dove for her own phone. There were bubbles under the protective covering. Her fingers trembled as she held down the power button. Nothing happened. She tried it again. Her jaw clenched at the blank screen.

"It's dead!" Callie cried, desperation welling inside of her.

That phone was her only connection to the real world. Her salvation in case of emergency. And now it was about as useful as a rock.

"Mine's dead, too." Lissa sighed, tapping the blank face of her own useless phone.

Penelope started to pull more things out of the pack. Lissa's sweatshirt, soaked. Her washcloth, soaked. The sleeves of crackers, an open bag of marshmallows, hot dog buns, trail mix, potato chips, all soaked. All ruined. The only food that had survived was some random pieces of fruit, the few hot dogs and mustard packets that were in the insulated bag, and a tube of peanut butter.

Callie's whole body shook, and not just from the cold. Dread was beginning to take over, like a horrible, slimy eel curling up around her rib cage. No phones, and dwindling food. What were they going to do?

Jeremy hung his head in his hands. "You guys, I'm so sorry."

Penelope was silent, her face ashen. But Lissa was all business.

"We still have the cereal and dried fruit in your bag, right?" she asked, promptly taking Jeremy's bag off her own shoulders.

"I have gum and M&M's in there," Jeremy said weakly.

"And I have a Snickers!" Callie announced, clinging to that one fact as if a chocolate bar could save her life.

"Oh, and a bag of Goldfish," Jeremy said, snapping his fingers.

"Goldfish?" Lissa said snidely. "What're we, four?"

Jeremy shoved himself up. "Hey! It's food!"

"Food we wouldn't need if you weren't so incompetent!" Lissa shouted back.

"You guys, don't fight!" Callie blurted, hugging herself to try to stop the shaking.

She realized Penelope hadn't said a word. Callie glanced at her friend to see her still pulling out item after waterlogged item in a growing frenzy. Then she fell back on her heels with the trashed map and compass in her hand. The glass front of the compass was smashed.

"That was my grandfather's!" Lissa lamented.

Penelope handed it to her and turned to her own bag, pulling everything out and laying it on the ground. Once all her sopping clothes, her plastic bracelet-weaving kit, and her toiletry bag were strewn over the rocks—not to mention their one roll of toilet paper, which now looked like a swollen diaper—she got up and raced down to the water's edge, her back to the others. Callie watched her, wondering if she was about to cry or scream. The iPod and headphones that had been in her pocket were probably toast, too.

"Pen?" Callie asked, her teeth chattering. "Are you okay?"

Penelope held a staying hand behind her. She headed first downriver, peering out at the water every few feet, then walked back up, checking the rocks and the dirt and the underbrush, looking, probably, for any food that might have come out of her bag while she was under.

"Nice job, genius," Lissa said to Jeremy. "Now we're down to half our food and we have no compass and no phones. All because you got spooked by a little bird."

"You don't have to keep blaming him, Lissa. It was an accident," Callie pointed out. Even though the tiniest part of her kind of blamed Jeremy, too. He couldn't have just kept walking and then looked back when he was safe on the other side of the bridge? But the act of standing up for Jeremy actually warmed her a bit, and if she was going to be choosing sides here, she'd be choosing her boyfriend's. If he had her back, she was going to have his. "And, to be fair, I wouldn't say it was a small bird."

"Thank you, Cal," Jeremy replied.

He wrapped his arms around her and, even though he was just as wet and cold as she was, Callie finally stopped shivering. Lissa groaned.

"You guys do know where you're going without the compass, right?" Callie asked, pressing her back against Jeremy's chest. "We can still follow the trail markers?"

"Hopefully," Lissa replied acerbically, giving Jeremy a look of death.

"Come on. You're just saying that to make him feel worse," Callie said.

"Oh, am I?" Lissa snapped. "Thanks, Callie. Nice to know you think I'm so evil."

Callie blinked, stung and uncertain. Maybe talking back to Lissa twice was one time too many, and she didn't want to get on Lissa's bad side. "That's not what I meant. I just . . . we *can* follow the trail markers, right?"

"In theory," Lissa said. "But it's not always a perfect system. Sometimes people come up here and mess with them. Take them down or destroy them. I'm not saying we're gonna get lost, but there's a reason we always bring the compass. It's our only plan B."

She looked down at the destroyed heirloom in disgust and shoved it into her shorts pocket. Callie pushed herself to her feet, her water-heavy clothes clinging to her skin. The last thing she wanted to do was anger Lissa even more, but she felt like she had to say what she was thinking.

"Maybe we should just go back the way we came," she suggested tentatively. She saw Penelope walking slowly toward them from where she'd been searching. She looked despondent. "Just to be safe. We can hike this trail another time."

Silently, Callie decided that whenever the girls rescheduled the hike, she'd conveniently come down with a nasty case of the flu. Or mono. Or a coma.

"I think my phone still works," Penelope offered weakly, pulling the big waterproof case out of her pocket and holding it up.

Jeremy scrambled to his feet and Callie's lungs expanded with hope.

"Yes! Omigod! Yes!" she cried. "Let's call home and tell our parents to meet us back where they dropped us off!"

"And you guys mocked me and my case," Penelope chided, taking the phone out and turning it on. She looked pleased with herself, but also distracted. "This case is gonna save us."

"Nope. No way." Lissa snatched the phone out of Penelope's hand. "We are not wussing out just because your boyfriend is a klutz," she added, whirling on Callie.

"Oh, because your boyfriend is so perfect?" Callie shot back, then instantly regretted it.

Lissa's face practically turned purple. "Zach might not be perfect, but he never would have let this happen."

"Really?" Callie demanded. "Then maybe you should have let him come with us!"

"Or *maybe* we shouldn't have let *him* come," Lissa snapped, pointing at Jeremy.

Before Callie could think of a comeback, Lissa turned and started shoving everything back into her dripping bag. Every inch of her vibrated, like she was fighting as hard as she could to keep her rage in check. Callie felt a lump in her throat. Jeremy studied the ground.

"It's only another seven miles to the trail stop," Lissa said firmly as she packed. "We should be there by the end of the day. We'll throw out everything we can't use and buy some more supplies when we get there."

Penelope fiddled with her woven bracelets as she eyed her phone, which was clutched in Lissa's hand. "Lis, come on. Don't you think we should—"

"No. I don't."

Lissa emphatically pressed down on the off button, then tossed the phone back to Pen, who, luckily, caught it.

"Well, let's at least double back to the end of the bridge," Jeremy suggested. They had veered a ways downstream chasing Jeremy. In fact, the bridge looked much farther away than Callie would have thought. "We'll pick up the trail again from there."

Callie nodded, thinking that was a safe plan. Meanwhile, Penelope looked forlornly down at her phone.

Lissa rolled her eyes, as if she simply couldn't take another minute of insubordination. "If we just cut diagonally through here, we'll meet up with the trail again and it'll be much faster. The shortest distance between two points is a straight line, isn't that right, Science Boy?" she said tersely, like she was explaining basic math to a twelve-year-old. "Now let's go."

She paused before turning away and looked Jeremy up and down. "And if you even think I'm carrying that soaking-wet bag, you're insane. It's all you."

Then she stomped off up the incline and disappeared from sight. Callie turned to Jeremy just in time to see him shoot a look after Lissa that could have felled that huge crane midflight. His jaw was set and his brown eyes narrowed; his nostrils flared. For a second he looked so different she hardly even recognized him.

"We'd better catch up to her," Penelope said with a resigned sigh, half walking, half crawling up the incline.

Jeremy shouldered the big bag and shrugged at Callie. Just like that, he was himself again.

"Sorry about your phone," he said.

"It's okay. I was due for an upgrade anyway," she told him.

They both smiled and then she let him walk ahead of her up the riverbank, casting one quick look over her shoulder at the spot from which the crane had taken flight. There was nothing there. Nothing but the silent, dark trees.

TEN

By the time they stopped for lunch, the sky had turned an ominous gray, with thick clouds crowding low. In the distance, thunder rumbled. Callie, still damp and shaken, sat at the foot of an ancient oak, munching on a handful of Goldfish and trying not to imagine what it was going to be like to hike through a thunderstorm.

Lissa silently cut up an apple with a Swiss Army knife and passed a couple of slices to each of them.

"Thanks," Callie said.

"No problem."

They were the first words anyone had uttered since the river. Jeremy shoved an entire apple slice into his mouth and looked away as his teeth crunched down on it.

"Okay, this has to stop," Callie said. She'd only come on this insane torture trip to bond with her friends, and that wasn't going to happen in complete silence. "We can't just spend the next three days not talking."

"What do you want to talk about?" Lissa asked, pulling her knees up. "The fact that we now have yet another embarrassing Jeremy story to tell?"

Jeremy huffed and Callie fixed Lissa with the most scathing stare she dared to direct at her. Lissa frowned back, and Callie dropped her gaze.

"Well, we definitely shouldn't tell any more scary stories," Pen spoke up from where she sat beside Lissa.

"True," Callie sighed. She thought back to her friends in Chicago, how they used to fill the endless winter evenings when it was too frigid out to leave the house. That gave her an idea.

There was a possibility that Lissa and Pen would think what she was about to say was dorky, but at that moment, she didn't care.

Callie took a deep breath. "How about we play a game instead?"

"Like what?" Penelope asked, delicately lifting an apple slice.

"Light as a Feather, Stiff as a Board, maybe? Or Truth or Dare."

Jeremy sighed. Callie knew his preferred games were things like Trivial Pursuit and Apples to Apples, but of course they didn't have any board games on them.

"How about I Never?" Lissa suggested, biting into her apple slice.

Penelope frowned but didn't say anything. Callie chewed on the inside of her cheek. It was no big surprise that Lissa would suggest I Never. Brave Lissa had probably done a bunch of exciting things that Callie had surely never done. And now her lameness was going to be exposed. But if it would end the silent tension, she'd give it a whirl.

"Okay," she said finally. "I'm in."

"Sure. Why not?" Jeremy said, clearly trying to be a good sport. He pulled the king-size bag of peanut M&M's out of his bag and ripped it open. "And every time we've done whatever the person says, we eat one of these."

"Now I'm *totally* in," Callie said, scooting forward.

"You're such a chocoholic," Lissa joked.

Callie shrugged. It was almost annoying how Lissa ate the perfect high-protein, low-carb, veggie-heavy diet and rarely indulged in anything bad for her.

"Shouldn't we preserve those?" Penelope asked. "Just in case?"

"He's got enough to feed an army, and we'll be at the trail stop soon," Lissa said, closing the conversation. "I'll go first." She crossed her long legs and leaned back on her hands. "I've never been to Europe."

Callie's heart did a brief happy dance. Maybe she wasn't so lame after all. She reached for the bag of M&M's and pulled out a red one. Lissa was wide-eyed.

"*You've* been to Europe?" she asked.

"Um . . . yeah. A few times." She popped the M&M into her mouth.

"A few times." Lissa looked around the group like she was somehow offended by this statement. "Wow. I had no idea you were so cultured."

It was amazing, how she could make that sound like a put-down. "My parents are both professors and they sometimes get asked to give lectures or teach classes abroad," Callie explained. "We spent a whole summer in Germany when I was ten and I've been to Spain and Portugal. I've been to Brazil, too, because I have lots of family there. Cousins and uncles . . ." She trailed off, wondering if she was boasting.

"Wow. That's really cool," Penelope said, fiddling with her bracelets. She glanced over at her iPod, which she'd laid on the grass in hopes of drying it out, no longer caring, apparently, if Lissa knew she'd brought it along. All of her bracelet-making supplies—various spools of thread and some sort of plastic loom—were laid out, too. "I don't even have any cousins, but if I did, I'd want them to live someplace exotic like Brazil."

Lissa and Callie looked at Penelope expectantly. Callie knew that Penelope had been to France with her family last year. It was one of the first things she'd told Callie about herself when they'd met back in January.

"What?" Pen asked.

"You didn't take one," Lissa said.

"Right. I forgot." Penelope laughed and brushed her fingers off before reaching for the bag. Jeremy looked down, scratching his neck as he held the M&M's out to her. He had a nasty bug bite right where his hair came to a point back there.

"You forgot spending an entire month in France?" Lissa asked. "That just escaped your mind?"

Penelope put the M&M in her mouth and rolled it around. "What? I was distracted by Callie's surprise internationalism."

"Okay. I've never snuck into the movie theater without buying a ticket," Jeremy interjected.

"Lo-ser!" Lissa sang, grabbing an M&M along with Penelope. Then they all glanced at Callie. It was her turn. She chewed her lip, and then thought of the obvious.

"I've never been camping before," she said.

Jeremy shook out three M&M's for himself, Penelope, and Lissa. "Like we didn't already know that," Lissa laughed.

"I just wanted to make sure you all got your sugar rushes," Callie joked.

"In that case, I've never lived in a big city," Penelope said, smiling at Callie.

Callie took an M&M, grateful to Pen for giving her that.

"Ugh, you're not supposed to make it so easy," Lissa groaned, glaring at Penelope.

To Callie's surprise, Pen glared back.

"I've never cheated on a boyfriend," Penelope blurted.

Silence.

Lissa's face tightened. Callie could practically feel the instant regret pulsating off Penelope. She'd said something Lissa clearly didn't want said.

Lissa slowly hinged forward, took a blue M&M, and held it for a second between her front teeth. Then she crunched into it and leaned back on her hands.

Wow, Callie thought. She and Jeremy exchanged a glance. She wondered who Lissa had cheated on. Zach? They'd been together a long time. Callie's stomach churned uncomfortably and she glanced at Pen, who was watching Lissa worriedly.

Lissa looked toward the trees, somewhere over Jeremy's head, and casually recrossed her legs at the ankle.

"I've never kissed someone that one of my friends had already kissed," she said.

No one moved. A single spider picked its way across the circle made by their legs. Lissa flicked it away when it reached her knee, and she looked right at Callie.

"You should be eating, rookie."

Callie blinked. "What? But I never—"

She automatically looked at Jeremy. His eyes were on the ground. Penelope's were, too.

"Wait a minute," Callie said, dread and realization spilling hot across her whole body. "You two—"

"Nice one, Lis," Jeremy said, getting up and shoving the M&M's back into his bag.

"Hey! She didn't eat!" Lissa protested, as if that was the important factor here.

Penelope pushed herself to her feet and grabbed her iPod, fumbling it into her pocket with shaky hands. Slowly, Callie rose from the ground, but immediately regretted it. Her knees were weak with nerves and her brain felt fuzzy, like she'd just done a flip and landed upside down.

Jeremy and Penelope had kissed?

When? How often? Had they been a couple? How was it possible that she'd been with Jeremy for almost six months and no one had said anything about this until now?

Suddenly Callie couldn't stop thinking about all the time Jeremy and Penelope spent alone together. Their families had dinner every other week. They'd spent a weekend at the Cape just this July. She imagined them talking about her behind her back, whispering about this big secret and how stupid Callie was for not figuring it out. Had they done that when she wasn't around? Had they kissed when she wasn't around? She felt tears start to well in her eyes.

"Callie," Jeremy said.

The sound of her name woke her from her stupor. The sadness and confusion she'd felt was now replaced with hot anger. Thunder cracked overhead, as if the sky was as furious as she was.

She swung her backpack onto her back, yanked on the straps, and tightened them with a zip. She didn't know where she was going, but she had to get away for at least a minute. She had to get away from the embarrassment that was coursing through her, away from Jeremy, away from Penelope, away from the betrayal.

She turned to storm off, but then stopped in horror.

She had almost walked face-first into the large wooden handle of a hunting knife.

ELEVEN

"Omigod, no! No!"

Callie staggered back and bumped right into Jeremy, which sent her whirling in the opposite direction. Thunder sounded again, this time so close it shook the ground beneath her feet.

"Callie, I'm sorry, but you don't have to—"

"Look!" she shouted, pointing at the knife. The handle was sticking straight out of a gray tree trunk, the blade all but swallowed by the meat of the tree. It looked old and used, the wood on the handle faded and cracked, but the gash in the tree was not. The wood around the point of penetration was bald white, untouched by rain or wind or scurrying animals. The bark had only cracked away recently.

"What is that doing there?" Penelope asked, adjusting her backpack as she joined them.

Callie took a sideways step, instinctively putting distance between herself and the liars. As she moved, something caught her eye and she stepped closer to the knife, narrowing her eyes. There were spots on the handle. Dark spots.

"Is that blood?" she heard herself say, though the high pitch of her voice was unrecognizable.

At that moment, the sky opened up and the rain began to fall. Fat, cold drops landed on Callie's bare arms.

"Don't freak out," Lissa said calmly, her hands out as if she were trying to soothe a rabid animal. "Anybody could have left that there at any time. People do some stupid, crazy stuff out here. Maybe someone got mad and stabbed the tree, then couldn't pull the blade out again."

"Oh. That's comforting," Callie snapped, no longer caring if she stood up to Lissa. "So there's a camper with violent anger issues wandering around out here somewhere. Awesome."

Callie turned on her heel and stomped off. The cool rain actually felt good on the back of her neck, but it was about the only positive thing she had going for her at the moment. She had never fought with her friends back in Chicago. Not about anything more important than what movie to watch. And Jeremy was her first boyfriend. This situation was not something she knew how to deal with. The only things she knew for sure were that her boyfriend and best friends were all traitors and liars, she was stuck in the wilderness and reliant upon said traitors and liars, there was almost no food to share between them, and now? A knife-wielding psycho. This day could not get any worse.

"Callie! Callie, please wait up! Let me explain!" Jeremy called out.

She walked faster. Her hair, which had just started to dry into its natural curls, was now plastered against her forehead. She pushed it back, fishing in the pocket of her shorts for a ponytail band.

"Callie."

Jeremy fell into step with her as the trail dipped slightly. The rocks beneath her feet were uncertain within the muddy terrain. The leaves on the trees seemed a brighter green as they shone with a fresh layer of rain, but everything else was gray. A swirling mist surrounded them. The woods themselves were denser here, crowding against the trail, threatening to suffocate her.

"Please don't be mad," Jeremy said. "Can you just hear me out?"

Callie clenched the ponytail band between her teeth while she attempted to gather up as many of her thick, wet curls as she could while still walking, the cold rain sluicing down. She removed the band from her teeth, tied her hair back, and let the band snap. "I don't really feel like talking right now, Jeremy."

Her heart felt bruised. Jeremy had always been so kind, so considerate. Before today she never would have been able to believe that he could do anything to make her feel this way. But now he had. She felt sick, sorry, stupid, and sad. She felt like she needed some time alone to think. If only she were home, safe in her own room. The stress of being out in the unknown was simply too overwhelming once emotional upheaval was added to the mix.

"What the—" Jeremy said.

Callie looked up and her shoulders slumped. Spread out before them was a huge, muddy expanse of water, its brown surface dotted by pockmarks from the rain. It swallowed the trail at their feet, and was so wide Callie couldn't see where, or even if, the trail picked up again on the other side. Spindly trees snaked up, their roots submerged deep below. A cloud of gnats traveled across Callie's line of vision, the tiny gray bodies within it a frenzy of nonstop motion.

Lissa and Penelope trudged up from behind. They both stopped abruptly.

"Well," Lissa said casually. "That's not good."

Something inside Callie exploded.

"Okay! That's it!"

She whirled around and shoved between the girls, starting back in the other direction.

"Where're you going?" Penelope asked meekly.

"Home," Callie replied firmly. "I'm going home." She wiped the rain from her face with both hands and stared them down.

"We can't let a little puddle stop us," Lissa said.

Callie barked a laugh. "You call that a puddle? That's a lake! Probably with frogs and snakes and who knows what else living in it. And I am not about to try going across it with a bunch of people who've spent the last six months lying to my face!"

Callie crossed her arms over her chest. The rain came down harder. Jeremy looked at Penelope, then they both quickly looked away, which made Callie want to scream. For a long moment, no one said a thing. Then Lissa turned to look out across the muddy water.

"There's a trail marker!" she exclaimed.

"What? Where?" Penelope stood with her toes at the water's edge and looked where Lissa pointed. "Oh, yeah! There is."

"I don't care if there's a trail marker," Callie replied. "I want to go home."

The second the words were out of her mouth, she regretted them. Her voice sounded petulant and whiny right when she wanted to be defiant and strong. One particularly fat drop of rain smacked into the center of her neck and snaked its way under the collar of her T-shirt, carving a long, frigid line down her spine.

"Callie, look. If we can get across the mess, we'll be at the trail stop in no time," Lissa said, approaching her. "You can get dried off, get some real food. And then, if you still want to go home, you can call your dad from their phone, or from Penelope's. Whatever. Just don't bail on us now. Please?"

Callie swallowed hard. She'd never heard Lissa's voice so soft and coaxing. For once, she wasn't ordering her around or telling her what was best. She was asking. Maybe this was her way of apologizing for what she'd revealed during I Never. If so, it wasn't enough.

Still. Callie glanced over her shoulder. Did she really think she was going to double back the way they'd come and sleep by herself in the woods tonight with no tent, in the rain? She was sure that if she did decide to go, at least Jeremy would come with her, but the thought made her throat close over. She couldn't even look at him right now.

Besides, after seeing that knife, she really did wonder if someone was following them, and hate it as she might, that whole safety in numbers thing was probably true.

Then she heard a laugh. A light, airy, but somehow sinister laugh just a touch louder than the sound of the raindrops pitter-pattering against the leaves. Her blood stopped cold.

"What was that?" she asked, turning.

The laugh sounded again. Lissa—brave, irreverent Lissa—grabbed her hand and held on tight. Callie's eyes darted around at the trees. There was no telling what direction the laugh had come from. She remembered how last night, Lissa had been standing right next to her and Callie hadn't even known. Her heartbeat thundered in her ears.

"Is that the laugh you heard before?" Lissa asked Jeremy.

"Oh, so now you believe me?" he hissed through his teeth.

"Do you think it's whoever left that knife there?" Callie asked tremulously. "Do you think the knife was, like, a warning?"

Another laugh—mocking, cruel. Callie's shoulders tightened.

"Who's there?" Jeremy shouted. "Whoever you are, come out." Silence.

"You guys," Penelope whispered, "maybe we should—"

They heard it again. A knowing chuckle this time, and louder—closer.

"He's right behind us," Callie whispered.

There was a crunch of leaves, a tumble of rocks downhill, and Lissa's eyes widened horribly.

"Run!"

TWELVE

Clutching hands, Callie and Lissa dove into the muddy lake with Jeremy and Pen right on their heels. Callie's feet sank so quickly she almost lost her balance, but Lissa clung to her, holding her upright. The water swirled up to Callie's knees. When she tried to lift her foot, the mud held tight to her boot, sucking at the thick rubber sole as if trying to swallow her whole.

"I can hardly move!" Penelope whimpered.

"Callie, are you okay?" Jeremy called from behind, but Callie ignored him.

She managed a step, then another, then another, but it was slow, slogging work. She gasped for air as she wrenched herself free of the mud, each step more difficult than the last. About a third of the way across, something slick brushed her shin and she screeched.

"What?" Lissa demanded.

"Something touched me!" Callie wailed. "There's something swimming around in here."

"Who cares? Just keep moving."

Lissa's fingers were clenched so tightly around Callie's that the knuckles felt like marbles against her bone. Lissa was moving faster than Callie, of course, their arms now outstretched between them as Lissa tried to drag Callie along. Callie's legs strained and quivered from the effort of trying to keep up. She looked over her shoulder, past Jeremy and Penelope, at the path from which they'd come.

No one was there, but Callie felt at every moment that some-one was going to come crashing through the woods, teeth bared, knife glinting in the rain. All she wanted to do was run. But she couldn't. She could barely take a step.

Lissa, Penelope, and Jeremy had been wrong. The Skinner was still out here. And he was coming for them.

Finally, Lissa let out a frustrated groan and let go of Callie's hand, racing for dry land. Penelope moved past Callie as well. The two girls were nearing the far side of the swamp.

"Cal. Are you okay?" Jeremy asked, coming up beside Callie.

"I'm fine," Callie snapped as she strained to lift her right foot. It suddenly pulled free and she fell sideways, careening into Jeremy. Tears filled her eyes, threatening to spill over.

"Here. Let me help you."

He went to put his arm around her, but she shoved him away. "I said I'm fine."

Jeremy's eyes were pleading. "Come on, Cal. Let me help."

Callie heard a branch snap and decided it would be better to accept Jeremy's offer than to get skinned alive by a psychopath. She locked her arm around him and he did the same to her. Together they found a rhythm for their steps and struggled slowly but surely to the far side of the swamp.

The second they hit dry-ish land, Callie detached herself from Jeremy. The rain had slowed to a mist-like drizzle and she could see more clearly across the water than she had from the other side.

Penelope had both hands pressed into a tree trunk as she gasped for air. Lissa paced back and forth, catching her breath, her gaze on the far shoreline.

"What is it?" Callie gasped, following Lissa's sight line. "Who's there?"

"There's no one," Lissa said, her hands on her hips. "Nothing."

Callie's brow knit. "But we all heard—"

"Yeah. We did," Lissa confirmed with a nod. "I think we should keep moving."

"Um, you guys?"

Jeremy had jogged ahead a few steps and was standing next to the trail marker they'd spotted from the other side of the swamp. It was a metal square that looked like it had been through a trash compactor, its green paint chipped away from the edges.

Callie's heart skipped a startled beat. "Wait. Isn't that supposed to be blue?"

"Yep. It most definitely should be blue," Jeremy said.

Penelope lifted her head. Wet wisps of her brown hair were stuck to her cheeks like dark veins. "We're on the wrong trail?"

"No," Callie said in a low voice. "No, no, no."

"We're lost?" Penelope asked, her green eyes filling with panic.

"No way. We're not lost." Lissa lifted her chin, but there was none of the usual bravado in her voice. "We're not. We're just—"

"On the wrong trail!" Jeremy shouted.

Lissa scowled but had no response. Callie's chest filled with an awful, prickling dread.

"We took the wrong path after the bridge, didn't we?" she said quietly. "We should have doubled back like Jeremy said."

"No," Lissa protested, shaking her head. "We cut right through the woods and found the trail."

"Yeah, well, clearly we found the *wrong* trail," Callie shot back. She pressed her face into her hands, holding back a wave of terrified tears. "And now there's some crazy, laughing psycho coming after us. What're we going to do, you guys? What're we going to do?"

She looked back across the swamp, wondering if whoever was out there knew they were lost. If that was why he was laughing. She wondered what he was planning to do with that knife.

"I can't take this," Penelope said shakily, ripping her backpack off and throwing it at the ground like it had betrayed her. When she took her cell phone out of her shorts pocket, Callie's heart leapt. Visions of rescue vehicles and clean towels and pizza boxes danced in her head. "Anyone have an issue with me using this now?"

Lissa pushed her hands into her hair. "Come on, Pen. You can't just—"

"Callie's right!" Penelope interjected, startling everyone with the sheer force of her voice. "There's some crazy person out there laughing at us! I'm not just going to stand here and wait for him to decide which one of us he wants to gut first."

"Hey there!" someone shouted. "You guys need some help?"

Callie spun around as a complete stranger materialized out of the woods.

THIRTEEN

Callie's heart fluttered around inside her chest like it wanted to escape. Not that she could blame it. *She* wanted to escape. Instead she ended up gripping Jeremy—the one person she *really* didn't want to be touching right then—for support.

The stranger was tall, with brown shaggy hair that fell over his ears. His face was tan and his arms strong, plus he had the widest calf muscles Callie had ever seen. There was a flannel shirt tied around the waist of his green cargo shorts, and sweat stains beneath the arms of his light gray T-shirt. As he got closer, Callie could see that he had a small white scar just above his right eye, and that he was young—not much older than her and her friends—and handsome. There was a well-worn gray backpack secured to his back with a sleeping bag tethered to it by a set of blue bungee cords. No tent, as far as Callie could see.

"Where did you come from?" Lissa asked the stranger, stepping up in front of the others.

The guy raised his hands. They looked like hard-worked hands, with short scraggly nails and dirt creased into the knuckles. It was a gesture of peace—of surrender, even—but Callie's fists clenched.

Someone had been laughing at them. Laughing in a sinister way. And this guy was the only person they'd seen since starting out on the trail the morning before. She could do simple math.

"Just out here for a hike like you guys. Except unlike you, I know where I am."

"How do you know we're lost?" Penelope asked, clutching her phone to her chest as she stepped closer to Jeremy.

Callie felt a flash of annoyance and jealousy. If Jeremy was going to be protecting anyone around here, it was going to be her. But even as she thought it, she felt stupid and childish. They were all in danger. They were all scared. Her love life, she could figure out later. If there was a later.

The guy chuckled. It didn't sound like the scary chuckle they'd heard earlier, but it was hard to tell.

"Because no one hikes this trail. Not anymore." He tilted his head toward the green trail marker. "Park service closed this one down ten years ago thanks to a series of mudslides. This is nothing," he said, gesturing toward the swamp they'd just crossed. "Parts of it farther up are completely wiped out."

Callie, Jeremy, and Penelope turned to glare at Lissa. Her ears quickly flushed pink.

"So we were right," Jeremy said. "This isn't the trail Zach told you about. We should have gone back to the bridge."

"And you know this how?" Lissa demanded of the stranger, ignoring Jeremy.

"I grew up on this mountain." The guy took a wide-legged stance. When he crossed his arms over his chest the muscles strained, tightening the hems of his sleeves. "My dad was a park ranger. My name's Ted, by the way. Ted Miller."

No one said a word. Callie and her friends looked at one another, wondering whether they should introduce themselves.

The corner of Ted's mouth curled up. "This is the part where you guys tell me your names."

"Did you hear a laugh a few minutes ago?" Callie asked, trying to test him.

His thick eyebrows rose. "A laugh? What kind of laugh?"

"Like a . . . taunting laugh," Penelope said quietly. "It wasn't you, was it?"

Callie's fingernails dug into her palms. One bit tighter and she was going to draw blood, but she couldn't seem to unclench. Fear gripped her chest, making it hard to breathe.

"Got no reason to laugh." Ted shook his head slowly. "I'm out here alone and it's not like the trees are telling any jokes." Now he did laugh, and it was a pleasant, jovial sound, nothing like what had set Callie's teeth on edge before. She managed to relax, ever so slightly. "So are you going to tell me your names, or should I just move on?"

Callie hesitated. But if this guy was going to ax murder them in the middle of the woods, it hardly mattered whether he knew their names or not.

"I'm Callie," she offered quietly. "That's Lissa, Penelope, and Jeremy."

"Nice to meet you." Ted gave Callie a friendly smile. "So, listen, I know the trails up here like the back of my hand. I can get you back to civilization, if you want."

"Really?" Callie squealed automatically.

"Oh, we want," Penelope said, then looked at Lissa and blushed, as if she'd spoken out of turn.

"I'm not sure, you guys," Jeremy said. "We don't even know him."

"Hey. Standing right here." Ted waved.

"Well, it's true, isn't it?" Jeremy asked pragmatically.

"Look," Lissa spoke up. "What we really want is to get to the trail stop. We know where we're going from there." She reached back and tugged the band out of her hair, combing her wet blond locks out over her shoulders. "Can you tell us how to get there?"

"The trail stop?" Ted extricated one arm from his backpack strap, then the other, letting it drop to the ground. He crouched over it and unzipped the top. Callie, Jeremy, and Penelope took an instinctive step back. Who knew what he had in there? "You mean the Twin Pines stop? You're at least fifteen miles from there."

"What?" Penelope breathed.

"Yep. How far did you guys veer off course?" He said this lightly, like it was some kind of joke. Then he pulled out a bulging bag of trail mix, tore it open, and held it out to Lissa. "Hungry?"

Lissa didn't move. Callie's stomach grumbled. There were peanuts in the trail mix. And raisins. And chocolate.

"I'll have some," she announced.

Jeremy shot her a betrayed look, but she ignored it. She'd had nothing but a handful of Goldfish, three apple slices, and a couple of M&M's since breakfast and had probably burned more calories hiking than she ever had in her entire life. She didn't see the harm in taking a bit of trail mix when it was offered. She reached in for a handful and stuffed it in her mouth. The chocolate melted on her tongue. It was as if she hadn't eaten in days.

Penelope was the next to step forward, then—grudgingly—Jeremy. Lissa took nothing.

"Listen, my cabin is a couple days' hike south of here. I can get you there and avoid the parts of the trail that are missing." Ted stood up and popped a few peanuts into his mouth. "We have a booster, so your cell phones will work and everything." He looked down at their feet, which were dripping with gloppy mud. "And showers."

Callie swallowed the rest of the trail mix. A couple days. That meant they could still make it back to civilization before Sunday—before her dad came to pick her up and before her mom got home. She wasn't at all confident that she could make it through a couple of days—especially not now that there was going to be some serious awkwardness between her, Jeremy, and Penelope. But what was the alternative? At least Ted had a direction for them to walk in—a destination. And a shower sounded like heaven to her.

"Come on, Lissa," Penelope ventured, fiddling with her bracelets. "At least if we go with him we'll know we're going the right way."

"Yeah, if he's telling the truth," Lissa shot back.

Ted lifted his hands again. "Hey. I'm just trying to help."

Jeremy looked away, his jaw set, like something had seriously angered him. What was that, exactly? Callie wondered, annoyed. The chance to get home in one piece?

"Hey!" Callie said, turning to Lissa. "If we go with him, you still have a shot of making it home in time for soccer practice. But if we go it alone, who knows how long we might be out here?"

"She's right," Penelope said, brightening. "There's no way you make starting forward if you miss the first practice."

Lissa's lips twisted to one side, and Callie knew she was deep in thought. Callie held her breath. Lissa couldn't really say no, could she? Not when there was literally no other conceivable course of action.

"Fine," Lissa said finally. Then she took a step to the side, giving Ted a wide berth. "Lead the way."

Callie almost wanted to high-five Penelope behind Lissa's back. They'd done it. They'd gotten Lissa the Great to cave. But Callie resisted. When Penelope shot a tentative smile at her, Callie looked away.

"Cool," Ted said. "Let's go."

He started up the trail and they all fell into line behind him. It wasn't until Ted was just cresting the small incline that Callie noticed the swipe of blood across the back of his shorts—four long smears. Like fingerprints.

FOURTEEN

"You can put that away, you know," Ted said, looking over his shoulder at Penelope, who was still clutching her phone hours later. The sun was starting to set, turning the sky an inky shade of blue. "You're never gonna get a signal out here."

"I can't help it," Penelope said, holding the phone close to her chest. "It's like a security blanket."

Ted pushed a low branch out of the way and held it for the rest of the group, like a doorman holding open a door. Callie kept staring at the bloodstains on his shorts, trying to get up the guts to ask him about them. Was she the only one who'd noticed?

"I've got a security blanket, too," he said as the group crept past him, one by one. "It's called a gun."

Callie's heart plummeted. He wasn't serious, was he?

"What?" Jeremy snapped.

Ted let the branch whip back into place behind them and raised his hands again. "Kidding. Chill, Little Man."

Jeremy glowered and Callie felt an odd little thrill of triumph. She was still no closer to forgiving Jeremy for his betrayal, for keeping his relationship—or whatever it had been—with Penelope a secret. So now it kind of made her feel gratified that someone was making him feel bad.

Which, of course, made her wonder if she was an awful person.

Following Ted, they came to a plateau in the mountainside and a wide, grassy area surrounding a glassy pond. The surface of the pond was so placid, it perfectly reflected the scenery around it—the mountaintops and trees, the clouds that had finally broken up into wispy curls.

"It's getting dark," Ted said. "We should set up camp here."

Callie sat down so fast, she misjudged where the ground was and collided with it rather ungracefully, but she didn't care. They'd been walking for hours, and her shoulder muscles were coiled into knots, her feet throbbing. She let her backpack drop off her shoulder and leaned forward, head between her knees. The blisters on her feet felt raw and wet and the very idea of washing them, drying them, medicating them, and rebandaging them exhausted her.

"This is pretty," Lissa commented offhandedly.

Callie lifted her eyes. The pond was surrounded by bright yellow wildflowers and half covered by floating lily pads. In the waning sunlight, dragonflies flitted from leaf to leaf, their wings beating so fast they were nothing more than a shimmering flicker. A tiny head popped up in the middle of the water—a frog, maybe—sending ripples across the surface, but it was gone before Callie could get a decent look.

Callie thought about how she could work this magical setting into one of her stories. Maybe in that piece about the girl who falls down a storm drain near Millennium Park in Chicago and discovers an underground world of urban faeries . . .

Jeremy shuffled over to her. Callie stared at the mud-caked toes of his boots. "Can we talk?" he asked quietly.

"Why?" She thought of last night—how beautiful the stars had been, how safe she'd felt with Jeremy, for a few minutes anyway. "So you can lie to me some more?"

"I didn't lie," Jeremy said haltingly. "I just—"

"Didn't tell the truth," Callie finished.

Callie pulled her book out of her bag and opened it to a random page, hoping Jeremy would get the hint and leave her alone. Now that everyone knew she had *Jensen's Revenge*, she didn't care anymore if they saw her read it.

Ted loped over, a large rock in each hand, and tossed them on the flat stretch of ground nearby, where they thudded and rolled.

"What's up?" he asked, his eyes glinting. "Are you guys, like, a couple?"

"Back off, man. It's none of your business," Jeremy said, his harsh tone surprising Callie. He wasn't usually so belligerent.

Ted raised his hands, which seemed to be his favorite gesture, and backed up. "Sorry, dude. How about you make yourself useful and help me find some more rocks so we can start a fire? It's about to get pretty darn cold up in here."

Jeremy looked down at Callie hopefully. She turned her face away, focusing on the book. She heard him huff.

"Fine," he answered.

The two guys marched off toward the waterline. Penelope was keeping a safe distance from Callie, as she had all day, setting up the girls' tent a few yards off.

"Can I talk to you for a second?" Lissa murmured, bending at the knee to nudge Callie's arm. Callie almost grunted. What was with everyone suddenly wanting to explain? If any one of them had done so six months ago, she wouldn't be miserable right now.

"I don't really feel like—"

"No. We need to talk."

Lissa turned and walked down the rocky shoreline in the opposite direction from the guys. Classic Lissa. No arguments allowed. Callie blew out a sigh, then put her book aside, got up, and followed, as Penelope watched forlornly after them. At the water's edge, Lissa stopped. She bent and plucked an orange wild-flower that grew near her feet.

"Listen, Callie, I'm sorry. You shouldn't have found out that way."

Callie's throat tightened. "Found out what? I don't even know what happened."

Lissa glanced past Callie, who cast a quick look over her shoulder. Ted was toting a few rocks back to the dirt patch, but Jeremy and Penelope were now standing close together, locked in some sort of heated debate. Callie felt her cheeks flush. She'd walked away for two seconds and Pen had made a beeline for Jeremy. If the two of them had something to fight over, then they had something between them.

"They went out for three months last year," Lissa told Callie.

"Three months?" Callie echoed, shocked. It sounded like a lifetime.

"Yeah, and it didn't end well," Lissa said. "He sort of broke her heart. That was why she and her family went to France. She said she had to get out of here. She even missed the last month of school. She had to make up the work over the summer."

Callie felt like she was going to throw up. "Why didn't anyone tell me?"

"Pen was embarrassed," Lissa said, plucking a petal from the flower. "She gets like that sometimes. She can be so . . . frail." She said it like a judgment, and ripped three petals at once. Callie bit her lip. "I don't know why Jeremy didn't tell you. You'd have to ask him."

Callie hated the warm squirmy feeling of jealousy inside of her chest. This morning she'd trusted Jeremy more than she trusted anyone other than her mom and dad, but now, that had been obliterated.

"If it's any consolation or whatever, I don't think Jeremy was as into her as she was into him," Lissa said. "And it's obvious he really likes you. Plus she's clearly over it. If she wasn't, there's no way she would have said yes when you asked if Jeremy could come with us."

Callie took a deep breath, letting this logic permeate the sour force field around her heart.

"But what do you think I should do?" Callie asked. "I can hardly even look at him."

"We could send his butt home," Lissa suggested.

"No," Callie said automatically. Lissa raised her eyebrows. "I don't want him to have to walk all the way back by himself. It's getting dark. I'm mad at him, but I don't want him to, like, get eaten by a bear."

Plus there was the issue of the laugher, who was still out there somewhere. She watched Ted as he unrolled his sleeping bag out in the open air. They'd decided to trust him, but there was still the inkling of a possibility that it might have been him laughing out there in the woods. And maybe he'd just been messing with them, but did they really want to hang out with a person who would do that—prey on a bunch of lost hikers? The very idea that they were potentially settling in for the night with the enemy made her vision blur. She closed her eyes, took a breath, and steadied herself.

"Besides, we don't even really know where we are," she couldn't help reminding her fearless leader.

Lissa shot her an admonishing glance, but then she smiled. "Well, then you have your answer. If you don't want him to get eaten by a bear, then you must still like him. Which means this is fixable."

Callie sighed, looking out across the pond. Another ripple appeared, dead center, but whatever had caused it never came to the surface. "I guess."

Lissa tore the rest of the petals off the flower and tossed the destroyed stem over her shoulder. "Come on. We'll make camp and you and your boy can have a chat when you're ready."

"Thanks, Lissa." Callie managed a small smile. Though she wasn't sure if she was ever going to be ready to speak to Jeremy.

"See? Told ya we needed to talk," Lissa replied, slinging her arm across Callie's shoulders.

As they walked back toward the others, Callie saw Jeremy and Penelope suddenly stop their conversation. Of course.

"Hey! What was that?" Penelope asked, looking past Lissa and Callie.

For a second, Callie thought Penelope was just trying to distract her. But then she saw it—a quick flare, like a flashlight going on and off, on the far side of the pond.

"There it was again," Jeremy said, alert.

"It's probably just some other hikers," Ted offered, whipping out a box of matches.

"I thought you said no one ever hikes these trails," Lissa said.

Ted smirked. "Well, you're here, and I'm here, so maybe we're about to have some company."

"Why does that sound more menacing than comforting?" Callie asked, hugging herself.

Ted held the match to his kindling tepee and sparked the fire, then shook the match out as he rose to his feet.

"Hey. The more the merrier, right?" He walked over to Callie and Lissa with a big smile and nudged Lissa's arm with his, making her blush. "Don't worry. I'll protect you."

Callie couldn't stop staring across the lake. Somehow, she didn't find that declaration comforting, either.

FIFTEEN

Callie sat up straight in her tent, dragging in a gasp so violent it stung her throat. For a split second she couldn't figure out what had awoken her, but then she heard it again.

The laugh.

It was unmistakable. A horrible, evil chuckle that surrounded her.

"You guys!" Callie hissed. "Wake up!"

Her journal—which she'd apparently fallen asleep with—slid off her lap, the thud scaring her, and she tossed it toward the back of the tent, out of sight. Callie grabbed at her friends, catching Lissa's arm and Penelope's calf in her grip. Lissa lifted her head, one eye squinted open. Penelope simply rolled over.

"What time is it?" Lissa asked, her voice raspy.

"I have no idea. I just heard—"

The laugh sounded again. It seemed to come from everywhere, from all around them, filling the air.

Lissa pushed herself up. "Pen! Wake up!" she whispered, and reached past Callie to shove Penelope's shoulder.

"Eeennnnh . . . what?" Penelope whined.

"That psycho's out there again, laughing," Lissa told her, curling her knees up under her chin.

"What?" Penelope was awake now, and sitting. Her hair staticked out around her head and some of it clung to her cheeks.

The laughter came again, this time louder, and Lissa and Penelope inched closer to Callie, sandwiching her between them, reaching for her hands.

"Do you think it's Ted?" Callie whispered.

"If it's not, then he's in trouble," Lissa whispered back. "He's out there without a tent."

Callie could feel it inside her cheekbones and her nose, in her eyes. If Ted was in danger, then so were they. So was Jeremy. These tents weren't exactly houses made of bricks. Any wolf worth its salt could blow their tents down in two seconds, then have three little girls for breakfast.

Callie, Lissa, and Penelope sat still, holding their collective breath as best they could while clutching hands. They waited. And waited. And waited some more. But the laugher was done. Either he'd gotten bored, or he'd found some other psychotic fun to have.

"What do we do?" Callie whispered.

Lissa released Callie's hand, leaving Callie's cold, clammy palm exposed. She crawled over to the tent's door and reached for the zipper.

"No! Don't!" Callie cried desperately.

"I'm just checking on Ted," Lissa hissed back. She unzipped the door half an inch and pressed her eye close to the opening. "He's fast asleep. It definitely wasn't him."

Cold dread pierced Callie's heart. Somehow, this was worse. An unknown enemy was more terrifying than one they sort of knew.

"So who was it?" Penelope asked, her eyes wide with anxiety in the dark of the tent. "Why are they doing this?"

Silence. No one had a clue.

"We should try to sleep," Lissa said finally.

"Like that's gonna be possible," Penelope said, but she released Callie as well. Callie remembered then that she was still mad at Pen. It had been easy to put that hostility aside when they'd felt that their lives were at risk. Callie sighed as Pen and Lissa lay back down on their sleeping bags, and were both asleep within minutes.

Callie lay down, too, but she couldn't sleep, even as her heart rate began to slow. Maybe the laugher was just a solo hiker who happened to be enjoying himself. Maybe he was listening to a really funny book on his phone. There could have been a million innocuous explanations for the laughter.

Unfortunately, Callie couldn't make herself believe a single one.

RECOVERY JOURNAL

- - - - - - - - - - - - - - - - -

ENTRY 3

- - - - - - - - - - - - - - - - -

Sometimes I find it amazing that anyone would ever go to sleep in the presence of another human being. People are completely vulnerable in their sleep. One could do almost anything to a person who is in a truly deep slumber. Tie them down, gag them, blindfold them, even cut them. It can take several seconds before a sleeping mind registers pain, and by that point, it's too late.

It would have been so easy on that night. So easy to take what I wanted. Two could have been disposed of before the third ever realized what was happening. And that boy. That oblivious boy snoring alone in his tent. He never would have seen it coming.

But that is exactly why I didn't do it that night. Why I had to control myself. Because the whole thing would have been so pointless, so . . . unsatisfying. They had to know they were about to die. I needed to look them in the eye while I did it.

I needed them to know why.

SIXTEEN

Callie scratched at an itch on her face. The sunlight was pink against her eyelids and the air inside the tent was warm and humid, but she didn't want to open her eyes yet. She felt as if she'd just fallen asleep five minutes ago. Her head was heavy, her arms and legs stiff, and when she lifted her hand to rub another itch on her ear, her fingers were clumsy with sleep.

Her nose prickled. She scratched it and rolled onto her side. Penelope made a noise, pinched and annoyed, and Callie reluctantly opened her eyes.

What she saw wrenched a scream from her very core.

Penelope's face was covered in spiders.

"What?" Lissa gasped, opening her eyes.

Callie sat up. Her entire sleeping bag was teeming with tiny brown spiders, their legs scrabbling and picking along the material.

No. Nooooo.

Callie jumped to her feet. She could feel them now. On her hair, down the back of her shirt, up her sleeves. She screamed and screamed and screamed, making a high-pitched noise she never would have believed could come from her own throat.

Then Lissa was sitting up and screaming, too.

"Oh my God! Oh my God! Oh my God!" Penelope was also wide-awake, swatting spiders off her face, arms, and shoulders. Totally pointless. There were so many of them that as soon as one was gone, another crawled up to take its place.

Lissa dove for the tent door and grabbed the zipper, shaking in a way Callie never would have thought her cool-as-a-cucumber friend could. A spider clung to the lobe of her ear like a gross, hairy earring.

"Open it! Open the door!" Callie screeched, still doing a crazy dance.

"I'm trying!" Lissa wailed.

"Callie!" It was Jeremy, shouting from outside the tent. "What's going on? Are you okay?"

Finally Lissa's trembling hand managed to rip open the door. She stumbled free and stood in the middle of the camp area, flinging her hands over her body again and again. Spiders fell off her and scattered like brown leaves off an autumn tree.

"Get them off me!" she screeched. "Get them off!"

Callie crawled out, quivering from head to toe. Jeremy's eyes widened at the sight of her. On the far side of the doused campfire from last night, Ted was just rousing inside his sleeping bag.

"Help! Do something!" Callie cried again, jumping around and shaking her arms like a panicked marionette. She didn't even know what she was doing, what she was saying. She only knew that she couldn't stop moving. She would have peeled her own skin off if she could have. "What do I do?"

Jeremy grabbed her wrist. "The pond! Get in the water!"

Penelope was out of the tent now, too, also screaming. Lissa sprinted right into the pond, taking a loud, gasping breath and diving under. Callie ran after her. The water was so cold her muscles seized up and her bones seemed to freeze on contact, but she didn't care. Her whole body went down and she pulled the band from her hair, shaking it out underwater. When her lungs couldn't take it anymore she surfaced and took in a huge swallow of air. In the water around her and Lissa were hundreds of struggling, drowning spiders.

Lissa looked around. "Where's . . . ?"

But at that moment, Penelope surfaced, too.

"What *was* that?" she demanded, her face red from the cold.

"Are you guys okay?" Jeremy shouted from the shoreline.

Slowly, Ted meandered up next to him, his eyes heavy with sleep, completely unalarmed as he patted his messy hair.

"We're fine!" Lissa shouted back, shivering in her wet pajama top. "Just freezing!"

"Not to mention bound for therapy!" Callie added as she and the other girls began to swim back to shore.

"So many spiders," Penelope said, gazing down at the water and trembling violently. "So. Many. Spiders."

Then Callie, Lissa, and Penelope looked at one another. Callie felt a bubble burst inside her chest, and before she could stop herself, she was laughing. Penelope and Lissa were laughing, too, doubling over. Callie laughed so hard she had to grab Lissa's shoulder for support. Tears squeezed from Lissa's eyes as she pushed her wet blond hair back from her face. Penelope pressed her forehead into Callie's shoulder and held her stomach, gasping.

Again, in a crisis, Callie had forgotten that she was upset with Penelope. Now, she remembered. But she didn't want to completely spoil the moment. Callie moved away ever so slightly and wrung out her thick dark hair.

"Did you *hear* the sound you were making?" Lissa crowed at Callie. "You sounded like a tortured kitten."

"Me? I think *you* actually growled," Callie shot back, splashing at Lissa.

"You guys, I'm not even kidding. I think I might have swallowed one," Penelope said, sticking her tongue out.

"Gross!" Lissa and Callie shouted at the same time, and Lissa splashed Penelope. They all laughed again.

"Well, at least I'm not the only screamer around here," Callie said.

Penelope sighed. "No, you're definitely not."

"Hey, I was only screaming because you were screaming," Lissa put in.

"Ugh." Callie shook her hair back from her face. "I wish I could take a shower right now."

"Well, we're already wet. Hey, Jeremy!" Lissa shouted. "Bring us some shampoo and soap!"

Jeremy crossed his arms over his chest. "Do I at least get a please?"

Callie eyed him, not wanting to admit to the fact that he looked so cute with his hair tousled from sleep. She kept silent while Lissa and Pen clasped their hands under their chins and chorused, *"Please?"*

Shaking his head, Jeremy went into his tent. While he was gone, Ted smirked at the three girls in the pond.

"Did you guys really freak out over a couple of spiders?" he asked.

"A couple? That was an infestation," Callie replied, shuddering again. "They were everywhere inside the tent. Everywhere."

Ted nodded as if this made perfect sense to him. But then, maybe it did. Maybe this kind of thing happened every day in his outdoorsy world. He seemed even more at home in the woods than Lissa, Pen, and Jeremy did.

Jeremy emerged from his tent with a small yellow bottle and a blue soap box, which he passed to Lissa. Callie was still avoiding his gaze. She turned to join Lissa and Penelope as they all washed and rinsed their hair, dunking one another under. Sudsing up her arms and legs had never felt better, even though she was half clothed. The shampoo smelled like pineapples and Callie smiled. Her hair was going to be crazy curly after this, but she didn't even care. Spider-free was all that mattered.

"That was awesome," Callie said when they had all rinsed off.

"And as an added bonus, we won't be hiking in a cloud of B.O. all day," Lissa joked.

Callie and Penelope rolled their eyes as the three of them struggled their way across the rocky, slick bottom of the lake back to Jeremy and Ted, who were waiting on the shoreline.

"Where did those spiders even *come* from?" Penelope was asking as the girls reached dry land.

"I bet there was an old nest in the corner of your tent or something," Jeremy theorized. "If some spider left an egg sac there it could have hatched overnight."

"Okay, Science Boy," Lissa groaned.

"Little Man's right," Ted put in with a yawn. "That's probably exactly what happened."

"If you say so," Lissa replied lightly, smiling at Ted, which earned her a sour glance from Jeremy.

Callie could feel Jeremy's eyes on her as she returned to the girls' tent. Lissa and Penelope started pulling out the sleeping bags and their backpacks, shaking them out onto the ground. Callie steeled herself as she grabbed her own backpack. There were still dozens of spiders inside the tent, crawling on the walls.

Callie felt ill.

Two nights down, she told herself. *Two to go.*

That was if Ted was telling them the truth. If he was really leading them back to his supposed cabin. If he really knew how long it would take to get there.

And if the laugher even intended to let them live that long.

Clenching her teeth, she pressed one knee into the floor of the tent, strained her arm to reach across, and grabbed her journal, glad that she had a chance to stash it away before anyone noticed it. As she emerged from the tent, Jeremy was right beside her.

"Are we ever going to talk?" he asked.

Callie's heart thumped extra hard. But she knew she had to do this. She couldn't spend the next two days avoiding him. Not out here. She opened her mouth to respond.

"Um, you guys?"

Penelope was standing next to the fire pit, looking down at the charred wood from last night's fire like it was oozing blood.

"What is it?" Callie barely choked out. "What's wrong?"

Penelope pointed down. Propped up around the pit in a circle, leaning against the rocks, were a bunch of tiny, rudimentary dolls made out of twigs and tied together with grass. Their arms stuck out at unnatural angles and a couple of the heads were bent to one side, but one doll—the one closest to where Ted was now standing—looked as if it had been crushed under a heavy boot. One arm was severed and the head lolled forward toward the ground.

Callie swallowed hard, fear mounting inside of her. "How . . . how did these get here?"

Lissa and Penelope both fixed her with meaningful stares. They were all thinking the same thing. The laugher had come even closer to their camp than they'd thought.

"I don't know," Ted said.

"You guys, there are five of them," Jeremy said, his voice tight. He pointed at each of the people standing around the circle as he counted off. "One." Lissa. "Two." Penelope. "Three." Callie. "Four." Jeremy. "Five." Ted.

They all stared at the crushed and mangled doll and Callie suddenly couldn't breathe. She knew they were all thinking the same thing—which one of them was *that one* supposed to be?

"You guys," Lissa said, her voice strained as she took a step back. "I think we should pack up and get out of here now."

For once, nobody argued.

SEVENTEEN

"Still no signal," Penelope said, shoving her phone into her pocket as they emerged onto a rocky hillside.

Callie paused, hands on her knees, and gasped for air. The pace had been a lot quicker so far this morning. Probably because everyone was freaked about the dolls.

"What's this?" Lissa asked, nodding at the terrain ahead. She pulled out a water bottle and took a swig, then offered it to Callie, who gratefully sipped at it.

"We've gotta climb down," Ted told them, rubbing his hands together.

"Climb down?" Callie stood on her toes. It wasn't the steepest drop-off, but it wasn't an easy hill, either. To test it, she booted a small rock over the edge. It bounced and rolled, then bounced some more, but she couldn't see where it eventually landed.

"Don't worry," Ted said. "We don't even need ropes. I swear."

He jumped down the first drop and landed on his feet right below them. Then he reached up a hand to Lissa. "Need some help?"

"Uh, no," Lissa said, as if the mere suggestion insulted her, then hopped down right next to him. Ted flashed a grin at Lissa, clearly impressed.

Lissa grinned back at him, then looked up at Callie, Penelope, and Jeremy. "Come on. We'll be fine if we stick together."

Penelope lifted a shoulder, then carefully climbed down to join Lissa and Ted.

"You guys go ahead," Jeremy called to the three of them. "I want to talk to Callie for a minute."

Callie's chest constricted and she shot a pleading look at Lissa, but she was too busy smiling coyly at Ted.

"Okay," Ted said. "Just don't hang back too much."

He turned and moved on with Pen and Lissa beside him, their boots crunching on gravel and dirt.

"Why'd you do that?" Callie asked, the sun hot and fierce on her face. "Lissa just said we should stick together."

"Callie, come on. You can't keep ignoring me," Jeremy said.

Callie clenched her jaw. Her friends were already halfway down the hill. She wanted to talk to Jeremy. Very much. But was now really the time—standing at the top of a treacherous slope that she had no clue how to navigate?

"All right, fine. But let's keep moving." After a moment's hesitation, she jumped down onto the first outcropping of rock and looked up at him. "Why didn't you tell me about Pen?" The minute the words were out of her mouth, she was worried she was going to cry.

"I thought *she* would tell you. I thought she *had*," Jeremy replied, jumping down next to her. "And then a month had gone by and you said something that made me realize she hadn't and then I just felt dumb and weird about it. And then the longer I waited the worse it seemed that I hadn't told you so I just kept not telling you and now I feel like the biggest jerk on the planet."

He sucked in a breath. Up ahead, Lissa and Ted's laughter carried back to them, echoing off the rocks.

"It wasn't intentional. I swear."

Callie rolled her eyes and tromped across the flat black rock to the next drop, this one shallower than the last.

"I thought you guys were like BFFs and I thought girls told each other everything," Jeremy rambled, following her. Callie hopped down and Jeremy did the same. He reached out and touched her forearm, an awkward spot. Callie kept walking. Lissa, Pen, and Ted had disappeared, obscured by a sharply jutting rock. Callie swallowed the lump in her throat as Jeremy kept talking. "Also, it was stupid. Me and Pen . . . we've known each other our whole lives and since we were, like, five, our parents had been joking about how we'd make a great couple. So last year, she kissed me at this party and I thought *Why not?*"

A picture of Jeremy and Penelope kissing in some random basement flashed through Callie's mind and suddenly she had to start moving again. This was why she'd been avoiding this conversation for so long. The details. She didn't want to be able to imagine the details. And Penelope was so pretty . . . of course Jeremy had liked her.

The next drop-off was the longest yet. Callie lowered herself down, carefully placing her foot inside a crevice. She scraped her knee on the way, but her feet landed firmly on the next flat plateau. Jeremy hovered above her.

"But it was all wrong and awkward," Jeremy went on. "Like dating my sister or something. It was nothing like it is with you."

Callie's heart skipped a hopeful beat. She waited for him to climb down next to her, then lifted her chin defiantly, not ready to give in. "What's it like with me?"

He laughed, but his cheeks colored. "You know what it's like."

Callie crossed her arms over her stomach. "No. I want you to tell me. What's it like with me?"

Jeremy shrugged like the answer was obvious. "It's perfect."

There was a long moment of silence. Jeremy's words ping-ponged throughout Callie's head, warming her heart, relaxing her shoulders.

"Come on, you two!" Ted shouted, making Callie jump. She looked down and saw that his hands were cupped around his mouth. Penelope and Lissa stood beside him. "Let's keep it moving!"

"Are we okay?" Jeremy asked hopefully, his brown eyes wide.

Callie blew out a sigh. There was still a part of her that wasn't ready to forgive Jeremy. She wished he'd told her about Penelope sooner. The fact that he'd chosen not to—this lie by omission—ate away at her. But she also didn't want to spend the whole rest of this trip angry. She had more pressing matters to deal with. Like the laugher in the woods, the creepy dolls. What she needed to concentrate on was getting out of here alive. So she could get back to civilization, burn these hiking boots, and make a solemn vow to avoid nature for the rest of her life.

Two nights down, two to go. Please, please let it be true.

"Yeah," she said finally. "I guess."

Jeremy's face fell. Clearly, this wasn't the enthusiastic response he was looking for, but it was the only response she had in her.

EIGHTEEN

As they walked on through a landscape of evergreen trees, Jeremy reached for Callie's hand and she let him take it, but she was still worked up inside.

Every few minutes she'd think of another opportunity he'd had to tell her the truth—like when they'd all hired a limo together for the spring dance in April, or when she'd helped him pack for that trip to the Cape with Pen's family in July, or even when he'd asked to come along on this trip.

Why *had* he been so gung ho to join them on what was supposed to be a girls-only weekend anyway? Had he been afraid that Penelope was going to spill their secret? Was his whole explanation for wanting to be here a lie?

Callie glanced up at his profile. He looked different to her somehow. Harder. She wondered if she was ever going to trust him again.

Ted, Lissa, and Penelope walked in a clump ahead of them, gabbing and laughing like old friends. Ted had found a large fallen tree limb somewhere along the trail and was now using it as a walking stick. Whenever he looked at Penelope, she'd fiddle with her bracelets or brush back her hair. Whenever he looked at Lissa, she stood a little straighter.

"They're both flirting with him," Jeremy said tersely.

"Does that bother you?" Callie asked.

Jeremy tensed. "What? No. But Lissa does have a boyfriend, doesn't she? And I know Zach comes off as this chill jokester dude, but he'd freak if he found out Lissa was into another guy. Besides, what do we even know about Ted anyway? Zip. Zero. Zilch. He just appeared and now we're following him like he's . . . I don't know . . . the pied piper."

Callie heard Penelope laugh, a light trilling sound that was echoed by the songbirds in the trees.

"You know what?" Callie said, releasing herself from Jeremy's grip. "You're right." She swiped her fingers beneath her eyes to clear the sweat.

"And?" Jeremy said, looking confused.

"I may not be great at making campfires or pitching tents or whatever, but you know what I am good at?" she said with a bright smile.

Jeremy smiled back. "I could name about a hundred things."

Callie smirked. Okay. He scored a couple points with that one. "I'm good at being a people person." She slapped his shoulder resolutely. "I'll be right back."

Callie jogged down the trail past Lissa and Penelope, who had fallen momentarily behind, and fell into step beside Ted. He glanced over at her, then did a surprised double take. Clearly he was expecting one of his two admirers.

"What's up, Caliente? Everything okay with you and the Little Man?" he asked.

Caliente. *Hot.* Interesting nickname. She tried to hold back the blush creeping its way onto her cheeks.

"Why do you keep calling him that?" Callie asked, cocking her head. "He's only like an inch shorter than you."

Ted grinned and, much to Callie's surprise, her heart did a flip-flop. His smile was undeniably charming—crooked, teasing, cute. "Therefore, *little*."

She rolled her eyes but couldn't seem to control the upward twitch at the corners of her lips. He was one of those guys. He was handsome and he knew it, and knew how to take advantage of it. Like making every girl fall for him so that they might follow him anywhere.

Except this girl, of course, Callie thought resolutely.

She trained her gaze on the trees up ahead. The ones on this stretch of trail were skinnier and spindlier, with matchlike branches sticking out of mostly bare trunks. They made the landscape around her seem half dead.

"So, it looks like we're going to be stuck out here for a while. Why don't you tell me about yourself?" she suggested.

"Why don't *you* tell me about *your*self?" he asked, a mischievous glint in his eyes.

"I'm serious!" Callie clucked her tongue. "We know almost nothing about you and here we are, following you through the woods."

He smirked, his blue eyes merry and teasing. "I'm not the Skinner, if that's what you want to know."

Callie's heart jumped. As far as she knew, nobody had mentioned the Skinner to Ted. How did he know about him? Was the legend that popular? Why would Ted's mind have gone there right away?

"Well, that's, um, that's good news," Callie said lightly, pretending his comment hadn't completely thrown her. "So . . . are you in school?"

He pushed a bare branch out of the way and it snapped off the tree. "Yep. Just finished freshman year at Syracuse."

Syracuse. A good college. Not easy to get into. So he had some brains to back up the brawn.

"How was it?" Callie asked.

"Fine."

Callie waited for him to elaborate. He didn't.

"That's it? Fine?"

"What else do you want me to say?" he huffed, almost as if he was sick of the question even though she'd only asked it once.

"I don't know . . . did you like your classes? Did you make a lot of friends?" Callie, for one, couldn't wait to get to college. She'd been dreaming of Northwestern—where her mom used to teach, back in Chicago—forever, and was still hoping to go there. The campus felt like home to her, and she also loved the fact that in college, it was considered cool to be geeky about certain things. At least, she hoped that was the case. Maybe she'd be able to write even more, to finally finish a story. Or even a book.

"Do I have a girlfriend?" he shot back, grinning that Cheshire grin again.

Callie shook her head, pushing a wayward curl behind her ear. "You really have a one-track mind, huh?"

"Can't help it," he replied, and used his stick like a golf club to knock a rock off the trail. "When I headed off for my camping trip, I didn't expect to end up hanging out with the three prettiest girls in upstate New York."

Callie blushed again, against her will. Even though she knew it was a line, even though she had a boyfriend, even though Ted was totally smarmy . . . he was still kind of winning her over. What was wrong with her?

"Somehow I can't imagine you being a one-girl type of guy," she countered.

"Well, I have been known to juggle a few different—"

Ted grabbed her arm so hard she let out a yelp of pain.

"Hey!"

"Nobody move," Ted said through his teeth.

Something stirred in the corner of Callie's vision and her heart caught in her throat. Not four feet from where they were standing, a long snake slithered onto the trail.

"Oh my God. What is that?" Callie whispered.

"It's a timber rattler," Ted replied under his breath. "And it'll kill you where you stand."

NINETEEN

Callie could actually hear the wet trail the striped snake made as it shushed over dry leaves. Her throat constricted and she clung to Ted's arm.

"Shouldn't we, like, back out of the way?" Penelope hissed, appearing behind them with Jeremy and Lissa.

"It hasn't seen us yet," Lissa whispered. "Keep still."

Jeremy's breath tickled the back of Callie's neck. The five of them were standing so close together she could feel the body heat coming off the others, could smell their sweat. Suddenly the snake paused and picked up its head. The threat was clear in the tension of its pose. Callie's knees began to quiver.

But the snake wasn't looking at them. It was all Callie could do not to glance over her shoulder to see what might appear more interesting to a deadly rattler than five humans. The snake held its stance for a minute. Callie couldn't breathe.

Then it quickly laid itself out again and slithered off into the trees, moving much faster this time, like it was bent on escape. Once it was gone, Callie's posture relaxed. She glanced over her shoulder toward the trail. Nothing was there.

Jeremy took a step forward. "Callie, are—"

"Are you okay?" Ted asked, turning toward her and gripping both her elbows.

Callie nodded. "Fine. I'm fine."

"All right. Let's give that thing a couple of minutes to put some distance between it and the path, and then we'll keep moving."

"Are there, um, a lot of those snakes . . . out here?" Callie asked.

"Not really." Ted reached up to squeeze her shoulder. "Seeing one of them is rare, so now that we have, we probably won't see another." He dipped his head to look her reassuringly in the eye. "Okay?"

She nodded. "Okay."

Ted let her go and blew out a sigh. "I think we're clear. Let's keep moving."

Callie shivered, shaking off the last of her terror, and reached for Jeremy's hand.

She caught air.

"Jeremy?"

When she turned to look at him, he was glowering at her, the same way he'd looked at Lissa when she'd teased him by the river yesterday. His chest heaved beneath his black *Star Trek* T-shirt.

"Jeremy, what—"

"Nothing," he said, trudging ahead of her, his hands balled into fists. "You heard him. Let's get moving."

Callie was so stunned by his sudden change in demeanor, she couldn't move. Tears stung her eyes and she gulped in the thick air.

When she finally turned to follow the group, they'd disappeared around a bend in the trail, and for half a second she experienced the mind-numbing terror of being completely alone. The trees around her were identical spindly sentries.

Move, she told herself. *Move!*

But, suddenly, she didn't know which way to go. Left was right and right was left. Had her friends gone uphill or down? She wildly scanned the ground for footprints, but her gaze was so blurred she couldn't make out a thing.

Move!

Callie heard a laugh—Lissa's laugh—and took off running toward the sound. Her face was wet with sweat and tears, her backpack slamming painfully against her spine.

What if I don't find them?

But then she came around the bend and nearly ran right into Lissa. Penelope, Ted, and Jeremy had walked ahead.

"You okay, Cal?" Lissa asked, looping her arm through Callie's.

Callie could hardly hear past the pounding of her heart. She felt light-headed and sick, scared and desperate and pathetic.

"Fine," she said, her voice cracking. "Totally fine."

She just wished it were true.

RECOVERY JOURNAL

ENTRY 4

The meek little twit seemed so innocent at first. So clueless. Not anymore. Maybe it was the fact that she was challenging herself, that she was "surviving," that made her so brazen. What a joke. She had no clue what it really took to survive. The kind of sacrifices a person has to make. The kind of pain one has to endure. Honestly, watching her attempt to flirt made me sick to my stomach. I almost felt bad for her boyfriend. Or I would have. If he wasn't such a gutless loser himself.

He simply stood there. Just stood there and watched it happen. Spineless.

He wasn't a man. He was never going to be a man. So it was obvious: He'd have to be the first to go.

TWENTY

The sun was high in the sky and Callie knew lunchtime was fast approaching, but she had no clue what they were going to eat. She'd added her Snickers bar to the collection of food that Penelope now carried in her pack so that they could split it when the time came. But a dark, insidious part of her wished she'd kept the bar for herself. She imagined sneaking off into the woods to devour the whole thing. Her mouth watered at the very thought of it.

"You guys! Up here!" Lissa shouted.

Callie's heart squeezed. What had they found now, a severed head or something? She looked over her shoulder at Jeremy, who had walked the last mile or so in silence behind her. He barely met her eye, then quickened his pace, skirting past her. Callie jogged to catch up.

What was the matter with him? She was the one who'd been wronged here.

The tree line abruptly stopped at a flat outcropping of rock that ended at a cliff—a sheer drop to nowhere. A huge hill rose up to the right, the slope covered with evergreens, and the blue sky above seemed endless. An enormous bird circled the yawning expanse.

"What kind of bird is that?" Callie asked, taken in by the majesty of it all.

"An eagle." Ted slipped out of his backpack. "Searching for its prey," he added in a menacing voice, then laughed.

Callie responded with a tight smile. Penelope walked up next to her and tugged her earbuds from her ears. They still hadn't talked about yesterday's revelation. Callie wasn't sure how she would, or even if she should, broach it, now that Jeremy had sort of explained. But she also wondered why Penelope hadn't said anything. Wasn't it up to her to apologize for keeping Callie in the dark?

Maybe upstate New Yorkers had a whole different set of social and friendship rules than they had back in Chicago. But if this was how things were going to be in her new life, Callie didn't think she could survive it.

"See that line of downed trees out there?" Ted said, pointing.

Everyone stepped closer to the edge of the cliff, and Callie's head and heart swooped, temporarily switching places. She was looking straight down at the tops of towering trees. It was surreal to have this vantage point when those same trees would have dwarfed her had she been walking beneath them. The realization of this made her dizzy and she took a step back, forcing herself to look up and follow Ted's sightline instead.

That was when she zeroed in on the destruction. Hundreds of trees had been felled and crushed, trunks and branches splintered and bleached white like gruesome, gnarled fingers clawing up through the earth. "That's where your trail would have led you eventually." He turned to grin at Lissa. "Aren't you glad you bumped into me instead?"

Lissa held his gaze for a second, then blushed and looked at her toes. *Blushed* and looked at her *toes*. So now Lissa Barton was bashful? Callie felt as if she'd just stepped through some kind of wormhole into another dimension.

And what about Zach? Callie remembered the painful game of I Never, how she'd learned that Lissa had cheated on someone. Would she cheat on Zach with Ted?

Callie bit her lip. If Lissa had caved and let Zach come on this trip, this little flirtation would not be happening. In fact, if Zach had been allowed to come on this trip, they wouldn't be in this situation at all. He'd hiked the trail they were supposed to be on. He would have known the second they made the wrong turn that had landed them here.

Out of nowhere, Callie felt an itch to dig out her journal and start a new story. One that involved a guy who looked a lot like Zach Carle leading a grinning bunch of hikers safely through the woods. No conflict, no love triangles, no snakes or spiders or creepy dolls. Just a happy nature story.

"So I guess that means you intend to lead us around it?" Lissa said finally, recovering herself.

"That is exactly what I intend to do." Ted reached over, twirled Lissa's ponytail once around his finger, and flipped it, letting it tumble back down her back.

Lissa smiled and tugged on her ponytail. Penelope took a quick swig from her water bottle and narrowed her eyes. Yeah. This was going to be fun.

"My cabin's north of the slide, so we'll be fine." Ted crouched over his backpack and got busy pulling out tools. A box of matches, a compass, and a thermos.

"What's all that for?" Lissa asked.

"You guys hungry?" Ted asked, standing up.

"Um, *yeah*," Jeremy said, sounding annoyed that Ted even had to ask.

"Well, I'm gonna go get us some lunch." Ted clapped Jeremy on the arm. "How about you see if you can get a fire started, Little Man? That should be simple enough for you, right?"

He tossed Jeremy the matches, which hit his *Star Trek* T-shirt right in its *USS Enterprise*, then bounced off onto the ground. Ted scoffed, then took off into the trees at a jog, leaping over a fallen trunk. Lissa bent to retie her laces, picked up the matches, and chucked them at Jeremy. This time, he caught them.

"You guys want to gather some firewood?" he asked, his jaw tight.

"For what?" Penelope lifted her shoulders. "Do you think he has a cooler of burger meat hidden out there somewhere?"

"I don't know, but the guy told me to make a fire, so I guess I'm making a fire."

He trudged over to the tree line and gathered a few sticks in his arms. Callie followed to help, keeping her distance, since she was still getting a cold-shoulder vibe from Jeremy. As she crouched to grab a broken branch, she cast him a quick look, wishing he would look back at her and smile, but he didn't. He just kept working, his jaw still clenched. Callie's insides felt hollow. What was happening with the two of them?

Finally Callie heaved a sigh and went back to drop her twigs on the dirt. Jeremy did the same. Lissa and Penelope had set up a circle of rocks for them and Lissa quickly built an expert tepee out of the kindling, which lit up quite quickly. Jeremy sat back on his heels, avoiding eye contact with everyone.

"What do we do now?" Callie asked, eyeing Penelope's backpack as if she could see the Snickers bar through the blue vinyl.

"Now, we eat!"

Ted appeared through an opening in the trees roughly ten feet from where he'd disappeared. He was holding two very large, very bloody, and very dead bunny rabbits.

TWENTY-ONE

"Oh my God," Callie blurted, jumping to her feet and half hiding behind Lissa. She wanted to gag. "Where did you get those?"

Ted strolled over with his chest out, looking proud of himself. Three smeared lines of red ran down the side of his shirt, as if he'd swiped his bloody hand there. *That explains the bloody marks on his shorts*, Callie thought. *I guess.*

"Traps I set up earlier. Lunch is gonna be a feast today," he crowed, tugging a small red tarp out of his backpack. He slapped the rabbits down on top of it and the bigger rabbit's head lolled to the side. Callie turned and pressed her face into Lissa's back. The top of her skull prickled and she wondered if she was going to faint.

"You're really gonna eat that?" Jeremy asked, rising to stand next to Lissa and Callie. Penelope hovered off to one side, clutching her skinny elbows with her hands.

Ted reached into his bag and pulled out a large wood-handled knife. The blade glinted in the midafternoon sun, sharp and sure. The handle looked almost exactly like the one that had been sticking out of that tree trunk yesterday afternoon. Callie stopped breathing.

"What the what?" Jeremy gasped.

Callie's vision clouded over with gray and black spots.

Dead kids. A boy covered in blood. The broken doll. That laugh in the woods.

Did they really know that laugh hadn't come from Ted? He could have been faking sleep last night when Lissa checked on him.

"Why do you have that?" Lissa asked, pointing to the knife, a mix of intrigue and fear in her voice.

"Survival of the fittest, baby." He flipped the knife over, catching it deftly by the handle, and smiled. "We don't have enough food to feed the five of us over the next day, so we gotta supplement with what the woods provide."

Callie pressed the heels of her hands into her temples. *The Skinner. The Skinner. The Skinner.*

"There's no way I can eat fresh bunny," Penelope said, her nose wrinkling.

Ted shrugged. "You gotta do what you gotta do."

"Can't argue with that," Lissa put in, hovering off Ted's left shoulder.

Callie stared at her friends. How could they just stand there and act like it was no big deal that a perfect stranger had just produced a deadly weapon as if from nowhere?

"Now *she* has got the right attitude," Ted said, pointing at Lissa with the knife.

Then he turned and, with one swift downswing, chopped the head off the first bunny. *Kling!*

Callie's stomach heaved and she tasted bile in the back of her throat. She turned around and shuffled toward the edge of the cliff, struggling to draw in breath. There was another loud *kling* as he beheaded the second rabbit. Callie braced her hands against her knees.

"Ew!" Jeremy groaned. "Ugh. That's nasty."

Callie hazarded a glance over her shoulder. Ted was crouched next to the carcasses, deftly skinning the first rabbit.

She slapped a hand over her mouth and turned away again.

The surviving boy. Half naked, dazed, caked in blood and mud. His friends skinned alive right in front of him. She could picture him so vividly, his hair matted, his eyes wild, his steps staggered.

Help, she heard him beg inside her mind. *Somebody help me.*

A hand came down on Callie's shoulder and she screamed.

"God, chill!" Lissa gasped. "What's the matter with you?"

"Don't tell me you're not thinking it," Callie said through her teeth, keeping her back to Ted and his work.

"Thinking what?" Lissa asked, though it was clear by the glint in her eye that she knew.

"Ted is very good with the skinning!" Callie hissed.

Jeremy moseyed over to join them. "Hey, I admit I don't like the guy, but he wasn't even born yet when those murders happened, Callie," he said in an uncharacteristically condescending tone. "There's no way it could be him. Besides, people skin animals all the time. It's kind of necessary if you're going to eat them."

Callie reluctantly turned to look back at the butchering station. Ted was working swiftly, nearly done with the second rabbit. He leaned past the carcasses, grabbed a couple of extra sticks from next to the fire pit, and started snapping off their excess branches. Penelope stood nearby the whole while, fiddling with her bracelets and watching intently. Maybe she was worried that she'd get stuck out here by herself one day and need to skin something. Meanwhile, Callie's decision to never venture out of civilization again had just been solidified. There would be nothing but concrete, steel, and brick for her from here on out.

"Get a grip here, Cal," Lissa said, crossing her arms over her chest. "He's not a murderer. He just . . . knows what he's doing out here."

She said it with a hint of respect, even attraction. Callie looked Ted over, trying to see *him* and not the knife. Yes, he was good-looking in a rugged way. But he wasn't really Lissa's type. Or Penelope's. Lissa had been with clean-cut, preppy Zach as long as Callie had known her. The only guy Callie knew Penelope had liked was standing next to Callie right now, and he was Ted's polar opposite.

Ted skewered the raw rabbit leg with one of his cleaned branches and set the skewer up over the fire, balancing it against one of the rocks so that the flames licked hungrily at the flesh.

"Whatever. I don't care who he is," Callie said with a sniff. "There's no way I'm eating that."

TWENTY-TWO

They fell one by one. It was the scent of the roasting rabbit that did it. It smelled so much like chicken, it was unbelievable. Lissa was the first to give in. She asked for a leg, sat down with her ankles crossed, and started gnawing on the meat like she was hanging out at KFC. Callie even saw her lick her lips. Once Lissa started eating, Penelope wasn't far behind.

"Oh my God, this is *so* good," Pen said, popping a bit of flesh into her mouth. "You guys have to try it."

Jeremy looked at Callie. His leg bounced beneath him. His eyes were desperate.

"Don't," she said even as her stomach caved in on itself.

"I have to."

He turned away from her and walked over to the fire. Callie sat back on her hands near the edge of the woods. She pushed her legs out, knocked the toes of her boots together, pulled her legs back in again. She thought of the Snickers bar in Pen's bag. Overhead, the circling eagle suddenly let out a cry and dove into the trees below. There was a loud rustle, another caw, then nothing.

Apparently the eagle had finally tracked down *its* lunch.

"You'd better get over here before I eat it all," Lissa chided, sucking on her finger.

"Seriously, Callie. It's really good," Jeremy said.

"Thanks, Little Man," Ted said with a self-satisfied smile.

"Don't call me that," Jeremy muttered in reply, which only made Ted's smile widen.

The breeze shifted, making the fire dance and sending the scrumptious scent of the cooked meat directly toward Callie. Her stomach was basically devouring itself in its desperation. Finally, she shoved herself off the ground and walked over to drop down next to Lissa.

"Give me a piece," she said reticently, holding out her hand. "A *small* piece."

"Ha! Knew you'd come around." Ted reached down and picked up a skewer. Callie couldn't tell what part of the rabbit it was, and she was glad. What she could tell was that the meat had been cooked to a charred perfection. She held her breath, sent a silent apology to all bunnies everywhere, and took a bite.

Her mouth nearly exploded with happiness. The meat was tender and slightly salty and really did taste almost exactly like chicken. She chewed slowly, carefully, waiting for a wave of disgust to hit her, but it didn't. She was eating. And it was good.

"Thanks for this, Ted," Penelope said with a shy smile. "You're officially my hero."

Ted beamed. Lissa reached for a nearby twig and cracked it, tossing both halves in the fire moodily.

"Can you guys imagine what Zach would say if he saw us right now?" Penelope asked, glancing at Lissa.

"Who's Zach?" Ted asked.

Lissa shot Penelope a warning look, but Penelope was reaching for her water bottle. "Lissa's boyfriend."

Callie bit her lip. Lissa was stone-faced.

"You have a boyfriend?" Ted asked, raising his eyebrows.

Lissa took a long gulp of water.

"Not that I'm surprised," Ted added, grinning. "I mean, look at you."

Lissa blushed again. "Thanks."

Penelope stiffened.

Callie felt hot on the back of her neck. This flirt-triangle thing could not end well.

"So. What *would* this Zach guy say?" Ted asked, folding his legs in front of him.

"Hmm . . . he'd say, 'You ate *what*?'" Penelope cried.

"And then he'd be all like, 'Dude. I'd totally eat that,'" Jeremy said, putting on a low, doofy voice that sounded almost exactly like Zach's.

"Oh my God! That's so him!" Penelope laughed.

"No it's not," Lissa said, but the red blotches on her cheeks betrayed her.

Callie tried to ignore the appreciative glance that passed between Penelope and Jeremy—a glance she wouldn't have even noticed two days ago. Instead, she took another bite of her rabbit. With the sun shining down on her face and her hunger sated, she felt a lot less grumpy than she had earlier and she refused to dwell on anything negative.

In fact, she felt kind of proud of herself. If someone had told her a week ago that she'd be eating roasted rabbit today, she would have laughed. But here she was, trying new things, doing what it took to survive.

RECOVERY JOURNAL

ENTRY 5

Sometimes people do amaze me. They amaze me with the depth of their stupidity, their ignorance. Their ability to rationalize their idiotic decisions. But mostly, I'm shocked by their naïveté.

They had no clue, out there on their own. No idea what they had gotten themselves into, how much danger they were in. That total confidence and assuredness in one's safety is mind-boggling to me.

But that doesn't mean I didn't relish it. That I didn't love every minute of it. It was so pathetic, yet so utterly, purely perfect. In this situation, the element of surprise would not be an issue. I had them exactly where I wanted them.

TWENTY-THREE

That night Ted led them off the beaten trail to an almost perfectly round clearing. Already stars were winking to life within the darkening sky. There was a used fire pit at the center of the packed dirt.

"Been here before?" Lissa asked, tossing her golden hair over her shoulder as she put down her bag.

"Use it all the time," Ted replied with a wink.

Jeremy heaved a sigh, dropped his bag, and lay down on the ground, using his backpack as a pillow. "I can't move."

"Well, I have to go . . . do my thing," Callie said. She wanted to get into the woods and back again before it got too dark. No more surprise guests and getting lost during her pee breaks, thank you very much. "I'll be right back."

"Don't you know you're never supposed to say that?" Ted asked.

"Say what?" Callie asked, hesitating.

" 'I'll be right back.' " He looked around at them. Everyone but Jeremy, who had his eyes closed, stared back blankly. "It's the last thing the characters in horror movies always say right before they get their guts torn out by the ax murderer."

Callie's insides twisted.

"What's the matter with you?" Jeremy asked, raising his head. "Honestly. Why would you say something like that?"

"What?" Ted threw his arms out. "I'm just joking around."

Callie paused at the edge of the clearing. Every tree seemed the ideal width for some wild-eyed psycho to hide behind. She had to pee worse than ever, but she couldn't make herself move.

"I'll go with you," Penelope offered.

"Um . . . that's okay." Callie wasn't sure if this was worse or better. She and Penelope hadn't been alone since the game of I Never.

"It's okay. She won't bite," Lissa said, as if reading Callie's thoughts.

Penelope's green eyes were round with worry, with fear of rejection. They looked almost too large in her small, delicate face. Callie thought back to what Lissa had said the day before, about how Penelope could be so frail, and she decided to take pity on her. And maybe it was time to finally have this out, as much as she was dreading it.

Besides, going into the woods alone was not an option.

"Okay," Callie said finally. "Let's go."

They stepped into the underbrush together, weeds tickling Callie's ankles. Penelope seemed to be walking heavily, stomping down with her feet, even pressing her toe down and wiggling her ankle here and there.

"What're you doing?" Callie asked.

"Making a trail so we can find our way back," Penelope said.

"Oh." Duh. Why hadn't Callie thought of that? She started to do the same, tromping through the woods loudly, brazenly, destructively. Somehow, it made her feel safer, like maybe she could scare away whatever might be waiting out here for her.

"I'm sorry I didn't tell you," Penelope announced.

She stopped and so did Callie. Already the trees had closed in around them. When Callie looked back, she couldn't see the others. The blood in her veins seemed to simmer with nerves. "Okay. So we're doing this now."

"It wasn't something I liked talking about," Pen continued, as if Callie hadn't spoken. She fiddled with her bracelets, twisting them tight. Somewhere high above their heads two birds chirped at each other. "So when you first moved here, it never came up."

"Okay. So what about after he asked me out?" Callie asked, raking a hand through her curls.

Penelope frowned. "I thought about telling you. I did! But you seemed so happy. Plus, it's not like we were in love or something. It was only three months . . ."

Her words trailed off and she glanced to the side, like she hoped some faerie would flit out from beneath the low-lying plants, wave a wand, and save her from this moment.

Callie wanted to say everything was okay. She could save them both from this endless awkward. But something held her back.

"I just feel so stupid. That I didn't know," Callie said, finding her voice. "It's like you guys all knew this thing, like you were all talking about it behind my back."

Penelope's eyes widened. "No one was talking about it. I swear. It was that much of a non-thing. Lissa and I never even said one word about it after you told us you and Jeremy first kissed. It didn't matter to me."

"But Lissa said you took the breakup—" Callie stopped herself, realizing she might have gone a step too far.

There was a shift in Penelope's stance. Almost imperceptible, but it was there. Her arms tightened over her torso; her knees bent a little closer together.

"That I took it hard? She said that?" Pen asked, her voice quieter.

"Well, I mean . . ." *Stop talking*, Callie told herself. *Just stop*. There was this weird fluttery feeling at the base of her throat, as if a tiny moth had gotten trapped beneath her skin. "She said it's why you went away."

Penelope pressed one hand against her forehead, as if steadying herself.

"I was just being melodramatic! It was my first relationship." She laughed harshly. "If you can call it that."

Callie stared at the washed-out heart motif on Penelope's pink T-shirt, unable to meet her eyes. This was Callie's first relationship, too. And it had been strained all day thanks to the secret her friends had kept from her.

"Anyway, I hope you'll forgive me," Penelope said in a rush, holding Callie's gaze. "Honestly, if I could go back and do it again, I'd tell you as soon as you moved here. I'd invite you over for some big sleepover and tell you every last thing about me, just to avoid this fight."

"It's not a fight," Callie said automatically.

"It's not?"

"No. It's just . . . I just wish I knew I could trust you guys," Callie said. "Back home, my friends were like my second family. We did everything together and knew everything about each other. And I guess . . . I guess I wanted to find that here, too, but now—"

"Omigod, yes! I want that, too. I mean, I don't want you to not trust me," Penelope said, taking a step forward. "That would kill me, if you didn't trust me."

Callie's brow knit. If someone had asked her, honestly, how she thought Lissa and Penelope felt about her before that moment, she would have said that she was sure they both liked her, but that they didn't truly care. They cared about each other first and foremost, which was natural, since they'd been best friends since kindergarten. Penelope's outpouring of emotion was surprising.

"Really?" Callie said finally.

"Yes! Really!" Penelope glanced past Callie's shoulder as if she was checking to see if anyone was listening. "Callie, I don't know if you realize this," she whispered. "But honestly? You're my best friend."

Callie laughed. She couldn't help it.

"I'm serious!" Penelope cried, looking offended.

"But you and Lissa have known each other forever," Callie said.

"Yes, and I'll always love Lissa, but lately I've been noticing our friendship is kind of . . . one-sided," Penelope said, her voice so low Callie could barely hear her. "I mean, she blows off half of what I say completely, and laughs at the other half."

Callie took a breath. She couldn't deny that assessment.

"But you listen. You don't judge. You're a good person, Callie. A good friend."

Callie's heart expanded inside her chest. She was so touched she felt tears sting her eyes. "Pen. That's so sweet. You're a good friend, too."

She reached out her arms and the two girls hugged. "Just don't tell Lissa," Penelope said.

Now they both laughed. "I won't," Callie promised.

They pulled away, and at that moment, a large branch cracked and a voice came from behind them.

"Don't tell Lissa what?"

TWENTY-FOUR

Jeremy stood two feet away, looking angry.

"Jeremy!" Callie breathed, relief flooding her heart.

"What *is* this?" Jeremy blurted. "You forgive her and not me? How is that fair?"

Penelope took a step back. "Um . . . I think I'll leave you guys alone."

She cast a wary look over her shoulder as she found the trail she'd made. Then she ran back to the clearing gracefully, like a leaping doe. Callie faced Jeremy, confusion and fear pounding behind her eyes.

"I don't understand," Callie said. "*You're* the one who's been rude to me all day long."

"Oh, please," Jeremy scoffed. "What do you expect when you're flirting with that jerk back there?"

Callie's jaw dropped. "Flirting?" she squeaked. "I was not flirting!"

But her face felt hot even as she said the words. Because maybe, possibly, she had been flirting with Ted. But only just a little.

"I saw the way he touched you after that snake took off into the woods," Jeremy said. "What were you trying to do, punish me or something? I thought I explained."

"I wasn't trying to punish you. I was just talking to the guy and then, yes, suddenly found myself in a life-threatening situation. He was only making sure I was okay."

"Yeah, well, that's my job," Jeremy said, deflating slightly.

"It's not your *job*," Callie snapped. "I can take care of myself pretty well, in case you haven't noticed." She paused, feeling her annoyance rise, then added, "And I'm sorry if Ted stepped on your testosterone or whatever. But that doesn't mean you get to blow me off for the rest of the day, when *you're* the one who's been lying all this time."

"Oh, so we're back to that?" Jeremy said, taking a step closer. "Do you even know why I volunteered to come out on this hike with you? You don't know even half the story about your friends, Cal. Penelope isn't—"

"Dude. What're you doing?" Lissa stepped up behind Jeremy. "This is supposed to be a girls' pee break, Science Boy," she said. She shooed him with her fingers. "Go find your own restroom."

Jeremy sighed and shook his head. "Fine." He looked at Callie. "I'll talk to you later. I mean, if you want to be bothered."

Then he turned around and was almost instantly swallowed by the trees.

TWENTY-FIVE

"So you were homeschooled?" Lissa asked Ted as they sat around the fire later that night. "What was that like?"

The two of them had settled in next to each other on Lissa's red blanket and seemed to inch closer with every passing minute. Callie sat directly across from them with her headlamp on, reading *Jensen's Revenge*. Jeremy played solitaire on his own blanket, while Penelope had perched herself on a rock nearby and extracted her bracelet-weaving materials from her bag.

Jeremy muttered something under his breath and Callie glanced surreptitiously over at him as he gathered up his cards. Her heart ached to fix things between them, but she didn't know how. Was he really angry at her for talking to Ted when he'd spent months keeping a huge secret from her?

With a sigh, Callie turned her eyes toward the sky, where millions of stars were crowded so densely they practically blotted out the dark. Never in her life had she seen so many stars.

Her stomach grumbled. For dinner, they had split Penelope's last two granola bars and each had a handful of dry fruit and M&M's, plus a cup of water.

Callie found her mind wandering to thoughts of hamburgers and fries and big, colorful salads. Ted had guaranteed they'd get to his next set of traps by lunch tomorrow. Callie was already salivating for more roasted bunny.

Which kind of made her want to strangle herself.

"My mom did most of the actual teaching, but my dad made sure I got in the physical fitness requirements," Ted was saying, cracking a large branch and tossing half of it into the fire, where it settled perfectly into the tepee formation with the others. "I could do twenty pull-ups by the time I was twelve."

"Show-off," Jeremy whispered.

"Wow! That's impressive." Lissa reached over and squeezed Ted's bicep. He pulled up his sleeve and exposed his black tattoo. It was a long dagger with blood dripping from the end.

Not a good sign, Callie thought, gripping the edges of her book.

"Thanks." Ted grinned, his teeth glinting in the firelight. "I was pretty proud of it."

"I like your tattoo." Lissa ran a fingertip down the length of the inked blade. "I'm going to get one as soon as I turn eighteen."

"Oh yeah? Where?" Ted asked.

"I was thinking the back of my shoulder." Lissa indicated the spot with her hand. "But I don't know what to get yet."

"Whatever you decide on, I'm sure it'll look good on you," Ted told her.

Callie fought the urge to roll her eyes.

"Do you think you'll ask Zach for his opinion before you decide?" Penelope asked pointedly.

Lissa's eyes flashed. "I know I didn't ask for yours."

Penelope huffed a sigh and slapped her plastic box of string closed.

"I think it's time for bed," she announced, shoving a bracelet into her pocket. She picked her way around the fire toward her tent. "Are you guys coming?"

"Since when are you the house mother?" Lissa asked, carefully folding Ted's sleeve down again. Callie noticed that Lissa's hand lingered on his arm.

"It's late," Penelope stated tonelessly.

"I *am* kind of tired," Callie said, stifling a yawn. "Maybe we should all call it a night."

Jeremy unfolded himself from the ground and shook out his blanket. Callie thought about saying something—maybe trying to ease the tension between them—but he turned away from her, which made her heart sink. Lissa didn't move a muscle.

"You coming, Lis?" Penelope asked.

Lissa's knee leaned against Ted's. She was looking at his hands as he cracked another branch.

"In a few minutes," she said.

"Fine," Penelope said with a sigh. "Do whatever you want."

Callie froze. That was the harshest thing she'd ever heard Penelope say to Lissa.

Now Lissa did turn, and glared at Penelope. "Don't I always?"

Callie felt a prickle down her spine. The last thing she needed right now was for Lissa and Penelope to turn on each other. It was about the only thing that could make this entire adventure worse.

But before she could think of anything to say to defuse the situation, Penelope had turned and yanked open the zipper to their tent, diving her head inside so fast, it was as if she was running for her life. Callie waved good night to the others—though Jeremy had already disappeared—then followed.

Inside the confines of the tent, Penelope's anger seemed to take up space. She was shoving things into her bag, yanking them back out, then shoving them back in again, and muttering something under her breath. Finally she found a paper Tylenol packet that looked soggy and half destroyed, ripped it open, and swallowed both pills dry. Her face screwed up in pain as the capsules traveled down her throat.

"You okay?" Callie asked, settling on top of Lissa's sleeping bag to give Penelope some extra room. She was about to offer to get some water, but they had almost no fresh water left, and they both knew they had to conserve some for the morning.

"Whatever, it's her funeral," Penelope said, in an acidic voice. She shoved a lock of light brown hair back from her scowling face.

"What do you mean?" Callie's mind's eye instantly flashed on the knife sheathed to Ted's belt. "You think Ted's, like . . . a bad guy or something?"

"No, but who knows? I mean, not necessarily, but . . . that's not even the point." Penelope stopped her frustrated reorganizing and sat down. "It's just . . . she always needs to be the center of attention. Every guy has to like her. Every girl has to either want to be her or be afraid of her. The world must revolve around Lissa Barton."

"I never thought you minded that," Callie said, picking at some dirt beneath her fingernails. "I mean, you always seemed fine with who she was. Everyone has always seemed fine with who she was. Except maybe Jeremy."

Penelope blew out a breath.

"I know," she said. "I just worry about her."

"Worry?" Callie couldn't have been more surprised if Penelope had just said Lissa was actually a brain-eating zombie in disguise. Lissa Barton was not the type of person anyone had to worry about. Ever. She could hold her own in pretty much any situation.

"Why's that?"

Penelope crawled inside her sleeping bag, lying flat on her back and staring up at the ceiling. Slowly, she folded her hands across her chest in a prim, pious way that made Callie randomly think of a body laid out in a coffin.

"I just worry that it's going to get her into trouble someday."

TWENTY-SIX

A twig cracked.

Callie sat up in the dark, her heart racing. Was that psycho back, getting ready to leave them more gifts around the fire? Her fingers curled into the puffy polyester of her sleeping bag as she held her breath. It was so pitch-black inside the tent, she couldn't see as far as her toes.

There was a soft crunch outside, then a pause, then a crunch, then a pause. Callie squeezed her eyes closed. Someone was walking alongside the tent, so close she was sure that if she pushed her hand into the vinyl wall, she could brush his leg through the fabric.

Crunch. Pause. *Crunch.* Pause. *Crrrrunnnch.*

Callie whipped around, grabbed her headlamp, and turned it on. The light illuminated the lumpy forms of Lissa and Penelope tucked inside their sleeping bags.

"Jeremy?" Callie called shrilly.

The footsteps stopped. Callie bit down on her tongue. Her back trembled. She clung to the strap on the headlamp, her palms tacky with sweat.

"Jeremy? Ted? Is that you?"

Lissa stirred, letting out a soft sigh as she rolled over in her sleep.

Silence.

"Jeremy, please," Callie whispered. "Please, if it's you . . . say something."

Callie gnawed at her lip. She could hear the person breathing. Could practically *feel* the rhythm of his breath. She bit down harder and tasted blood.

Don't hurt us, she thought, her shoulders curling in on her. *Please, please, don't hurt us.*

Then, suddenly, the footsteps started again, much faster this time. Callie was sure that whoever it was meant to dive into their tent, but instead the footsteps took off. Seconds later she heard a rustle of branches, and then, nothing. Nothing but her own ragged breathing.

A single tear spilled down Callie's cheek as she tried to get hold of herself. Part of her wanted to wake up the girls and tell them what had happened, but what was the point now? The time to wake them, she realized, would have been when she'd first heard the footsteps.

Measuring her breathing as best she could, Callie slowly got onto her hands and knees and inched toward the tent door. She closed her eyes, said a quick prayer, and ever so carefully unzipped the door until a small flap fell forward toward her. The crickets were so loud it was like being at a sold-out stadium show. Callie squinted into the darkness and saw that Ted was still in his sleeping bag. He snorted and rolled over. Alive.

Callie let out a breath and glanced toward Jeremy's tent. She was wide-awake now. There would be no more sleeping. And, suddenly, she wanted more than anything to just make up with Jeremy. He was right after all. She'd forgiven Penelope. If she could forgive Jeremy, too—and explain that she had zero interest in Ted—then the rest of this awful trip would at least be slightly less awful.

An owl hooted. Callie gathered up all her courage, unzipped the door the rest of the way, and stepped out into the night.

TWENTY-SEVEN

Wait a minute. What am I thinking?

The second Callie was out in the open air, she realized what a target she was. Two minutes ago she'd heard someone creeping outside her tent and now she was coming out and being all like, "Hey! Here I am! Hope you have your knife, cuz I'm ready to be slaughtered!" What was wrong with her?

There was a noise deep inside the trees, a great, swooping *whoosh*. Callie yelped. She ran for Jeremy's tent and, with nothing to knock on, grabbed the poles and shook the whole structure as hard as she could.

"Jeremy! It's me! Wake up!"

There was a long moment of silence. Callie looked over her shoulder. The eye-level branches in the trees right behind the girls' tent rustled. Oh, God. What was it? What was out there?

"Callie?"

"Open the door! I need to talk to you," Callie hissed.

It seemed to take forever, but finally, Jeremy unzipped the door. Callie practically hurled herself inside.

"What's the matter?" Jeremy asked.

"I heard something," Callie said, breathless. She felt much better now, being inside, being with him. Even if the walls were made of flimsy cloth, at least there was something between her and the outside world. And if she couldn't see the trees, it was harder to imagine the many creatures that could be out there watching her. The prying eyes. The rusty, bloody weapons.

"Why're you up?" Jeremy asked with a yawn.

He sat down on the far side of the small tent. As far away as he could get from her inside the close space, Callie noticed.

"I couldn't sleep," she said sheepishly. "I heard footsteps outside my tent."

"It was probably Ted," he said acerbically.

"No. When I looked out he was sleeping." Callie sat up on her knees, her headlamp hanging around her neck and illuminating her lap. "There was someone out there, Jeremy. I swear."

Jeremy huffed a fed-up sigh. "The Skinner does not exist, Callie. Not anymore. Can't you just get over it?"

"But someone *is* following us, Jeremy. Who left those dolls around the fire?"

He clenched his jaw and looked away, unable or unwilling to answer that one.

Callie's face burned with hot indignation. "And why do you keep talking to me like that?"

"Like what?" he asked.

"Like I'm five years old and stupid?" she shot back.

"I'm not." Jeremy's jaw dropped. "I mean, I didn't."

"Yes, you did. And you did it earlier, too. I already have Lissa talking down to me. I don't need you doing it, too."

"You know, that's what I don't get. If you don't like the way Lissa talks to you, then why do you follow her around like a puppy dog?" Jeremy retorted. "Why did you even come on this trip you clearly don't want to be on?"

Callie felt like she'd been punched in the chest. *A puppy dog?*

"I thought it was cool that I came on this trip. That I'd do that for my friends," she whispered harshly. "At least that's what you said two days ago."

"Yeah, well, that was before," he said, looking away.

"Before what?" she asked, not sure she wanted to hear the answer.

"Before it became totally clear that they mean more to you than I do."

Callie stared. *They don't*, she thought. *You mean more to me than anyone.*

But something stopped her from saying it. Things had changed between them on this hike. Callie had seen sides of Jeremy she didn't recognize. If *he* cared about *her*, he should have been doing everything he could think of to make things right between them, not snapping at her for having a conversation with the guy who was saving their butts. Not criticizing her for the way she acted around her friends.

"Wow." He let out a breath. "Way to not deny it."

Callie made a move for the door. Her eyes were full of tears. "I'm going back to bed."

"I should've never come on this trip," he said.

Callie looked over her shoulder at him. "Well, then maybe you should go home."

He lay down flat on his back and folded one arm over his eyes. She could see nothing of his face.

"I would if I could," he said. "Believe me."

Callie kept gulping air, but it felt like she was taking in mouthfuls of water. Each one made her choke. She didn't want to say the words that soured the tip of her tongue, but she had to. She knew she had to.

"Are we breaking up?" she asked.

Jeremy didn't move. "Yeah," he said quietly. "I think we are."

RECOVERY JOURNAL

ENTRY 6

People today. It's as if nothing truly matters to them. Nothing is sacred. Nothing is precious. This "live in the now" attitude might work for some desperate thrill-seeker types, but it's simply destructive. That's all there is to it. And that night . . . that night is a night I will never forget because of how sick they made me. They disgusted me. Sneaking out in the dead of night. As if they were somehow safe. Safe among one another, safe in the woods, safe in the world. They had no respect for themselves.

And people with no respect for themselves don't deserve to live.

TWENTY-EIGHT

"Well, you don't have to be such a jerk about it!" Penelope shouted.

Callie's eyes popped open. It was light inside the empty tent, but not bright, and she could feel the humidity clinging to her skin. It was going to be another long, hot, gray day.

Three nights down, one to go, she thought instantly.

Callie rolled over onto her side and her nose hit something hard. Her journal, open facedown, the uncapped pen next to it. She noticed that the skin on her cheeks felt dry and tight, and suddenly realized why. Her heart clenched as everything that had happened the night before came rushing back to her.

The footfalls outside her tent. The conversation with Jeremy. Then lying here between her sleeping friends, silently crying, the tears streaming down the sides of her face and pooling in her ears.

Jeremy had broken up with her. Or she had broken up with him. Who knew? What mattered was, they were no longer a couple. Six months, done. Just like that. After she'd gotten control of her sobbing, she'd decided to write about it, and had scrawled six pages about how angry and sad and confused she was. Getting the words down on paper had allowed her to finally fall asleep. She could only hope Pen and Lissa hadn't snuck a peek at the journal when they'd woken up earlier.

Trying to breathe past the tightness in her chest, Callie shoved her journal into her bag, then rooted around for a ponytail holder. She quickly plaited her curly hair into a passable braid and sighed, her back slumping.

She and Jeremy were no longer a couple.

How was she going to explain this to everyone?

"Calm down, Pen. He was just making a comment," Lissa snapped from outside the tent.

"Stop telling me what to do!" Pen replied.

Yeah. That didn't sound good. Callie unzipped the tent and peered out. Ted and Lissa sat on one side of a small fire, bent over a sleeve of crackers and the tube of peanut butter, the sight of which made Callie's stomach grumble. Penelope hovered beside them, one hand massaging her right temple. Jeremy peeked his head out of his own tent. He and Callie locked eyes and Callie felt like she'd been shot.

"I'm just saying, there's no point in making a fire when we have nothing to cook," Ted said as Callie climbed out of the tent. The air was as thick as honey.

"Well, I was bored!" Penelope whined. Her hair was pulled back in a haphazard bun and her eyes were hyperalert, like she had downed too much coffee. "You guys all slept so late. What did you want me to do, go out hunting?"

"Now *that* would have been useful," Ted joked.

Callie stepped around to the side of the tent where she'd heard someone walking last night. She crouched to inspect the ground. There was nothing. No footprints, no broken twigs or crushed grass. But the earth was wet. It had rained at some point overnight. Maybe the weather had cleared the evidence. Callie stood and walked toward the fire just as Jeremy approached from the opposite direction.

"You were only up so early because you went to bed so early," Lissa said to Penelope, sandwiching two crackers around some peanut butter and taking a bite. "If you weren't so lame—"

"Where'd you get the crackers?" Jeremy asked.

"Ted had them," Lissa said. "You want?"

"Oh, hey! You're up!" Penelope brightened when she saw Jeremy and Callie. She bent over her weaving supplies and stood up with two bracelets, one in each hand, which she held out to them. Callie saw that one was thick, and the other thin, but they both were made of the same color string. Blue and aqua. Jeremy's favorite color and hers, woven together in perfect harmony. "I made you matching bracelets," Pen said with a smile.

Neither Callie nor Jeremy moved, so Penelope stepped forward and shoved the bracelets into their hands.

"I just want you guys to know how much I support you. I think you make a great couple and I'd hate it if what happened the other day . . . you know . . . got between you."

Callie stared down at the colorful bracelet, her eyes so full of tears she might as well have been swimming underwater.

"Put them on!" Penelope prompted.

Jeremy shifted from foot to foot, his heavy boots crunching pebbles on the ground. "Um . . . actually . . . we broke up."

"What?" Penelope gasped.

"When?" Lissa demanded.

"Last night," Callie said. She looked around at the three of them. Penelope stunned, Lissa confused, Ted unconcerned. "In the middle of the night. I went to his tent and . . ."

"Dude. When a cute girl sneaks into your tent, you're not supposed to break up with her," Ted chided, popping another cracker into his mouth.

Jeremy shot him a look of death and handed the bracelet back to Penelope. "Thanks anyway. That was nice of you." Then he turned around and crawled into his tent.

"Sorry, Pen." Callie handed her bracelet back, too, then returned to her tent and zipped the door closed behind her. She tried to cry quietly, but she was sure the others could hear her sniffling as she pressed her face into her sweatshirt.

"Well," Lissa said finally. "This isn't gonna be awkward."

Callie let out a sob as tiny raindrops began to pitter-patter the roof of the tent.

TWENTY-NINE

"This is all my fault," Penelope whispered to Callie as they set out for the day's hike. "I'm so sorry."

"No. It's not," Callie assured her, watching Jeremy's back as he speed-walked ahead. Ted was out in front of Jeremy, and Callie and her friends were walking slowly, trying to get themselves some privacy.

"It's actually my fault." Lissa gripped both backpack straps tightly. "If I hadn't said anything during I Never, you guys would be fine right now. I'm such a jerk."

Callie and Penelope both gaped at Lissa. Had she just said something negative about herself?

"What?" Lissa said with a smirk. "It's not like I'm gonna go throw myself off the next cliff we come to. Chill."

Callie managed a smile—a small one—and looked at the sky. The rain had come and gone, but it was completely overcast. The sky looked white.

"I'm glad you said something during the game," Callie told Lissa, even though it wasn't entirely true. Half of what she'd written last night had been her going back and forth about whether she would have erased the knowledge of Pen and Jeremy if she could have. But the truth was, she'd never know if she would have been better off clueless. She knew what she knew now and there was no reversing it.

Lissa lifted her eyebrows skeptically.

"No. I am. I mean, it stinks right now. It hurts. Like, it's-very-possible-that-we-left-my-heart-back-at-the-campsite kind of hurts."

Lissa chuckled, but Penelope fixed her with a concerned look. She placed her small hand against Callie's arm in a comforting way, and it did make Callie feel better. Just slightly, but still.

"But it's better to know than to be kept in the dark," Callie went on forlornly. "And if Jeremy and I can't handle it . . . we can't handle it."

Lissa took a deep breath, watching the guys as they crested a small hill and gradually disappeared down the other side. "That's very mature of you, Callie."

Callie smiled. "Thanks."

"But just know if you want me to dead-leg him right now, I will."

"Lissa," Penelope scolded.

Callie laughed. But she wasn't angry at Jeremy, really. Just sad. And the idea of him falling over on the trail didn't exactly bring the happy.

"Thanks," she said. "I'll think about it."

"Was that what you were writing about in your diary last night?" Penelope asked tentatively.

Callie's stomach clenched. "You saw my journal? You didn't read it, did you?"

"What? No!" Penelope's eyes went wide and her hand fluttered to her chest. "Callie, I would never. I just saw it next to your sleeping bag, that's all."

"Did *you*?" Callie asked Lissa, her head light with panic.

Lissa crossed her heart and shook her head. "I swear."

Callie willed her pulse to calm. She would die if anyone ever saw what was in that journal. Simply die.

"Good. I mean, thank you. I just . . . I write personal things in there, you know? Thoughts, feelings . . . stories," she admitted, scrunching her eyes and waiting for the mocking.

But it didn't come. When she looked at her friends again, they didn't seem horrified or even surprised.

"I get it," Penelope said. "Your secret's safe with us. Right, Lis?"

"Of course," Lissa replied.

Penelope shot Callie a private smile, clearly thinking about the other day when Callie had said the same thing to her. Callie's heart felt warm. She and her friends *were* bonding. Just not over the fun, carefree stuff she'd hoped to bond over.

When they got to the top of the hill, they paused. The guys had stopped in the middle of the trail for a water break, so Lissa and Penelope pulled their bottles out, each offering to share with Callie. She took a swig from Pen's bottle and wiped her mouth with the back of her hand.

"You guys? Since we're all down with the honesty . . . there's something I want to say," Penelope announced. She shifted from foot to foot, like she was trying to find solid ground. Callie tensed. *Oh, God*. What if she was about to admit that when she'd woken up early this morning, she *had* read through Callie's journal?

"Okay. Spill," Lissa said with a laugh in her voice.

"I think I might like Ted. Like, like him like him." Penelope looked directly at Callie as she said this, clearly terrified to meet Lissa's eyes. Callie's lungs flooded with relief, but in the next second, her heart thumped with dread. She held her breath, waiting for Lissa's reaction.

"Really?" Lissa asked.

Pen's gaze flicked in her direction. "Yes. Really. Is that okay? I mean, I know you like him, too."

Lissa's brow knit and she gave Penelope a dubious look. "What? Please! I have Zach." She looked down the hill, where the boys were readjusting their gear. "Ted's cute and all, but it's not like I was going to ask him out or anything. If you *really* like him, you should go for it."

Penelope's jaw dropped in surprise. "Really?"

Lissa laughed, her head thrown back, like this was hands down the funniest conversation she'd ever had. "Of course! Come on, Pen. Like I would ever let a guy come between us."

She looped one arm around Pen's neck and dragged her close, knocking Penelope off balance. Even so, Penelope was beaming. For the first time in a couple of days, Callie realized she looked like herself again.

"Hey, we're down one couple. Maybe you and Ted'll pair up and we'll come out of this with a new one. It's the circle of life," Lissa joked, taking another swig of water as she released Penelope.

Down one couple. It sounded so simple for something that felt so completely world-ending.

"I don't know. I still can't believe you and Jeremy broke up," Penelope said to Callie.

Jeremy looked over at them, as if he knew he was being talked about. Callie expected him to glance away quickly, embarrassed or ashamed or whatever, but he didn't. He just stared, his expression hard. Callie's stomach suddenly felt hollow.

She'd thought she knew him. Really knew him. But now she wondered if she ever knew anything about him at all.

THIRTY

"Hear that?" Ted asked, a bright smile on his face as he paused in the center of the trail.

Callie held her breath and listened. Penelope leaned toward Ted. Birds chirped merrily in the trees, but there was also a more insistent sound, like a pleasant gurgle.

"Water?" Lissa asked, her eyes lighting up.

Ted nodded. "Water."

He walked at a fast clip down the hill and the rest of them followed. Callie was careful to keep her distance from Jeremy. Within minutes they had come to a burbling stream fed by a waterfall. Callie gasped at the beauty of the water tumbling over the sudden drop and frothing at its base.

Lissa dropped her bag and knelt at the water's edge to splash her face and suck some of the liquid from her palm.

"You really shouldn't drink that until Ted purifies it," Jeremy warned.

"It's just snowmelt. I'm sure it's fine," Lissa replied, splashing her face and the back of her neck. "What do you think the Native Americans used to drink?"

Jeremy pushed his hands into the side of a tall boulder, pressing one heel back to stretch his quad muscle. "Native Americans didn't have to deal with the thousands of pollutants we have today."

Callie looked away. How could he be acting so normal and

chatty? She'd feel much better if he was being quiet and broody, like her.

"Native Americans didn't have to deal with the thousands of pollutants we have today," Lissa mocked, pitching her voice so high she could have been a cartoon mouse. "When I want a science lesson, I'll ask you for one."

Jeremy flung his bag down right next to Lissa, so close she jumped up. Then she teetered, and Callie thought she might fall into the water. But Ted reached out to grab her. Callie found herself gripping Penelope by the arm.

"What the heck was that?" Lissa demanded.

"I'm so sick of your attitude!" Jeremy shot back.

"Oh, really? Well, I'm sick of your face!" Lissa replied.

"Lissa!" Callie blurted, then realized that, technically, she wasn't supposed to be defending Jeremy anymore.

"You guys, please don't fight," Penelope said, closing her eyes and bringing her hands to her head. "I have a headache and this is really not helping."

"Great! Now you're causing Penelope actual physical pain," Lissa chided Jeremy, getting right up in his face. "Nice work."

"She didn't say it was my fault," Jeremy replied. "Maybe it's the incessant sound of your know-it-all voice that's doing it."

"You guys, please," Callie said quietly.

"All right, all right!" Ted stood between Lissa and Jeremy and held up his hands. "Penelope's probably dehydrated and hungry. That could give anyone a headache."

Callie noticed that Penelope was trembling. "It's not a migraine, is it?" she asked her friend. Her aunt Lola got migraines a lot and always needed to lie down in her room with the lights off to get over them.

Pen shook her head. "I just . . . I feel all fuzzy."

"Let's sit down, then," Callie said. She gently took Penelope's hand and led her over to the water, helping her sit down on a dry rock near the edge. Penelope let her pack slip off her shoulders, then put her head between her knees. She cupped her hands in the water until she had gathered a pool between her palms, then brought it to her face. Water leaked out between her fingers.

"You okay, Pen?" Lissa asked, coming over.

Penelope lifted her face. Her skin looked ashen. Tiny droplets of water clung to her long eyelashes. "Is there anything to eat?"

"I'll get you some trail mix," Lissa offered, shooting Jeremy a dark look.

"I've got a couple of traps set up near here," Ted told them. "Maybe I could get a real lunch together."

"That sounds like a plan," Lissa said as she crouched in front of Penelope with about an ounce of trail mix nestled in her hand.

"Lissa, you stay here and keep an eye on Penelope," Ted said. "Get a fire going if you can. Caliente and Little Man, you come with me." Ted turned back toward the trees, but Jeremy didn't move.

"Stop calling me Little Man," he said tersely.

Ted paused and turned around again, very, very slowly. His chin was lowered, his brow shadowing his eyes. "You gonna start with me, too? Because I don't think you want to go there."

Callie's heart skipped a beat. Ted sounded like he meant business. Jeremy's hands curled into fists. For a second no one moved. Callie held her breath. The last thing they needed right now was a brawl.

"Forget this," Jeremy said finally.

He grabbed his backpack from the ground and stormed off,

disappearing into the trees. He was gone so fast, it was as if the woods had just gobbled him up.

"Jeremy!" Callie shouted. "Where're you going?"

But there was no reply. There was nothing but the hissing of the water, and the low, eerie creak of the trees in the wind.

THIRTY-ONE

"I'll go with you guys," Lissa offered, capping her water bottle after filling it in the stream. "Pen, you'll be okay here by yourself, right?"

Penelope nodded and laid herself out on the ground, using her backpack as a pillow. She closed her eyes, wisps of her light brown hair tossed over her face by the breeze. "I'm just gonna rest."

"I don't know. Shouldn't we wait for Jeremy to get back?" Callie asked, biting her lip worriedly.

"He's probably just blowing off some steam," Ted said, re-adjusting the knife sheath on his belt. "He'll be back in a minute."

Callie stared at the still trees where Jeremy had disappeared, then slowly looked over at Penelope. "You sure you're all right out here alone?"

"It's fine. Go." Penelope waved weakly. "If the Skinner shows up, he can have me."

Okay. That just seemed like inviting trouble.

But Lissa turned around and clapped her hands. "All right, then! Let's go get lunch."

"Follow me," Ted said, heading in the exact opposite direction from the one Jeremy had chosen. Callie glanced over her shoulder for some sign of Jeremy, but there was nothing. She hoped he knew what he was doing out there. She hoped he'd be back by the time they were. She still cared about him, even though she was angry. She wished she could just take back the last few days and start over.

But there was no starting over.

"Want a sip?" Lissa asked, offering Callie her water bottle.

"Sure. Thanks." Callie tipped her head back and let the cool water sluice down her throat. When she righted herself again, she felt dizzy and grabbed Lissa's arm.

"You okay?" Lissa asked.

"Lost, dehydrated, starving, and stuck in the woods with my ex-boyfriend? Sure. Why wouldn't I be okay?" she joked, then sighed. "Sorry if I've been kind of out of it today."

"Please." Lissa smirked, stepping over a fallen birch. "None of us are handling this situation very well. Except for Ted the Adventurer."

Callie let out a short laugh. "I like that. He does seem pretty cool about being out here, like it's just another challenge to conquer or something. Guess that's what happens when you grow up on a mountainside."

"Son of a psycho!" Ted shouted suddenly.

He had stopped a few paces ahead of them.

"Or maybe not," Callie said.

"What's the matter?" Lissa jogged over to Ted, and Callie quickly followed. He was standing in a tiny patch of dirt, staring down at his trap. It was empty.

"Oh. You didn't catch anything?" Callie asked, her heart sinking.

"No, I didn't catch anything because the trap was destroyed!" Ted shouted. He crouched over and picked the trap up, then threw it down again with a loud, metallic clatter. Callie had no clue what a rabbit trap was supposed to look like, but she could tell now that the cage part was dented, and there was some kind of spring mechanism that was lolling free when it probably should have been tensed. "What kind of jerk does this?"

"So there *is* someone else out here," Callie said, her pulse quickening.

"Well, clearly!" Ted shot back. He stood up and faced them. "Honestly, who would do this?" he demanded again, looking at Callie and Lissa with accusing eyes. "I'm serious! Tell me! What's the point of messing with someone else's traps? It's not like you get anything out of it! People suck, you know that?" He leaned back and bellowed toward the sky with clenched fists, the tendons on his neck bulging. "You suck!"

Callie was frozen in fear. She'd never seen anyone have a fit like this in her life. Lissa stepped in front of her.

"Ted, just chill," she said in a low, soothing voice. "We still have the Snickers bar and some cereal and peanut butter. We'll figure something out."

"It's not that," Ted said, whirling on them. "I just hate these people who traipse up in here like they own the place—like they have any frickin' clue—and just take what they want, *do* what they want. Who do these people think they are?"

Ted slowly approached Lissa until his nose was mere millimeters from her face. Callie's breath was short and shallow as she hid behind her friend's shoulder, wishing she wasn't such a wuss. Every doubt she'd had about Ted in the past forty-eight hours suddenly blared inside her mind.

Who is this guy? Where did he really come from? What does he want with us?

Ted took in a breath, then backed off and shook his head. "Sorry. I'm sorry," he said, holding up his hands. "Clearly this is something I've obsessed about a lot. It's not your fault. It's theirs. The idiots who have no respect for nature or for other people. You guys are pretty cool. I know you're not like that."

He returned to the trap and crouched next to it again, muttering to himself. Lissa cleared her throat and inched forward.

"Is there . . . I mean . . . is there anything we can do?" she asked. "Jeremy's pretty good with machines and electronics and stuff. Maybe he could fix it."

"They trashed the spring load. The whole thing's useless."

For a long moment, Callie and Lissa simply hovered there, waiting, as Callie wondered why they weren't just going back to the stream to rejoin Pen and hopefully Jeremy. Her stomach roiled angrily.

"Let's go back," Lissa said finally.

"Shh . . ."

Ted crossed his legs and laid his wrists across his knees with his eyes closed. Callie stared at Lissa.

What is he doing? she mouthed, wide-eyed.

No clue, Lissa mouthed in reply.

Just then a small brown bird flitted up and perched atop the broken cage of the rabbit trap. Ted's eyes opened and without warning, his hand shot out and grabbed the bird. There was an ugly crack and Callie felt like she would gag.

"Did you just—" Lissa didn't have to finish her sentence. Ted dropped the lifeless bird on the ground, its neck snapped.

Ted looked Lissa and Callie coolly in the eye and a shiver went down Callie's spine. "Survival of the fittest."

THIRTY-TWO

"You're looking a lot better."

Ted reached around Penelope's back and kneaded her shoulder. She blushed, dipping her head forward and smiling. Over a small fire, the carcasses of two small birds popped and hissed. Lissa, Callie, Ted, and Penelope had already eaten two of them.

Jeremy still had not returned.

"Thanks. I feel a lot better," Penelope said.

Ted jostled her slightly, pulling her in toward his side and hugging her. "See? I told you food and water would do it."

Lissa took a swig of water, staring pointedly into the flames. Callie kept her eyes trained on Ted. Because a) she couldn't believe he was flirting so blatantly with Penelope when it had seemed clear for the last two days that he favored Lissa, and b) she was slightly nervous that at any moment he might reach over and snap Penelope's neck.

She also couldn't stop thinking about the vandalized trap and what it meant. Was the laugher still out there, possibly very close by? Callie shivered in the blistering heat. And where was Jeremy? What had happened to Jeremy?

"You're sure staring a lot this afternoon, Caliente," Ted said suddenly, swiping his grease-stained fingers on his shorts. He took the last two birds off the fire and laid them down on his tarp to cool. "Don't tell me *you're* crushing on me now."

The way he said it was so egotistical, implying that he knew both Lissa and Pen were crushing on him already. Which, of course, they were, but still.

Penelope shot Callie a curious look, but Callie shook her head to tell her no. She was not crushing on anyone. Pen relaxed back on her hands, message received.

"I'm not staring," Callie told Ted.

He cleared his throat. "Listen, I'm sorry if my survival tactics have made you guys uncomfortable," he said. "But you gotta do what you gotta do."

"Where'd you learn to do—that?" Callie asked, the words tumbling from her mouth. She was hoping there was some reasonable explanation for what she'd witnessed. That he wasn't just one of those kids who, at a young age, started killing small animals for sport until he gradually escalated to serial killing.

"What?" Ted asked. "The birds?"

"Yeah." Lissa pushed herself to her feet. "That was really . . ."

"Cool?" Ted supplied, lifting one eyebrow.

Callie fidgeted. "I would have said 'disturbing,' but whatever you think."

Ted's face hardened, his lips all but vanishing as he sucked in a sharp breath. "I spent every summer since I was eight at a survival camp out west," he said. "They taught us how to do everything from building our own shelters to foraging for edible plants to killing anything that moved." Ted pushed a long branch into the ember pit and a flame suddenly burst to life. "And, by the way, I haven't heard anyone thanking me for providing lunch."

"I said thank you!" Penelope protested, her cheeks reddening.

Lissa walked over to the water, bent at the waist, and let her hair trail into the stream. After a few seconds she flipped her head back, spraying cold droplets across the ground. A few fell in the fire, hissing and smoking. Ted looked at her appreciatively.

"Thank you, Ted," she said flatly.

Penelope's face tightened at the shift in Ted's attention. She looked away, resting her cheek on her knees.

"What was this survival camp called?" Callie asked, testing him.

"Why? You thinking about trying it?" Ted asked, tearing his eyes off Lissa and leaning back on his hands.

"Maybe. You never know," Callie said, lifting a shoulder. She was trying to act casual, but her mouth was dry. She couldn't help noticing he'd deftly avoided answering the question. "The apocalypse could come tomorrow and then anyone left would have to live off the land, right?"

Ted laughed as Lissa rooted around in her bag for a comb.

"Girl lives for her post-apocalyptic novels," Lissa said in a jeering tone.

"No, she's got a point." Ted stood up and walked slowly around the fire until his hiking boots were perpendicular to Callie's stretched-out legs. Smatters of blood—some dried, some fresh—peppered the toes. "The meek will definitely *not* be inheriting this earth."

The sun was directly behind his head, casting his face in perfect shadow. Callie shielded her eyes, but the glare was so bright it stung. Finally, she looked at the fire again, purple Ted-shaped dots marring her vision. Ted sat down next to her. His knee pressed into her leg and she fought the urge to move away. She didn't want him to know how intimidated she was. Showing weakness seemed like a bad idea.

"So what kind of survival skills you looking to learn?" he asked. "Maybe I could teach you something."

Callie shrugged. "I don't know. What if a bear walked into this clearing right now?" she asked, forcing herself to look at him. His face was close to hers. "What would you tell us to do?"

"Get up slowly and move away from the food and the water," he said. "A bear comes wandering in here, it's because the scent of cooking meat attracted him. He wouldn't be looking to pick a fight with us. Best thing to do would be to let him have what he wants, then wait for him to move on."

For a long moment he held her gaze, and Callie's heart tripped. She found, to her surprise, that she couldn't look away. His eyes were so blue in contrast with his dark hair, and the irises had much darker blue lines through them. She'd never seen eyes like that before.

"The survival school was called Camp Outback," he said in a low voice. "You should tell your little boyfriend to try it. It might turn him into a man."

"He's not my boyfriend anymore," Callie heard herself say.

And Ted slowly smiled.

"You guys?" Penelope said, looking past Callie's shoulder.

Callie whirled around. Jeremy was standing right behind her and Ted. She hadn't even heard him walk up. Suddenly she realized what he was seeing—her and Ted sitting side by side, Ted's face hovering so close to hers. Her heart pounded like she'd just been caught cheating.

But she hadn't been cheating. And besides, she and Jeremy weren't together anymore.

"What's the matter?" Jeremy spat, glaring at Ted. "Two girls aren't enough for you?"

"Uh-oh, Ted. Don't anger Science Boy," Lissa teased. "He's going to sic the entire Galactic Empire on you now."

Jeremy shook his head and took off up the trail. Callie jumped to her feet and jogged after him.

"Jeremy, wait up!" she called, reaching for his arm.

He stopped and turned so abruptly that Callie collided with him.

"What *was* that, Callie?" Jeremy demanded as Callie staggered back, feeling stung.

"Nothing! He was just . . . telling me about survival camp," she sputtered.

"Yeah. Did he have to be all up in your face to do it?" he demanded. "And call me less than a man in the process? Who does he think he is?"

"Jeremy—"

"And Lissa!" he interjected. "I could *kill* Lissa!"

"Jeremy, calm down," Callie said, her heart hammering.

"Calm down? Are you serious? Calm down?" He brought his fists to his temples and paced back and forth. "You're flirting with him! Don't even try to deny it this time."

Callie's stomach burned. "We broke up, remember?"

"Less than twenty-four hours ago! And it's not like I really wanted to. But you . . ." He paused and heaved a breath. "How heartless are you? All three of you. I bet none of you would even mind if I disappeared right now."

A breeze rustled the trees and Callie saw something move. She turned, letting out a gasp, and saw a shadow disappear behind a thick tree trunk. This time she saw the brim of a baseball cap and, as clear as day, the bulbous hump of a backpack.

"Someone is definitely out there," she said to Jeremy, the certainty of it shaking her to the core.

"What? Not this again," Jeremy said bitingly. "There *was* someone out there—the guy you're busy cozying up to."

"No. He broke Ted's trap," she whispered, nearly desperate with terror. "He's still messing with us, Jeremy."

"Callie, come on. You're just trying to change the subject."

She groaned. "Jeremy. Listen to me. How do you explain the laughing and the knife and the—"

"Ted. All Ted. He was following us the whole time until he finally decided to make an appearance!" Jeremy shot back. "He could have made those dolls himself and left them there while we were sleeping to freak us out."

"But the flash across the pond couldn't have been Ted," Callie whispered furtively. "And the person I heard creeping around the camp last night? Ted was asleep. And someone is out there now, Jeremy. I know it."

"Callie—"

"Fine. You're so sure there's no one watching us? Why don't you just go take a look?"

Callie set her jaw, her arms tight across her chest. Jeremy gazed off into the trees. Suddenly, half a dozen birds startled from the underbrush, cawing and swirling their way into the canopy overhead. Callie saw his Adam's apple bob. He was as freaked as she was.

"Forget it. I'm not going to indulge your little distraction tactic," he said.

Callie narrowed her eyes. "Then I'm going back." She started down the hill, her steps shaky.

"Go ahead," he replied. "But you should know that you're not only embarrassing me by throwing yourself at that guy, you're embarrassing yourself."

An angry heat climbed up the back of Callie's neck. She turned to Jeremy, fuming. "You know what? Don't bother coming near me again."

"Fine by me," he shouted.

And she didn't look back to see if he followed her.

RECOVERY JOURNAL

ENTRY 7

It was a very interesting day. He finally stood up for himself. That was tantalizing. I loved watching him and his twit of a girlfriend fight. Dissension is so much more intriguing than harmony. I feel a thrill whenever someone so much as raises their voice, so that argument in the woods . . . it was a high, I must tell you, and I knew the moment was nearing. I could feel it. I had done a good job so far of keeping myself in check, of holding back, of controlling my . . . urges. But it wouldn't hold much longer. The fighting only made the craving that much worse. I needed a release.

But after that scene on the trail, I started to rethink my plan. He could still be worth something to me. Perhaps he wouldn't be the first to go after all.

THIRTY-THREE

"I just don't understand why we stopped here," Jeremy said that evening.

Callie sat back against the wide trunk of a towering tree, her book open in her lap, though her concentration was so broken she'd read the same line at least fifteen times. She watched Jeremy shove one of his tent rods into its sleeve. The sun had just dipped below the trees, bathing the world in a pinkish glow.

"We stopped here because I happen to know that there's not another suitable spot to camp for five more miles, and it was starting to get dark," Ted said through his teeth. He dropped a rock into the circle he was making for the fire pit. It clacked loudly like an exclamation point and threw up a spark.

"Oh, right. Sorry. I forgot. You know everything," Jeremy said drily.

Callie pressed her lips together. It wasn't just the many gnarled roots that made this spot less than ideal. The area was also way too tight for five people. Especially with everyone snapping at one another.

Lissa rummaged around inside the girls' tent while Penelope sat against another tree, rubbing her temples with both hands.

"I never said I know everything," Ted grumbled.

"Maybe not, but you imply it every time you open your mouth," Jeremy replied, yanking at the zipper on his tent.

Penelope dropped her hands. "He does have a point, Ted. Maybe you should—"

"Nobody asked you to chime in," Ted snapped at her. "Why don't you just sit there and look pretty? The men are having a chat."

Callie wanted to speak up, to tell Ted he was being a ridiculous chauvinist, but Lissa beat her to it.

"What did you just say?" she demanded, emerging from the tent. She had a battered New York Yankees cap pulled low over her forehead.

"Oh, so suddenly I *am* a man? What changed your mind? Realized you were totally outnumbered?" Jeremy asked bitterly.

"You can't talk that way," Lissa said snidely, squaring off with Ted.

"I was just kidding!" Ted said, throwing his arms out. "God! Take a joke!"

"I don't even know why we need a fire." Lissa walked over and kicked a rock into the center of the circle. "It's not like we have anything to cook."

"And that's my fault?" Ted snapped.

"She didn't say that," Penelope barked, the heel of her hand pressing into her forehead.

"Guys!" Callie shouted at the top of her lungs, standing so quickly her book hit the ground. "Stop!" She was so pent up with anger, fear, hunger, and exhaustion, she could hardly see straight.

Everyone turned to look at her.

"This situation is bad enough without all of us fighting over stupid things," she said.

"You're the one who wanted to trust this guy, Cal," Jeremy said. "Don't look at me."

"Hey! I didn't *have* to help you guys," Ted spat.

"No one asked you to!" Jeremy shot back, his face growing red.

"That's it!" Callie shouted. "Forget the fire. I say we break up the Snickers bar five ways and everyone turns in for the night. The sooner we get to sleep, the sooner we wake up and get moving again. Deal?"

No one said a word. Callie shook from the exertion of taking charge, but she also felt kind of proud of herself—especially when no one protested. Penelope pushed herself up unsteadily and walked past Callie. She fished the Snickers out of her bag and handed it to Lissa. The sight of the chocolate made Callie's stomach rumble. Lissa held out an open palm to Ted and he handed her his knife. Glancing around in the rapidly waning light, Lissa's eyes settled on Callie's book, lying forgotten in the dirt. Lissa walked over to it, crouched down, and used the back as a cutting board.

"Hey!" Callie protested.

"Got any better ideas?" Lissa asked, lopping off the end of the bar. Callie was amazed at how comfortable Lissa seemed wielding that big knife.

"Here." Lissa walked over to Ted and slapped a piece of chocolate into his hand, then passed the knife back to him. She gave Jeremy his share, then turned to the girls. "Ladies? Let's eat."

She led the way to the tent and crawled inside. Callie looked over at Jeremy, but he simply slipped inside his own tent, resolutely zipping the door closed behind him. Not even a quick "good night."

"So that's it?" Ted asked as Callie and Penelope followed Lissa. "No fire, no stories, no nothing?"

"Sorry, Ted," Penelope said, her posture slumped. "You'll have to entertain yourself tonight."

She glanced at Callie as she said this, and Callie's pulse fluttered. Clearly Jeremy wasn't the only one who thought Ted and Callie had been flirting earlier. Was Pen mad at her? When this trip was over, was she going to have a single friend left?

"You are so boring," Ted sighed.

Lissa stuck her head out of the tent. "You want me to take your share back? Because I will. Don't be such a jerk."

For the first time since they had met him, Ted looked momentarily unsure of himself. He clearly didn't like the fact that Lissa was putting him in his place. Then he set his jaw and the swagger returned.

"Take it," he said, and chucked the one-inch square of chocolate at her. Luckily, Lissa was a born athlete and her reflexes kicked in fast enough to catch it. "I don't need any help from you."

Then he turned around and walked into the woods on his own. No flashlight, no matches, no nothing. The girls watched him go, mute and still, as the darkness descended around them.

THIRTY-FOUR

Callie waited for Ted to reappear, but he didn't. What was with these guys and the dramatic exits? Overhead, two black birds chased each other from tree to tree, but something about the way their wings moved didn't seem right. When Callie squinted, she realized they weren't birds, but bats. Her whole body shuddered.

"Do you think he's coming back?" Penelope said finally.

"Who cares?" Callie said in a moment of bravado, knowing full well that if he didn't come back, they were in very serious trouble.

"Yeah. We don't need him," Lissa said, and held out his piece of chocolate between her thumb and forefinger. "And we've got extra Snickers!"

Callie managed a wan smile, but then the bats took flight again and she ducked inside the tent, accidentally kicking Lissa in the shin.

"Ow!" Lissa protested.

"Sorry," Callie said as Penelope joined them inside.

"Whatever. I have so many bruises at this point I can't remember where half of them came from."

Lissa rubbed her shin as they sat in a circle at the center of the tent, knee to knee to knee, holding their chocolate. Caramel oozed out onto Callie's palm, and her mouth watered. They were finally going to eat the Snickers. If they didn't get to Ted's cabin tomorrow, there was no telling when they'd see real food again.

"Ready?" Lissa said finally.

"Ready," Callie and Penelope said.

Lissa tossed her whole piece into her mouth. Penelope took a very small bite. Callie bit off half, and the second the chocolate touched her tongue she wanted to die. She'd never tasted anything better in her life. She chewed it slowly, then ate the second piece, feeling sad and thirsty as it went down.

"Oh, shoot."

Callie opened her eyes. Pen had dropped what was left of her portion on her leg. She picked it up and ate it, then swiped at the chocolate stain on her shorts.

"Great. Now I have to change."

"We're all dirty. Can't you just deal?" Lissa asked, holding up her hand to show them the dirt caked beneath her short, polish-free nails. Most attempts at cleanliness had gone out the window two days ago.

"I can sleep in dirt and sweat, but I'm not gonna sleep with food on me," Penelope said. "What if some wild animal smells it?"

"Yeah. We should wash that out," Callie said.

She grabbed a water bottle from Lissa's bag and dabbed some onto the chocolate stain while Pen changed into cotton sweat shorts. Once Callie had rubbed the spot mostly clean, Penelope took her shorts and hung them outside on a hook next to the tent's door. Then they settled in again and Lissa held Ted's piece of Snickers out in her flat palm, over the polyester of Callie's sleeping bag.

"What do we do with it?" Penelope asked, fiddling with her bracelets. Her face looked thinner somehow—sunken—as if she hadn't eaten a thing in weeks. In the dim gray light of the tent, Callie saw that there were purple splotches under her eyes.

"You can have it if you want," Callie offered, though her stomach pinched as she said it.

"No. No. We'll split it," Penelope said.

"You can't split a piece of chocolate that small into thirds. It'll just fall apart." Lissa leaned forward. "I say we each take a bite. Pass it around."

"I don't want your germs," Penelope said, scrunching her nose.

"Whatever. We're gonna die out here anyway. Might as well live on the edge," Callie said, feeling reckless. She plucked the chocolate square from Lissa's hand and took a bite.

Lissa and Penelope both cracked up laughing.

"This trip has turned you dark," Lissa said, patting Callie on the shoulder. "I like it."

Callie shrugged, then handed the remainder of the bar to Penelope. She took a bite and handed the end to Lissa, who inspected it, her eyes narrowed.

"Hogs," she joked. Then she popped the last bit into her mouth.

Callie laughed and leaned back on her hands. Penelope winced, as if suddenly hit with a new wave of pain, but she didn't say anything. She and Lissa both looked as perfect as ever, just slightly more dirty—their hair darkened with sweat and grime. There was a scrape on Lissa's right arm and purple bruises dotted her legs, but otherwise, she was still Lissa. And Pen was still Pen, graceful as a ballerina. Callie wondered how she looked, then decided not to care.

This was what this trip was supposed to be about. At least, this was how Callie had imagined it. She and her two best friends hanging out, bonding, sharing chocolate bars and jokes and secrets and stories. She hadn't expected the fighting and hunger, the fear and uncertainty. She hoped that when it was over, this was the moment she'd remember. Not her fights with Jeremy or Ted snapping the birds' necks or the shadows in the woods.

"What?" Penelope asked, her eyes wary. "Why're you looking at us like that?"

"Nothing. It's stupid." Callie dusted off her hands.

"Tell us!" Lissa said.

Callie felt warm all over and scratched at a bug bite on her elbow. "Just . . . I like this. Us. Hanging out. Do you realize that the three of us have barely been alone together this whole time? I mean, except when we're asleep."

Or when you're *asleep while I tremble with terror*, she amended silently.

"Well, you had to go and bring Science Boy," Lissa said, stretching her arms over her head.

"Lissa," Penelope chided.

"Sorry. No. You're right." Lissa let her arms drop. "Science Boy is not the issue. I mean, yeah, Ted has been a nice distraction for some of us . . ."

Penelope winced again.

"Pen? Are you okay?" Callie asked.

Penelope drew in a deep breath. "Sorry. Yeah. It's just that this headache doesn't want to go away. I should have brought more Tylenol with me, but oh well."

She squeezed her eyes like she was trying to squash the pain, then opened her eyes. They wavered for a second before focusing on Lissa. "Sorry, I'm good. What were you saying, Lis?"

"Just that Ted obviously doesn't compare to you guys," Lissa finished. "No offense, Pen."

"No, it's okay," Penelope said, her bottom lip wobbling a little.

"I might have been slightly wrong about him. He was so obnoxious out there just now."

Lissa nodded. "So like I said before—let's not let the guys . . . either one of them . . . get between us. Let's not let them ruin this trip for us. What's left of it, anyway. Deal?"

"Deal," Callie said.

Penelope smiled, blinking away the tears in her eyes. "Deal."

Lissa turned and crawled into her sleeping bag. Outside, the sky had gone so dark that it was hard to see inside the tent, and Callie and Penelope bumped elbows and shoulders a few times, giggling as they slipped into their own bags. When Callie finally laid her head down, she was surprised by how tired she felt. As she started to doze off, she realized she was smiling. Deep inside she felt a tentative hope springing to life.

Tomorrow they would be at Ted's cabin. Tomorrow she would shower and eat real food. She'd call her dad and he'd come get her. She'd get to see her mom, at last. Tomorrow she would walk out of this with her friends, knowing their relationship was stronger than ever.

THIRTY-FIVE

Callie raced through the woods, her lungs on fire, too terrified to look over her shoulder. The thing was gaining on her. She could hear its breath, feel its black claws reaching for her, grazing her sweat-matted hair. The underbrush bit at her ankles, trying to trip her and drag her down. But then she felt an itch on her arm, another on her face. It was an army of spiders. They plucked their way up her legs, dropping from the trees into her hair and down her shirt. And still, the thing gained.

She opened her mouth to scream and the claw came down on her shoulder, sharp nails digging into her soft skin. Callie whipped around to face it, but it wasn't a thing at all. It was Ted. He wore a battered baseball cap, and in his hand was his hunting knife, blood dripping from the tip.

"Survival of the fittest," he said calmly.

And then he raised the knife.

Callie awoke with a start, her breath so short her vision went fuzzy. Outside the tent was an orange glow, and Callie heard the pleasant crackling of a fire. She pressed her lips together to stifle a whimper and gripped her sleeping bag.

It was a dream. Just a dream.

Callie unzipped her sleeping bag, trying to cool off. She glanced at Penelope, who was curled up on her side, sleeping stilly for once. When Callie rolled over to see Lissa, she wasn't there.

The breath caught in Callie's throat, and then she heard Lissa's laugh. Callie sat up straight and edged toward the door of the tent. Then came Ted's low-pitched chuckle. Ever so carefully, Callie unzipped the tent until she could peek through a tiny slit. The fire burned just a few yards away. Lissa sat with Ted, basking in its glow, her head on his shoulder. They looked like a couple that had been coupled forever.

So much for claiming that her relationship with Zach mattered. So much for thinking that Ted was a jerk. So much for her stepping aside so Penelope could have him. So much for friends being more important than guys.

With a sigh, Callie zipped the door closed again and lay back on her sleeping bag, wondering idly if sleep would ever come, and whether, after experiencing that awful nightmare, she even wanted it to.

THIRTY-SIX

"Callie! Callie, *wake up*!"

Callie was aware of a sharp ache in her left shoulder. She pried her eyes open to look at Penelope, who was squeezing her arm.

"What?" Callie groaned, rolling over. Her shoulder radiated pain across her back and she reached up to knead the muscle. She must have slept on it for hours without moving.

"Lissa's not here," Penelope whispered.

Callie turned to look at Lissa's sleeping bag. The front was folded down and rumpled and her backpack had fallen over across it. Had she never come back inside after her midnight rendezvous with Ted?

"What time is it?" Callie asked, still trying to blink the sleep from her eyes.

"Six a.m.," Penelope replied.

"Omigod, are you kidding?" Callie moaned. "*Why* did you wake me up?"

"Because!" Penelope sounded exasperated. "Where is she?"

"I don't know!" Callie whined, sitting up. Somehow she didn't feel like sharing the cozy scene she'd witnessed the night before. "Maybe she woke up early. Maybe she went out to pee."

"Or maybe she snuck out in the middle of the night to go be with Ted."

Bingo.

Callie looked at Penelope. Her hair was pulled back in a loose ponytail and her eyes were bright with suspicion. Her skin had a sweaty sheen to it that made it seem green in the soft light.

"So what if she did?" Callie asked. "Can I go back to sleep now?"

"That doesn't bother you?" Penelope demanded as Callie lay back down. "After that whole speech she made last night about how we're more important to her and we shouldn't let the guys come between us? We practically made a pact."

Callie took a deep breath and blew it out. "Pen, I know you've been friends with Lissa longer than I have, but if there's one thing I know for sure about her, it's that she's going to do whatever she wants to do."

"Well, I'm gonna go find her." Penelope reached over to unzip the tent. Callie noticed that Pen already had her hiking boots on and tightly laced. She'd also changed back into the cargo shorts they'd put out to dry the night before. "I'm tired of letting Lissa do whatever Lissa wants to do. She has to start considering other people's feelings."

Callie rocked herself up onto her elbows. "Really? You're going to do this right now?"

"I have to. If I don't do it now I'm gonna chicken out." The look she gave Callie at that moment was so vulnerable, so hopeful, that Callie knew she couldn't just stay there and go back to sleep. She had to have Penelope's back.

"Okay, fine."

Callie whipped the sleeping bag off her legs, shoved her toes into her flip-flops, and followed Pen out into the humid morning air. The sun was up, but dim and hazy behind a layer of clouds. Everything seemed still except for one slim, curling line of smoke still snaking up from the center of the pit. On the far side of the clearing, Ted lay dozing in his sleeping bag, alone.

Penelope slowly turned around until she was facing Jeremy's tent. A crow cawed in a nearby tree.

"You don't think she's . . ."

"No," Callie said, staring at the square green structure. "No way."

She walked over to the tent and peeked through the mesh window. Jeremy was splayed across the top of his sleeping bag in red sport shorts and his Innovators Club T-shirt. He was, thank goodness, alone.

"So where is she?" Callie asked, a tiny inkling of fear beginning to work its way up her spine.

"Lissa!" Penelope shouted, startling Callie so much she jumped. "Lissa, where are you?"

Ted sat bolt upright in his sleeping bag, instantly wide-awake.

"What's going on?" he asked.

"Lissa's gone," Callie told him.

"What do you mean, gone?" Jeremy asked from inside his tent. He sat up and gazed through the window, letting out a huge yawn.

Callie walked around Jeremy's tent and paused. "Lissa!" she shouted. "If you're out there, answer us!"

The others began to shout as well, staggering their cries as they fanned out across the clearing.

"Lissa!"

"Lissa, this isn't funny!"

"Lissa, come on! Where are you?"

Slowly, they walked toward the center of the clearing, meeting around the fire pit. The dying smoke made Callie feel like choking. Her heart was in her throat now. She stared at the rocks around the fire and thought of the dolls, one of them crushed and torn.

"She can't have just up and left," Ted said as Jeremy walked up beside him.

Suddenly, the images from Callie's nightmare came flooding back. The terror of the chase, the composed, calculating look on Ted's face as he raised the knife for the kill—

"You were up with her in the middle of the night," Callie said to Ted. "Where is she?"

"Wait, what?" Penelope blurted. "I was right?"

"She went to bed around one o'clock," Ted replied calmly. "Last I saw of her, she was crawling into the tent."

"But her sleeping bag doesn't look slept in," Callie replied, a suspicious edge to her voice.

Ted lifted his palms, utterly unruffled. "All I can tell you is what I know. She went into the tent at one and I passed out. Next thing I know, you two are shouting for her."

Callie's fear seemed to harden inside her chest. "You guys, what if whoever's been following us took her?"

She waited for Jeremy to tell her she was imagining things. For Ted to laugh it off. They didn't. The fear tightened its grip.

"Where *is* she?" Penelope said under her breath.

Suddenly an awful, bloodcurdling scream split the air. Callie jumped and grabbed on to Jeremy without thinking. No one breathed. Then the scream came again, and two large birds took off into the sky.

"It was just a bird, you guys," Ted said, exhaling. "Just a bird."

Callie released her grip on Jeremy and set her jaw. "We have to find her," she said. "Now."

THIRTY-SEVEN

"Lissa!" Callie shouted, her voice cracking. Her eyes flooded with tears. "Lissa, please! Where are you?"

"Lissa!" Penelope called out in the distance, her voice almost like a bird's song. "Liiiisssaaa!"

Callie could make out the top of Penelope's head as she navigated the wilderness, ducking and sidestepping the branches and spiderwebs. Jeremy was nowhere to be seen, but Callie knew he was about twenty yards beyond Pen. Or at least, he should have been, if he was keeping to Ted's plan. Mr. Survival Camp had suggested they fan out to cover the most ground, but keep one another in their sights for safety. No one had argued.

Off to Callie's right, Ted walked slowly and silently like a predator, scanning first the ground, then the space directly in front of him, then the sky, methodical and precise.

If he did know where Lissa was, he was putting on a good show. Callie's empty stomach twisted painfully. She pressed her hand into the trunk of the nearest tree. She was exhausted and starving and thirsty, her mouth so dry her tongue kept sticking to the insides of her teeth. It wasn't even six a.m. and already the air was hot enough to have soaked the back of her T-shirt with sweat. But this was nothing. Nothing at all compared to the terror coursing through her veins. Every tree trunk looked the same. Every leaf was a copy of the ten thousand leaves she'd passed in the last five minutes. There were no colors other than green and brown. No sounds aside from the birds twittering in the trees. And Lissa . . . Lissa was nowhere.

But she had to be *somewhere*, didn't she? People didn't just disappear. How could she have snuck off without anyone hearing? And why? Where would she go?

Something was very wrong. Callie could feel it in her bones. Lissa wouldn't just bail on them. But part of her wanted to believe that was exactly what Lissa had done. Because if she had, that meant she was okay. It meant she was a jerk, but okay.

"Callie? You all right?" Ted called out.

She rubbed her slick palms against her hips.

Don't let him see your weakness, she told herself.

"I'm fine!"

"Keep moving, then. You fall too far behind and you'll get lost, too!"

"Right! Sorry!"

Callie turned and stepped over a dip in the ground. "Lissa!" she shouted.

She looked up at the branches crisscrossing overhead, and the second she did, her foot hit something hard. Her stomach swooped as she fell forward, throwing out her arms. Her wrist jammed against a rock and sent splinters of pain up her arm. She turned over, then froze.

There was a hand. A slim white hand, lying four inches from her toes. A hand with dirt caked under its nails.

THIRTY-EIGHT

Callie screamed so loudly she felt her tonsils vibrate. Her eyes trailed up to the wrist, then the arm. She saw the blue Mission Hills High basketball T-shirt Lissa had gone to bed in the night before. Saw the skin of her neck, red and raw and torn. Saw her hair—her beautiful thick blond hair—tangled and matted with dirt and flung carelessly over her mouth. Callie leaned forward and crawled to her friend, pushing aside a large fern frond, and there were Lissa's eyes. Blue and staring. Dead.

"Lissa!" Callie screamed at the top of her lungs. "Lissa! No!"

She grabbed Lissa's shoulders and shook them, but Lissa's head only lolled around like a rag doll's. Bile rose up in Callie's throat and she scuttled back on her hands and heels, then turned over and heaved into the underbrush. She gasped for breath, coughing, sputtering, bracing her hands against the ground.

She's dead. Lissa's dead.

Footsteps rustled the growth all around her. Callie had just scrambled to her feet when Ted appeared. He took her by the shoulders, gently but firmly.

"What? What is it? What's wrong?" Ted asked.

Callie shook her head. There was no air. She was going to pass out if she didn't get air. Ted had killed Lissa. She was suddenly sure of it. He was the only person out here she didn't know. The only one who could ever hurt her friend.

"Can you breathe?" Ted asked.

Callie shook her head again. He bent her down so that she folded in half and her face was touching the tall fronds at her feet. Was this where he would take out the knife and skin her alive? When he was done, would he go after her friends?

"Breathe!" he said. "You can do it. Just suck in one good breath."

Callie closed her eyes and concentrated. Finally her windpipe opened and she gulped in oxygen, coughing and gasping, then coughing again. When she finally got control of herself, she stood up, clinging to Ted's arm. Horrified with herself, she let him go and staggered away until she hit the side of a tree.

"Lissa." Callie pointed at the ground, her finger shaking uncontrollably. "Lissa . . . Lissa . . . Lissa."

Ted's eyes went wide when he saw the body, and he took a halting step back. His hands flew up to cover his mouth. "What happened?"

Callie stared at him. He seemed legitimately shocked. Suddenly she didn't know which way was up. Had Ted done this? Was he just a good actor?

Or was it the laugher? Was he out there right now, watching them? Deciding which one of them would be next?

Callie's eyes darted fretfully across the trees, but she saw nothing. Her mind turned over and over and over, trying to make sense of everything, trying to piece out everything she'd seen and heard and suspected, but it was all white noise. Nothing would come into focus.

Lissa was dead. Lissa was *dead*.

"What do we do?" Callie asked, letting out a sob. "I don't know what to do."

Ted fell to his knees at Lissa's side. He lifted her wrist and checked her pulse, then reached for her neck. His hands were so steady, Callie realized. Like he'd done this before. He leaned in closer before falling back on his haunches. For a long moment, he didn't say anything. The birds in the trees flitted about from branch to branch and sang like nothing was wrong in the world. Ted pushed his hands into his dark hair.

"What did . . . I mean . . . how did she . . . ?" Callie asked.

Ted's hands fell. "It looks like someone strangled her."

A horrible, desperate sound escaped Callie's lips. Some part of her had known this. Had seen it—the marks on Lissa's neck— but it hadn't sunk in until Ted spoke the words aloud.

Suddenly, there was a loud cracking noise directly behind Callie. She whirled around, just in time to see a huge, hulking guy charging toward them through the trees. Callie's heart all but stopped beating.

This is it, she thought. *This is how I die.*

THIRTY-NINE

"Dude. What is going on?" the guy demanded.

Callie blinked a few times, trying to focus her terrified, weightless mind.

"Zach?" she whispered.

It was him. Lissa's boyfriend. Tall, broad, handsome, sunburnt, baseball cap pulled over his wavy blond hair. He was wearing a blue New York Giants T-shirt that clung to his defined chest and arms. The backpack on his back was army green and bulbous, with a sleeping bag tucked up underneath.

It was Zach, Callie realized, both relieved and furious at once. *Zach was the shadow I've been seeing in the woods. He's the one who's been following us.*

"You're freaking me out, Callie," Zach said. "Why do you look like you've just seen a ghost?"

"You know this guy?" Ted asked, turning to face Callie.

Callie was speechless. If Zach had been following them all this time, did that also mean he was the one who'd left the knife and the baby doll and the other dolls for them to find?

Suddenly, Callie was more terrified than ever.

"It was you," she said to Zach, breathless, backing up.

"Me what?" Zach asked, his brow creasing.

"You stole that doll from Lissa's house and ruined it and left it for us to find," Callie said in a rush. "You're the one who's been stalking us, laughing to creep us out. You're the one who's been sneaking around our camp, messing with our heads!" Callie looked behind her and saw Lissa's limp foot inside its hiking boot. "You killed Lissa!"

Zach laughed. "Good one," he said jovially, rubbing his hands together. "You almost had me for a second."

"Why?" Callie screeched, tears filling her eyes. "Because she wouldn't let you come on this trip? Because you were jealous? What kind of psychopath are you?"

Zach calmly took a step toward Callie and put a big hand on her shoulder. "Callie, dude. Chill. Where's Lissa? Did she figure out I was here? Is she about to jump out and try to scare me or something?" He shook his head, laughing, ever the jokester. "Man. I knew she'd figure out it was me. What's she got planned for payback?"

"Zach! *This is not a joke!*" Callie shouted. "Lissa is dead. She's right there!"

Trembling, Callie turned and pointed. Zach looked down and the life seemed to drain from his face. He took two shocked steps back and pressed his body against the trunk of a tree, where, ever so slowly, he sank to the ground. It was as if he'd gone boneless.

"Omigod. Omigod. Omigod," Zach said over and over again. "Lissa. No. I—I thought you were . . . I thought you were joking. I didn't . . . I didn't do this, Callie. You have to believe me."

"Why would I believe you?" Callie cried. "You just appeared from thin air! How did you know where we were if you haven't been following us?"

Zach bent his head into his hands. He sobbed—two short, bleating wails—then looked up with wet eyes. "I have been following you. And yes, I've been messing with you," he said through his tears. "But I was just having a little fun. I wanted to teach her a lesson for leaving me out. I'd never actually hurt her. Oh my God . . . Lissa . . . Lissa . . ."

"Then who *did this*?" Ted demanded, turning his palms out at his sides.

Zach looked up at him, and his expression hardened. "Maybe *you*?"

"You don't even know me," Ted said.

"Exactly." Zach hauled himself to his feet, drying his nose with the back of his hand. "Dude comes in outta nowhere, starts flirting with my girl. How do any of us know you're not some serial killer?"

Ted thrust his chest out. "You think *I'm* the bad guy? At least I offered them help when they needed it. You must have known they were off track this whole time and what did you do? You tortured them! Some friend."

"What did you do to her, *Ted*?" Zach shoved Ted with both hands. Callie felt a bolt of fear. Ted stumbled back but caught himself, regaining his balance. "Yeah, I know your name. I know all about you. I've been watching, remember? I saw the way you've been looking at Lissa. I saw you two by the fire last night," Zach went on angrily.

"You guys, don't," Callie said desperately. She still couldn't grasp that Lissa was dead. They had to do something. They had to call the police.

"Oh really, *Zach*?" Ted replied, shoving Zach right back. "Is that why you killed her?"

"Dude. You are *so* gonna regret that," Zach said. And then, he threw a punch that drilled Ted in the jaw so hard the impact echoed for miles.

Callie screamed. Zach and Ted ignored her. The two of them threw themselves at each other with such force she was surprised they didn't crack open their skulls.

"Stop!" Callie shouted, tears streaming down her face.

They didn't listen. They were nothing but a furious tangle of throws and blows and kicks and grunts. Callie turned in the direction where Penelope and Jeremy should have been. How were they not hearing this? How had they not heard her screams?

The green tangle of branches seemed to stretch in front of her like the endless, mind-boggling reflection in a funhouse mirror.

The world had gone still. Suspended. As if tensing itself for whatever might come next.

Callie swallowed hard, a painful lump lodged inside her throat.

She was standing here with her friend's dead body while two guys tried to make each other the next victim. Was she really going to wait for one of them to succeed, then turn his venom on her? Gathering up all her courage, Callie dove into the woods, alone.

RECOVERY JOURNAL

ENTRY 8

I made sure to be nearby when they found the body. I wanted to hear her scream, and she didn't disappoint. It was so deep, so anguished, so primal. I can still hear it now, and whenever I think about it, I shiver. It was perfect. Everything I went through before, during, and after the act was made worth it by that one scream.

To this day, it remains so very, very worth it.

But I still had so much to do. Her fear had made her stronger— more alert, less naïve—but that didn't bother me. I had gotten what I wanted, but it had only made me want more.

And I get what I want. No matter what sacrifices I have to make. I always get what I want.

FORTY

Callie hurtled through the woods. Jeremy and Penelope had to be out here somewhere. They had to be. Unless Zach had found them first and snapped their necks before coming after her and Ted.

Oh, God, what if that was what had happened? If so, she'd just left Ted alone with a murderer.

Desperation surged inside Callie's chest. She didn't know what to believe, who to trust, where to go. A sharp branch nicked her cheek and immediately stung as the cut filled with salty tears.

Please let Jeremy and Pen be okay. Please, please let them be okay.

Callie heard a crack behind her and whirled around, throwing her arms up in front of her face to defend herself.

"Hey. It's just me. You blew right past us."

Jeremy. He was standing not ten feet away. Penelope sat on the ground next to him hugging her knees. Callie had never been so happy to see anyone or anything in her entire life.

"You're okay!"

She staggered toward Jeremy, falling into his arms, forgetting entirely about the lie, their fights, their breakup. All that mattered was he was here. He was alive. Callie started to sob, tears soaking the front of his T-shirt as her body convulsed. Jeremy put his arms around her and held her close.

"What is it? What's going on?" Penelope asked.

"Didn't you hear me screaming?" Callie asked, pulling away and wiping her eyes.

"Yeah, we did, but Pen twisted her ankle and I couldn't leave her," Jeremy said. "We figured you just saw another snake or something. Why? What . . . ?"

He took a step back as he finally got a good look at Callie. She had no clue what he saw, but whatever it was drained the color from his face.

"What happened?" he whispered.

"We found Lissa," Callie said, gasping for breath.

"You did?" Penelope cried, sounding relieved.

"She's dead." Callie's voice cracked. "You guys, Lissa's dead."

"What?" Jeremy cried, bending at the waist like someone had punched him.

"No. You're joking," Penelope said tonelessly. "Where is she?" she asked, her voice growing frantic. "*Lissa?!*" she called out.

"I'm not joking," Callie said, glancing around. "Ted thinks she was strangled. She had these marks around her neck and—"

Penelope looked up at Callie and something seemed to break inside her eyes. Suddenly they rolled back and she slumped sideways onto the ground.

"Penelope!" Callie shrieked. "Pen!"

"She fainted," Jeremy said, crouching in the muddy earth next to her. He gently tugged Penelope away from the fallen tree trunk where she was propped and laid her flat on the ground. "She'll be okay."

"Jeremy, you're not going to believe this, but Zach is here," Callie said, grasping his arm.

"Zach?" Jeremy blurted, his brown eyes wide. "Since when? How?"

"He's the one who's been following us. He admitted it. Then

he accused Ted of killing Lissa. When I left, the two of them were beating the pulp out of each other."

"Well, if he's been following us . . . watching us . . . maybe he saw what happened to Lissa last night," Jeremy suggested.

"Or he killed her himself," Callie replied.

Jeremy sat back, hard. He looked like he'd lost the will to exist. "Callie, what do we do? What do we do?"

Callie looked in the direction from which she'd come. "We have to try to call the police," she said. "Pen has her phone on her. Check her pockets."

Jeremy quickly patted his hands over the many pockets in Penelope's cargo shorts. "It's not here."

"No way. She's kept it on her this entire time," Callie said. She sat down and reached for the flap pocket, shoving her hand inside. It was empty.

"Zach must have stolen it," Callie said.

"Or Ted," Jeremy added acerbically.

Callie heard someone tromping through the underbrush. She grabbed Jeremy's arm again and turned. It was Zach, appearing from behind a stand of wide trees with a bloody lip and a swelling eye. The second he saw Penelope, he froze.

"Oh, God. She's not—"

"She fainted," Jeremy said, rising to his feet. "*What are you doing here, man?*"

"Dude, chill," Zach said, touching a dirty bandanna to his lip. Standing next to Jeremy, he looked like a brick wall, his shoulders broad and his posture perfect. He looked indestructible. "I'm sorry about everything I did, but I did not kill Lissa." His voice broke on her name.

"Where's Ted?" Callie asked, her throat tight.

"That loser? He's on his way back to your camp. Said he'd wait ten minutes if you guys still wanted his help, but after that, we're on our own," Zach told her. He spit a wad of blood and saliva near her feet. "But I don't trust that dude as far as I could throw him. We gotta get out of here and away from him."

"But we have to stay with Ted," Callie said. "He's the only one who knows where we're going."

"Or maybe he's leading you guys right into some psycho trap," Zach replied, his low voice fierce.

"Zach, you said you were watching Lissa and Ted last night by the fire. Ted said she went back into her tent around one o'clock. Were you watching then?" Callie asked, still wondering if Zach was the bad guy. She hoped his response would convince her one way or the other.

Zach nodded, looking shaky. "Yeah, I saw her go in and zip up the tent. Part of me wanted to step right up to Ted and confront him, but I didn't. I just went back to my camp and fell asleep," he explained. "That's where I was when you started screaming just now. I didn't see anything else, I swear."

Jeremy hung his head and groaned. "I can't take this anymore."

"What do you think we should do, Higgins?" Zach asked. "You're the smart one."

Jeremy suddenly seemed to inflate. The person who had been mocking him all this time had been silenced, and replaced by someone who respected his opinion.

"Do you have your phone on you?" Jeremy asked hopefully.

Callie's heart expanded. Of course! Why hadn't she thought of that?

"Yeah, man, but it died yesterday," Zach said.

The word *died* made Callie's body tense as she pictured Lissa's corpse. She heard herself let out a moan. "We're never getting out of here," she whispered.

"Yes. We are," Jeremy said. "We're going to wake up Pen, and then you guys are gonna take us to Lissa. Zach and I will carry her and we'll catch up with Ted."

"Dude," Zach said, disagreeing.

"We have to stick with him for now and just hope he's telling the truth," Jeremy insisted.

"Are you sure?" Zach asked.

"Yeah. But I say we keep him on a very short leash."

"You got that right."

Zach bumped fists with Jeremy, and Callie swallowed down her nausea. How could Jeremy be so casual with him? After the way he'd stalked them and scared them? And she still wasn't convinced that he hadn't hurt Lissa. What was it her dad was always saying when they talked about the criminal law classes he taught? Motive was the most important factor in any murder. Find the motive, and you'll find the killer.

As far as Callie could see, the only person in these woods with an actual motive to kill Lissa Barton was Zach Carle.

FORTY-ONE

After an endless slog through the woods, Callie and Penelope finally emerged into the clearing with Zach and Jeremy close behind.

The two boys were carrying Lissa's body between them.

Don't look back, don't look back, Callie told herself. If she didn't look at Lissa, then maybe it wouldn't be real.

Penelope's ankle still hurt, so Callie supported half her weight and together they staggered to the nearest tree. Penelope had been holding back tears the whole way, gasping and gulping them down, but the second her butt hit the dirt, she began to sob. Ted, meanwhile, hovered nearby, watching them with a cold, detached eye. He had a cut on one cheek and the other was badly bruised. He'd wrapped his wrist with a torn-up T-shirt.

"What now?" Callie asked the guys without turning around, still determined not to look at Lissa's limp form hanging between them. She bent down and kneaded Penelope's shoulder, her throat so tight she was sure her own sobs would start up again.

"Could you get my blanket?" Jeremy asked.

Callie went to his tent and retrieved the large, plaid wool blanket he'd been sitting on near the fire for the past few nights, which she then smoothed out across the dirt. This time, she couldn't help but watch as Jeremy and Zach gently laid Lissa down on top of it. One of Lissa's arms fell, crooking at her side. She looked like she was sleeping. Tears filled Callie's eyes, and she quickly closed them, turning away until she got hold of herself.

"How much farther do we have to go?" Jeremy asked Ted, his chest heaving after the effort.

"So we're going to stick together?" Ted asked stonily. "You've decided I didn't kill her?"

"We're gonna let the cops decide on that," Zach replied, his large hands on his hips. "But we realize you're our only hope of getting out of these woods."

"Great. So I'm innocent by convenience," Ted snapped.

"Let's just get back to civilization and then we can figure out what's going on," Callie put in, shocked she was able to keep her voice steady.

Ted took a deep breath. "Fine. We still have a few more miles to cover. I don't know how we're going to carry her the whole way."

"We can't just leave her here," Penelope blurted, wiping her eyes.

"No. We can't," Zach agreed, his voice thick.

"No one said we would." Ted grabbed his canteen and took a swig of water. "We just need a better plan."

"We have to build a stretcher," Jeremy said. "Something light-weight but strong enough to hold her." He glanced around at Callie and Penelope, his eyes oddly bright. "Either of you know how much she weighs?"

"One twenty," Penelope replied, sniffling.

"Okay, that's not too bad."

"I can't believe we're even talking about this," Callie said, holding her hands over her eyes. "What're we going to tell her parents?"

"We can figure it out later," Zach said, all business. It was so strange seeing him this way, without the easy smile, the jovial one-liners. "Right now we've got work to do. Where do we start, Higgins?"

Jeremy turned in a slow circle, surveying their campsite with narrowed eyes. He was so bright-eyed. So focused. It made something squirm inside Callie's stomach.

"What are you thinking, Jeremy?" Ted asked, stepping up next to him and offering him the canteen.

It was the first time since they'd met that Ted had called him by his name. Jeremy took a swig of water, then handed it back. Callie suddenly understood why her ex-boyfriend seemed so animated. To him, this was a physics problem. Something he could handle. Something he could solve. He was clinging to it because it gave him a distraction—a way to make sense of the situation. And the other guys were recognizing him as their leader.

"We can use my tent," Jeremy said. "The vinyl can supposedly withstand seventy-five-mile-an-hour winds. If we tear it up and double or triple fold it, it should hold."

It should hold. The weight of Lissa's corpse on the material. Callie pressed her hands to her stomach and glanced at Penelope, who looked ill.

"All right. We have a game plan," Zach said, clapping his meaty hands together like he was in a football huddle. Like he was the player and Jeremy was the coach. "Let's do this."

Keeping her eyes on the ground, Callie slowly crossed the clearing while the three guys got to work breaking down Jeremy's tent. *Jensen's Revenge* still lay near the fire pit where Lissa had left it last night after using it as a cutting board. There were little flecks of chocolate scattered over the gushing quotes from reviews of the first two books.

Lissa had touched that book. Just last night. A few hours ago, really. She'd been alive and vibrant and *here*. Now she was gone. Forever.

It took all Callie's self-control not to turn around and stare at Lissa's body.

"You okay?" Callie asked Penelope as she sat next to her.

Their eyes met and Callie realized what a stupid question it was. She picked at a patch of dried mud on her leg, noticing the stubble that stuck up from underneath it. She couldn't believe that just a few days ago she'd been obsessing about how she looked to Jeremy. It hadn't even crossed her mind to brush her hair in the last twenty-four hours.

"I mean your ankle. How is it?"

"Not good," Penelope replied. She pulled her knee up and rested her chin on it, staring across at where Lissa lay. "I've never seen a dead body before. Have you?"

"Just my mom's aunt Rosa at her wake," Callie said, studying the grass. "But it was a long time ago and she was really old and I didn't know her. This is . . . it's just . . ."

Her throat welled so swiftly she couldn't continue.

"I keep waiting for her to wake up," Penelope said, her voice quiet. "Sit up and tell us it was just a prank and laugh. God, I'd pretty much kill to hear her laugh."

"I know what you mean," Callie said. She turned her face to the side and lowered her voice. "Do you think it was Zach?"

"Zach? Please. You know him. He's like Mr. Popular and the class clown rolled into one giant man-boy," Penelope said. "He could never hurt anyone. Not outside the football field."

"Then what? There's someone *else* out here? Some random psychopath?" Callie asked, her heart pounding. Penelope's face tightened, like she was trying to communicate something silently. Her eyes flicked toward the spot where Ted was standing, not five feet away. Callie licked her dry lips with her dry tongue. "You think it was . . . ?"

She couldn't even finish the sentence. Yes, she'd had the same thought. Many times. But Ted . . .

"I was alone with him out there. I could hardly even see straight after we found Lissa," Callie whispered as Ted tore the tent fabric with his knife. "If he's the killer, wouldn't he have attacked me then, instead of calming me down and picking a fight with Zach? And then he waited for us here when he could have taken off."

"Unless . . ." Penelope bit her lip and fiddled with her bracelets. "Unless he's toying with us. Lulling us into a false sense of security. I bet this cabin of his doesn't even exist."

"Pen . . ."

"It's classic psychopath behavior," Penelope countered. "He makes us trust him, makes us rely on him, so that when he turns on us, it's this big, sick surprise."

"How do you know anything about classic psychopath behavior?" Callie asked.

"Don't you ever watch TV?" Penelope turned away, like she was annoyed at Callie's lack of crime procedural knowledge.

Questions itched at the tip of Callie's tongue, but she didn't dare ask them, fearing the answers would make her feel more terrified than she already did. Instead, she focused back on the guys.

The three of them were working together quickly, mostly silently, fashioning a stretcher out of two long branches, the poles from Jeremy's now destroyed tent, and the torn-up fabric. Every now and then Jeremy would bark an order at Ted, or Zach would make a suggestion, and the three of them would make the adjustments. It was surreal to watch—especially Jeremy and Ted. It was as if they were two guys who'd worked together their entire lives instead of a pair of strangers who had mostly rankled each other for the last three days.

They really want to get out of here, Callie thought. *They're just as scared as we are.*

It couldn't have been Ted. He was too shocked when they found Lissa's body. There was no way he could have faked that, was there?

Her gaze traveled to Zach. Even though he wielded all kinds of power at school, he'd never been anything but nice to her. She couldn't imagine him hurting Lissa when she really thought about it. But she also couldn't imagine him doing what he'd already admitted to doing—following them, taunting them, torturing them. If he was capable of that, what else was he capable of?

Slowly, Callie dragged her gaze toward Lissa, lying motionless on the blanket. She thought about her friend, how difficult and prickly she had been. Now, Callie would have given anything for another moment of Lissa's cruelty, if it meant that she was okay. But she wasn't okay.

Callie felt grief and shock battle inside her as she watched Ted and Jeremy carefully lift Lissa up onto the stretcher. Then Zach and Jeremy each took an end, crouching between their make-shift handles.

"Ready?" Zach said to Jeremy. "One, two, three."

The two of them stood and the weight of Lissa's body sat heavily inside the vinyl, an awkward, slippery load suspended down beneath the branches. Callie's throat constricted. They were going, and Lissa was coming with them.

FORTY-TWO

The sky was growing darker when Callie and Penelope rounded a bend and came upon an empty fire pit in the middle of a long, flat stretch of trail. It looked as if someone had given up trying to find a suitable camping spot and simply crashed. Penelope let go of Callie and limped over to a large pine tree, collapsing against the trunk.

"What're you doing?" Ted asked as the boys caught up with them.

"I can't anymore," Penelope sputtered. "I'm sorry, but I just . . . I can't take another step."

Callie stood up straight for the first time in hours and rolled her shoulders back. Her side hurt from bending toward Penelope, and she'd developed a nasty crick in her neck. The day couldn't have been any longer—hobbling over rough terrain with Penelope while watching Lissa's body sway between whichever duo was carrying her at that moment.

Callie thought about her parents. She longed to see them like she'd never longed for anything. By now, her dad must have been waiting for hours in the state park parking lot where they'd agreed to meet. *All* the parents had been waiting for hours. By now, they knew their kids were lost. Had they sent out a search party? Had they called the authorities? Callie wondered if her father had left to pick up her mom at the airport, or if he'd sent someone else. A neighbor, a colleague, a cop? Did her mom also know that Callie was missing?

And what were Lissa's parents going to do when they found out their daughter was dead?

"How far to your cabin, Ted?" Callie asked. The question tasted tart on her tongue, because she knew that every last one of them doubted the existence of said cabin, at least a bit. But the idea of it was all Callie had to cling to.

"I'd say another three-quarters of a mile or so," Ted said, bending his knees to lower Lissa to the ground. Jeremy did the same, then walked a few paces up the trail to where Zach was standing. "I was hoping we could get there today, but . . . maybe we should make camp for the night. If we start fresh in the morning, we can be there in less than an hour."

Jeremy scoffed, hands on his hips, shaking his head at the ground.

"What?" Ted asked.

"Does this cabin even exist, or are you just playing some kind of twisted mind game with us?" Jeremy snapped, his eyes wide.

"Um, I'm not the one coming off as twisted right now," Ted said, raising his hands with an incredulous look on his face. "Am I right, ladies?"

"Dude, I'd watch what you say," Zach warned, crossing his arms over his broad chest.

"My ankle hurts," Penelope whined.

Callie brought her hands to her head and turned away from Jeremy, Ted, Penelope, Zach—and the body. She felt like she was a bottle of soda and some stupid kid was shaking her up, bringing every bit of fizz inside of her to the top, just ready to blow.

"Do you actually know anything about this mountain, or was that all bragging to impress the girls?" Jeremy demanded.

"You're such a jealous little twit," Ted said snidely.

"Where's the cabin, Ted?!" Jeremy shouted, getting right in his face. "What are you getting out of this? What's the point of lying? Are you the one who killed Lissa? Are you planning to pick off another one of us tonight?"

"Jeremy!" Callie gasped.

"What?" Jeremy said. "Everyone suspects him. It was time someone said it."

Ted whirled on Jeremy, his eyes wild. "Shut up right now, Little Man." He spit at Jeremy's feet and suddenly, Callie saw something snap in Jeremy's eyes.

"No! Don't!" Callie shouted.

But it was too late. Jeremy flung himself at Ted, tackling him to the ground with one hard shoulder to the stomach. Penelope screamed as Jeremy reared back, his fist cocked to punch. But Ted was too fast. He brought his fist down like a sledgehammer into Jeremy's chest. Jeremy's face went slack. The whole thing went down in about two seconds while Zach just stood there, watching.

"What is the matter with you?" Callie shouted at him as she raced to Jeremy's side.

"What?" Zach said, palms up. "He was handling it."

Callie put her hands on Jeremy's shoulders. His eyes were wide, terrified. "Breathe! You have to breathe!" She whirled around to glare at Ted. "You knocked the wind out of him!"

"Whatever. He started it."

Jeremy sucked in a ragged, gasping breath and then coughed. Callie helped him sit up as he gulped for air.

"You're okay," she told him. "You're okay."

He nodded and pushed himself to his feet. Callie went with him, her hand still on his back, but she flinched away when she saw the look in his eyes. The awful glint was back, the same one she'd seen when he'd glared at Lissa that day by the river.

"Jeremy?" Callie said uncertainly.

He didn't respond. Instead, he let out a guttural cry and rushed at Ted, his fists clenched. Ted reached behind him, beneath the shirt that was tied around his waist. There was a flash and suddenly, Callie heard a click. Jeremy stopped in his tracks. Ted was holding a gun out straight in front of him with both hands. The barrel was trained directly on Jeremy's face.

FORTY-THREE

"You have a *gun*?!" Jeremy demanded, reeling backward. "I thought that was just a joke."

Callie's heart was in her throat as she looked back and forth between the two of them. Any fear she'd felt over the past few days paled compared to this. Jeremy. She couldn't let Jeremy die. The desperation pumping in her veins was almost too much to bear.

She loved him. Her whole chest filled with the realization. She loved him and she had to stop this.

"It's no joke, dude," Ted said.

Zach skirted sideways toward Callie, but Callie couldn't move. What was she supposed to do? Tackle Ted? That didn't seem like a good plan, considering it might make the gun go off. But what? One twitch of Ted's finger and Jeremy's life would be over.

"Is that thing loaded?" Penelope asked, sounding alert for the first time in hours.

"Do you really want to find out?" Ted replied, keeping his sights on Jeremy.

His snide tone made something inside Callie break, and the combination of anger and fear that rushed forth was uncontrollable.

"I don't believe this!" she cried as Jeremy slowly worked his way toward Callie in a wide arc around Ted, who followed him the whole way with the gun. "First you whip out a butcher's knife big enough to take down a rhino, and now you have a gun? How are we supposed to trust you after this?"

Ted lifted a shoulder. "It's a good question. How about you tell me why I should trust you? All I know about you people is what I've seen the past couple of days, and one thing is totally obvious—you and Lissa clearly hated each other, Little Man. So you tell me. How do I know *you're* not a murderer?"

Zach's gaze darted to Jeremy, his eyes sharp, as if this was the first moment it had occurred to him that any one of them could have done this—not just Ted. And that reality hit Callie square in the chest, too. She knew that she and Jeremy and Pen were innocent, but she could suddenly see this whole thing from Ted's perspective. To him, they were strangers. Complete and total ciphers. And clearly the fact that he was outnumbered had him totally wigged.

She had to talk him down. She had to make him feel safe. She had to get him to put the gun away.

"You don't," Callie said.

Jeremy turned to her, the depth of his hurt plain on his face. "What?"

"I'm just saying, none of us *really* knows," Callie said slowly. "Either there's someone *else* out there stalking us," she said, looking pointedly at Zach. "Or one of us did it. But even if one of us did, it's not like that person's ever going to admit it. Right?"

The air was thick with suspicion as they all looked around at one another.

"So for now, we just have to try to coexist," Callie said. "There's nothing else we can do."

She took a deep breath and looked Ted in the eye. "Please, Ted. Don't do anything rash. Do you really want to go to jail just because you stopped to help out a few lost campers? Because you tried to do the right thing?"

Ted blinked. He finally lowered the gun and Callie blew out a relieved breath. Jeremy was okay. For now.

With his free hand, Ted rubbed his brow, pinching the skin between his fingers.

"Look, Callie's right. It's pretty clear none of us trusts anyone else," he said. "And it's not getting any lighter out here. I say we make a fire, eat what's left of the peanut butter out of the tube, and get some sleep."

Sleep. Yeah, right, Callie thought.

"Unless you have some food on you," Jeremy said acerbically to Zach.

Penelope's wavering eyes widened. "Yeah! You must have something to eat, right? I can't believe you've been following us all this tim and didn't come out just to offer us something."

Zach looked a little green. "Actually, I'm all out. I didn't plan to be here as long as I was."

Ted rolled his eyes.

"Whatever. I don't need to eat anyway, but there's no way I'm sleeping," Jeremy said. "Not with you toting two deadly weapons."

"Fine, then we'll stay up all night and keep a good, suspicious eye on each other," Ted replied sarcastically. "Whatever. Let's find some wood."

Callie tried to catch Jeremy's gaze, but he turned away from her, his shoulders hunched. With a sigh, she took to the other side of the clearing, picking up broken branches and cradling them in her weakened arms. Her whole body felt shaky. But her fear had become a living thing, creeping its way around her chest, springing up and down on her heart, using her ribs as a jungle gym. It had taken up a gleeful, alert residence and she was certain it was never going to leave.

What if one of these people really was a killer? If Lissa, always tough, always brave, hadn't been able to defend herself, Callie had no chance. For the first time ever, she was forced to truly consider her weakness, her lack of size, her total cluelessness about self-defense.

She felt like she knew nothing of value. Like she'd spent her entire life up to this point wasting her time studying, writing stories without endings, reading fantasy novels, doing her nails, and texting pointless photos and memes to her friends. All that time she could have been lifting weights, training, taking karate or Krav Maga or boxing or anything. Anything that could actually save her life.

She tromped back to the fire pit and deposited her kindling next to the rocks, then sank to the ground. Ted eventually got the fire going and passed around first the tube of peanut butter and then his bag of trail mix. Callie took her portion and ate it slowly, piece by measly piece, rolling the granola and nuts and chocolate and raisins around in her mouth. No one pitched a tent. They simply rolled their sleeping bags out around the fire like spokes on a wheel and sat, watching the flames, watching one another.

Callie did want to stay up all night. She couldn't imagine sleeping, not with Lissa's corpse close by, not with fear and mistrust coursing through her.

Zach seemed primed to avoid sleep, sitting straight up with his legs folded in some kind of yoga pose, staring unblinkingly at the fire. But eventually, Penelope leaned back on her elbows, then lay flat, and then she fell asleep. Before long Callie felt herself start to nod off. She'd close her eyes and drift for a moment and every time begin to dream of Lissa, which would then startle her awake.

"Cal, lie down and get some sleep," Jeremy said finally. They were the first words he'd spoken to her in hours. He crawled over to her, unzipped her sleeping bag, and gestured to her to get in. "I promise I won't let anything happen to you."

Callie looked into his eyes and saw just Jeremy. The Jeremy she had trusted and loved. The Jeremy she'd invited on this trip to keep her company, to have her back, if things didn't work out with the girls. He couldn't be a murderer, could he?

She looked at Ted and Zach, both stoic and silent, the fire casting odd, distorting shadows across their faces.

What did it matter, anyway? She wouldn't be able to defend herself even if she was awake. Being asleep actually wasn't going to make much of a difference.

"Okay," she said quietly, giving in, giving up. "Thank you, Jeremy."

He smiled wanly at her. She crawled inside her sleeping bag and fell into a dark, dreamless sleep.

RECOVERY JOURNAL

ENTRY 9

Fear is such an insidious thing. It can take hold in an instant, but is the hardest thing to shake. It can inspire suspicion where there should be none and fracture even the tightest bonds.

It can also be a very useful tool. Especially when one wants to divide and conquer. Add a bit of fear to the mix and suddenly, everyone's out for themselves, everyone's watching their own backs. But they never know which way to look, really, which way to turn. In trying to protect themselves, they scatter their attention. They become unable to focus. Unable to see what's right in front of them. Or behind them. Or next to them.

They forget that the greatest danger often lies within.

FORTY-FOUR

The sunlight woke Callie and she sat up, surprised. Somehow, she'd slept right through the night. Her eyes went directly to Lissa's body, still wrapped in the torn-up tent. So it wasn't a nightmare. Yesterday had actually happened.

Swallowing down a lump in her throat, Callie looked at Jeremy. He was passed out, too, on top of his own sleeping bag, but something was wrong. His legs were covered in reddish-brown muck, some dried, some wet, and his fingers were dark with it, too. Her eyes slowly trailed up to his face, which twitched in his sleep. There was a smear of red across one cheek.

Blood. There was no denying it. Jeremy was covered in blood.

Callie shoved herself out of her sleeping bag and scuttled backward. Penelope was nowhere to be seen. Ted and Zach were gone, too. She was alone. Alone in the woods with a boy who had bathed himself in blood and then somehow, disturbingly, fallen asleep without a thought of washing it off.

What did you do, Jeremy? Callie thought, covering her mouth with one hand. *What have you done?*

Callie gripped her shirt in her hands and twisted it, looking left and right.

The only other person in sight was Lissa. Lissa's dead gray hand reaching out from within her shroud.

Jeremy rolled over and moaned. Callie tore off down the trail. She still wore her hiking boots from the night before, which was good, but her legs were weak, her head light. She'd barely eaten in two days. As she staggered up the dirt path, she realized she had no clue where she was going. Had she taken off in the direction from which they'd come? Her head swam.

"Focus, Callie. Focus," she whispered, closing her eyes. She heard a whisper, or possibly a breath, and froze. The air was thick and warm like milk bubbled over a fire, but a cold finger of fear grazed the back of her neck. She opened her eyes again. Nothing.

"Penelope?" she whisper-shouted. "Pen? Are you out there?"

There was a crack. One clean break of a branch.

"Callie!" Jeremy called out, his voice reedy. "Callie? Where are you?"

An awful, strangled sound escaped Callie's throat and she took off running again. She shoved twiggy branches away from her face, their sharper points tearing at her arms, but she kept going.

"Caaaallieeee!" Jeremy sang. "Caaaaallieee!"

I don't want to die, Callie thought, searching the trees wildly as they flew past her. *I don't want to die, I don't want to die, I don't want to die.*

Every moment she hoped to see some sign of Penelope or Zach or Ted, but at the same time she dreaded she'd trip over one of them like she had Lissa. The memory of that horror snaked its way through her chest and clung to her heart as if trying to stop its beating.

Please let them be alive. Please let them be okay.

"Caaallieeee! Where are you?"

Callie stopped. His voice seemed to come from in front of her now, rather than behind. She whirled around. Had she already passed that tree? There was an ugly, angry gash through its center, like someone had tried to chop it down, but given up. She was certain she'd seen it before. Where was she? Where was Jeremy? She started to run again when someone stepped out of the trees. She collided hard with his body and cried out, sinking to her knees in fear.

"Please don't hurt me. Please. Please don't hurt me!"

"I'm not gonna hurt you."

Callie looked up. It was Ted. He reached down to help her up. Callie's lungs flooded with relief.

"You're alive!" she blurted, throwing her arms around him.

"Of course I'm alive. I just went to do my business and I saw you tear by." Ted gently pushed her away, keeping his hands on her shoulders. "Take a breath. Are you okay?"

"No! No, I'm not okay! I just—"

At that moment Jeremy came moseying around a bend in the trail, scratching at the back of his hair, which was matted and scraggly.

"Callie. What's going on? Where'd you go?" he asked with a yawn.

Callie took two steps back from him—from the both of them. "Where's Penelope?" she demanded. "Why are you covered in blood?"

Jeremy gestured over his shoulder with one thumb. "Pen is back at the camp. She and Zach were using the 'bathroom.'"

He splayed his fingers, studying the backs of his hands, which were crusted with dried blood, then flipped them over to look at his palms.

"Oh, that." He gave a rueful snort. "I got up to pee in the middle of the night and tore up my calf on a sharp branch. I made some mud and smeared it all over to stop the bleeding."

Ted bent for a better look at Jeremy's leg, and when he stood up, he was wearing an impressed, thoughtful frown. "Not bad, Little Man."

Jeremy seemed nonplussed. "Thanks."

"So. We all made it through the night, then," Ted said, knocking his fist against his open palm. "That's good news."

"Yeah. So let's break camp and get to this 'cabin' of yours already," Jeremy said, with a dubious lilt to his voice. "Callie?" he added. "You okay?"

Callie flinched. She was shaking from head to toe, and she couldn't believe she'd doubted Jeremy. Just yesterday she'd realized she still loved him—that she was holding on to hope for them—and the sight of blood on him was all it took to send her careering into the woods? She had to get a grip on herself.

"Sure," she replied. "Fine."

She brushed past the guys, hoping they wouldn't notice that she was starting to come apart. Because Callie could feel how dangerously close she was to cracking, and if she did, it wouldn't be good. Not for anyone.

FORTY-FIVE

"There's not gonna be a cabin." Penelope's voice was hoarse as she gripped Callie's side and limped along next to her. "You know that, right?"

Callie ignored her and took a step, bracing her torn and battered foot as best she could against the steep incline of the hill. She had last tended to her feet the night they'd split the Snickers bar. By now, all the new Band-Aids had detached thanks to the sweat and the grime. There was a good chance that, after this trip, Callie's feet would never be the same again.

Up ahead, the guys rested Lissa and her stretcher down on the ground and fished out their water bottles.

"Did you notice that Ted's bungee cords are missing? Yeah. He used some of Lissa's rope to tie up his sleeping bag before," Penelope went on, as if giving voice to all the paranoia Callie herself had felt. "I bet he used the bungees to strangle Lissa and then threw them into the trees and now he's taking us to some remote ravine so he can strangle us, too, and toss our bodies over. Or even better, an old slaughterhouse with the crusty ancient tools hanging from the ceiling."

Callie gulped, trying with every fiber of her being not to cry or shout or scream. *Fifteen more minutes. Fifteen more minutes of walking and we'll be able to call home.* Last night Ted had said it would take them less than an hour to reach the cabin, so Callie had started a countdown on her watch, clinging to the hope that he was telling the truth.

"Or maybe he's actually found the Skinner's lair," Penelope suggested, cocking her head as if this was the most intriguing idea yet. "He said he knows these hills like the back of his hands. Maybe he's—"

"Shut up, Penelope," Callie said finally, as they neared the bottom of the hill.

"What?"

"I said, shut up!" Callie shouted. "Please! Please! Please! Shut up!"

Out of nowhere, it began to pour. For a split second they were dry, listening to the water tap at the highest leaves in the highest trees, and then fat raindrops battered Callie's face and shoulders. She slid the rest of the way down the hill to level land, dragging Penelope with her. At the bottom, Pen fell to her knees and Callie reached down to yank her up by her sleeves.

"Ow! What's wrong with you?" Penelope blurted.

Callie laughed. She couldn't help it. She was losing it. Bit by bit. She was losing what was left of her mind. "What's wrong? Are you serious? What's *wrong*?"

Up ahead, Jeremy and Ted lifted the stretcher, but the now wet branch instantly slipped from Jeremy's grip. He dropped one side and Lissa's body came tumbling out, side over side, rolling across the ground and coming to a stop right at Callie's feet.

Her skin was gray and her eyes had peeled open. There was a milky film across her retinas. Penelope screamed.

Callie felt her stomach heave and she turned around, vomiting onto the wet ground behind her. She didn't even know there was anything in her stomach to expel.

"Penelope, stop!" Jeremy shouted against the high-pitched screech Pen was producing. "Stop!"

"Put her back in. Please. Put her back in," Callie said, holding one hand to her mouth and keeping her back to the body. "She'll stop if you put Lissa back in the tent."

The guys did as they were told, struggling with the limp, heavy form of her friend in the pouring rain. Cold raindrops soaked Callie's shirt and trickled down her arms. Her hair was plastered to her cheeks and forehead and water dripped from her chin.

"Oh, God," Jeremy said as they wrestled the body onto the stretcher. Callie could hear the tightness in his voice, as if he was barely holding back his own nausea. "Oh, God, oh, God, oh, God."

"It's done," Zach said finally.

Penelope did stop screaming then. She pressed her face into her knees and cried. Her skinny back swayed, the bones of her spine like a curved comb beneath the thin, wet layer of her T-shirt.

Zach threw his pack on the ground and untied his sleeping bag.

"What're you doing?" Callie asked.

"I'm going to zip Lissa up inside this," he said, unfurling the bag. "She's starting to . . . attract flies."

Callie's stomach twisted again. She had to look away as Jeremy bent to help Zach with this new task. It was impressive, how well they were dealing with this whole thing—how they were pressing on and doing what needed to be done.

"We're almost there, Penelope," Ted said, standing near the stretcher, pulling in a ragged breath. "I promise you. This is all gonna be over soon."

FORTY-SIX

"We're here!" Ted shouted.

The first glimpse Callie got of Ted's cabin was the very top of the chimney, a wide rock structure with a waterfall of rain running down one crumbling side.

"I don't believe it," Jeremy cried. "I don't believe it! The cabin's real!"

"Of course it's real," Ted snapped.

The three boys hoofed it a bit faster up the rest of the trail, their boots splashing mud with each step as thunder rumbled in the distance. Callie felt such a rush of excited, relieved adrenaline that her head became weightless. She automatically upped her pace, forcing Penelope to sprint-hop the rest of the way with her. The cabin did exist. They'd made it. They were safe.

The house was rustic, fashioned of red wood logs and aging shingles, but it was also huge. Much bigger than Callie had imagined. There was a dirt driveway leading up to a two-car garage, a wide porch that stretched the length of the house and around the corner, and a large balcony off the second floor. On the back of the roof sat a satellite dish, and the mere sight of technology made Callie laugh a manic laugh.

They could call the police. Their parents. They could go online. They could reach the rest of the world.

Ted and Jeremy walked up the three steps to the porch and laid Lissa down carefully, the soles of their boots squeaking on the dry wood. Ted retrieved a key from underneath a worn green mat and walked inside. Penelope grabbed the railing and hopped the last few steps. Zach held the door open for her.

"We made it," Jeremy said.

Rain ran into Callie's eyes, but she didn't care. The terror of the last few days was melting away. Her first instinct was to hug Jeremy, but she hesitated. Could you hug a person you'd just broken up with? Did extreme situations allow that kind of thing?

"Yeah," Callie said quietly. "We did."

Then she turned sideways and slipped awkwardly past him into the house.

The first floor of the cabin was one wide-open space composed of a sunken living area, a massive dining table, and a large kitchen at the back. The air inside was cool and dry and smelled like tangy citrus—some sort of air freshener that instantly soothed Callie's nerves. Just the feeling of being safe indoors made her want to cry euphoric tears.

Ted, Zach, and Penelope were rummaging through the kitchen cabinets and pulling out random packages of food. Callie sat on the entryway bench and untied her boots, then peeled off her socks. Her feet were mottled white and red, her blisters angry and raw. She sighed and tossed her balled-up socks onto the floor.

Against the wall across from her was a wire basket full of athletic equipment—golf clubs, a baseball bat, a couple of tennis rackets, a basketball. Those objects looked so odd to her in that moment. Like part of a life she'd never thought she'd return to.

"You okay?" Jeremy asked, joining her as he took off his shoes as well.

"I'll live," she replied. Then nearly choked on her own saliva. Lissa's dead body was right outside the door.

"Come on." Jeremy's eyes were soft with sympathy. "Let's get something to eat."

They walked across the hardwood floor past a wide staircase with a banister made of raw branches, and across a plush rug that felt like heaven to Callie's feet. They joined the others at a large marble island in the kitchen. Penelope was munching on a pretzel stick and a baby carrot—one in each hand—while Ted downed a bottle of Coke like he'd never had a drink before in his life. Zach reached for a bag of cookies and tore them open, shoving two in his mouth at once as he handed the bag over to Callie.

For a second, Callie just gazed around. There was another set of stairs from the kitchen, curving upward around a corner, and a back door leading out to what looked like a stone patio. Beyond it was a quaint garden that had been flattened by the rain, and then the woods. Always the woods.

"Shouldn't we be calling the police?" Callie asked, staring down at the blue cookie bag. The very thought of eating made her stomach turn, even though she knew how badly she needed food. "We have to tell them about Lissa."

"Callie's right. Where's the phone?" Jeremy asked.

Ted glanced around as if he wasn't sure, then picked it up from a cradle on the counter, right next to his gun. Callie hadn't seen him take the weapon out, but the sight of it tossed there so casually sent a shiver of apprehension through her.

"Cal, let's go upstairs and take showers," Penelope said excitedly, walking around the counter and grabbing Callie's hand. "Ted, there are bathrooms upstairs, right?"

Ted only chugged more of his Coke.

Callie's skin actually ached at the wonderful thought of hot water rushing over her. "But we need to call first," she protested.

"We'll do it," Zach said, reaching for the phone. Ted watched him, still wearing a suspicious expression. "You guys go ahead."

"Come on!" Penelope pulled on Callie's hand. It was like she'd regressed from a half-dead old dog to a peppy puppy in a snap. When Callie didn't move, Pen groaned and headed for the stairs on her own, disappearing onto the second floor. Callie watched her go as she finally reached for a cookie, knowing she should try to choke something down.

There was some thought forming at the back of her mind and she grabbed at it, trying to bring it into focus, but it wouldn't come. She was too tired. And her adrenaline was quickly wearing off. The idea of a shower and maybe a nap sounded like heaven. After the police arrived.

"I'll be right back," she told Jeremy as Zach began to dial. Then slowly, heavily, she dragged herself up the stairs.

The second floor was dark. With the storm still raging outside, it could have been night. Callie glanced up and down a long hallway, listening for Penelope or the sound of running water, but there was nothing. She pushed the cookie into her shorts pocket and decided to go right, running a hand along the wall in search of a light switch.

"Penelope?" she called out. "Pen!"

The first door Callie came to was ajar and she pushed it all the way open, flicking on the light. She gasped so quickly she almost choked. A huge stuffed bear—claws extended, fangs bared—angled toward the door. The thing had to be seven feet tall and its glassy eyes seemed to stare at Callie. Hanging from every other wall were several severed, stuffed heads of deer, fox, moose, and one feral cat.

This creepy place belongs to Ted's family.

Callie backed away and didn't bother turning out the light, but closed the door behind her.

"Penelope!" Callie shouted. "Where are you?"

Hurriedly, Callie opened the next two doors. The first was a bathroom done in grays and whites, but there was no sign of Penelope. The second was a bedroom with walls painted a deep, grotesque red and a black lacquer bed at its center with four posters draped in red fabric. Callie backed away from it, freaked. It looked like the kind of place some vampire would sleep.

Did Ted really live here? Where were his parents?

A door creaked and Callie whirled around. The fourth hallway door swung slowly on its hinges and suddenly, an awful thought occurred to Callie.

What if Ted *had* left someone behind? Someone who'd been lying in wait all this time? Maybe he wasn't the Skinner, but he could have been the Skinner's son. Or grandson. Maybe Penelope was right. Maybe he'd lured them right back to the Skinner's lair.

From the corner of her eye, Callie saw the staircase that led back down to the kitchen. Ignoring the swinging door, she sprinted down the hall. She was halfway to the stairs when she heard the gunshot.

FORTY-SEVEN

"No!" Zach shouted as Callie hovered just above on the stairs. She could see a sliver of the tiled floor below. "Nonono please!"

The gun went off again. Callie's heart stopped and she covered her mouth with both hands to keep herself from screaming. Suddenly Zach's body slumped into view. He lay back on the tile, staring right up at her. For a split second, his dark eyes registered total shock, and then they fluttered closed. A bullet hole in his upper chest oozed blood down into his armpit. He still held the phone in his lifeless hand.

Callie whimpered. What was happening? Who had killed Zach?

"I know you're there, Callie. You might as well just come down."

Callie's jaw fell open. She tried to breathe, but it came in short, panicked, fluttering bursts.

"J-Jeremy?" she gasped.

Her head pounded, making everything around her go sideways. Not Jeremy. No. It couldn't be Jeremy.

"Come down. No one wants to hurt you. I promise."

Jeremy's voice sounded strained—tight and hoarse. She squeezed her eyes closed. It couldn't be Jeremy. The sweet boy she'd kissed in the back of the bus, the boy she'd held hands with, studied for finals with, spent hours in his backyard talking about life with. It couldn't be him. It simply couldn't.

I don't want to die. I don't want to die. I don't want to die.

"Callie."

Now he sounded impatient.

Maybe he wouldn't hurt her. Up until a couple of days ago, he'd loved her. She was sure of it. If she could just make him remember that—keep him calm until the police got there—maybe everything would be all right.

Wait. Had they even called the police?

"Callie!" he shouted.

Slowly, Callie tripped forward.

Lying at the foot of the stairs, Zach's legs draped over his, was Ted. His eyes were closed, one hand still clutching the neck of a broken Coke bottle. The wound on his chest pulsated blood across his gray T-shirt.

"Omigod," Callie gasped, her hands flying to her mouth. "Omigod, omigod, omi—"

Jeremy stood on the far side of the island, a pleading look in his eyes. Sweat poured down the sides of his face and dotted his forehead.

"I'm sorry," he said.

"Jeremy, what did you do?" Callie whispered.

Then, suddenly, the light in Jeremy's eyes went out. His mouth dropped open at an unnatural angle.

"Jeremy?"

Callie watched, disbelieving, as his knees buckled and he slumped, lifeless, to the floor. His skull made a sickening thud when it hit the hardwood. Standing behind him was Penelope, holding Ted's gun by the barrel in her small hand.

FORTY-EIGHT

"Penelope?" Callie gasped.

Pen tossed the gun in the air deftly and caught it, the business end now pointed at Callie's chest. A rush of relief collided with a wave of dread inside Callie's chest, making her dizzy. Jeremy was innocent. He was not the bad guy. But he was also unconscious on the floor.

And Penelope—Penelope had the hungry, focused eyes of a rabid hyena stalking its prey.

You're my best friend, Callie remembered Penelope saying to her. *You're a good person*. Was that really just four days ago? What had happened to her? To them?

"What . . . ? I don't . . . What did you do to Jeremy?" Callie demanded. Her brain seemed to be two steps behind her mouth. Penelope could never hurt Jeremy. She could never hurt anyone. Yet there she was, standing over his body with a weapon in her hand, and Ted and Zach, they were gone. One shot for each of them. Gone.

"I threatened to shoot him so he'd get you down here and then I knocked him out. Don't worry. Jeremy will be fine. Unlike those two," Penelope said, taking a few steps toward Callie. The gun trembled ever so slightly in her hand, but she never took her eyes off Callie's face. She seemed utterly, eerily calm. Determined. "I told Ted I'd let him go, but he had to try to be the hero and take his gun back. Guess his survival skills weren't exactly what they were cracked up to be."

This isn't real. This isn't really happening. Is it? Penelope had killed Ted?

"And . . . and Zach?" Callie's voice broke.

Penelope rolled her eyes. "He was calling the police. I had to stop him. Besides, after what he did to us in the woods? He deserved it. And I couldn't let him go back to town and tell everyone it was me, could I? Jeremy will keep my secret. I know he will. Deep down in his heart, he still loves me. But Zach. Whatever. Like the world needs another pathetic former football star."

Callie's brain was falling all over itself trying to make sense of what she was hearing, of the cold, calculating look on the face of the friend she thought she'd known. If Penelope had shot Ted and Zach in cold blood, did that mean . . . ? But she couldn't have. Not Lissa. Lissa was Pen's best friend. They were never apart. They loved each other.

"Penelope, you didn't . . ." Callie breathed. "How could you—"

"Come on, Callie. Let's not drag this out," Penelope said. "At least you won't have to struggle. Lissa struggled. She struggled a *lot*."

And there it was. The truth. Penelope had killed Lissa. She'd somehow lured her into the woods and *strangled* her. The very thought of the planning that must have gone into it, of the two of them struggling, of Lissa's confusion and desperation and fear, made Callie's vision go dim. She couldn't take in a full breath and her gasps were ragged, pathetic. Tears streamed down her face. She was about to die. Her best friend was going to kill her.

"How could you do this?" Callie cried, holding her hands up in front of her. "How could you kill Lissa?"

She backed toward the patio door behind her, her mind reeling, knowing that the bodies on the floor lay between her and freedom.

Penelope shrugged. "She lied to us, Callie. She said she cared about us more than she cared about Ted. And then I watched her. I watched her sneak out of the tent and go to him. She waited until she thought we were asleep, and then she turned her back on us. She was nothing but a liar in the end, cheating on her boyfriend. She deserved exactly what she got."

Callie glanced over her shoulder as she backed toward the door. She had to lift one foot to step between Ted's lifeless legs.

"Please don't hurt me," Callie said as calmly as possible. "I didn't do anything. I'd never do anything to hurt you."

Penelope laughed, leaning forward with one hand to her thigh as she kept the other steady, holding on to the gun as if she'd held one every day of her life.

"Are you serious? You stole the love of my life!" Penelope seethed. "Did you really think you could take him from me and I wouldn't care? That I wouldn't ever do anything about it? Wait. Of course you did. Because that's who I am. Who I always was. The doormat. The sweet yes girl. Lissa's little sidekick. Well, not anymore. I'll never play her sidekick again. And after today, after I kill you, I'll never be disrespected again, either."

"Nobody disrespects you," Callie protested, trying to puzzle a way out of this. Trying to imagine what she could say to make her unhinged friend see logic.

"Everybody disrespects me!" Penelope roared, making Callie jump. "You, Jeremy, Lissa, Zach, Ted, everyone at school, my parents, my doctors. No one thinks I can handle myself. No one understands that I am who I am and I'm not going to change, no matter what therapies they send me to, no matter what drugs they pump into me. There's nothing wrong with being yourself, right? Isn't that what they're always telling us? Well, then why can't I just be me?"

Callie's brain was on fire. Penelope wasn't making any sense. Drugs? Therapy? Doctors? Who in the world *was* this person?

"Penelope, you don't have to do this," Callie said desperately. "It's not too late."

Penelope's face turned to stone.

"It is for one of us." And then she pulled the trigger. The shot was so loud Callie felt her heart actually stop. Then the window frame in the door behind her shattered and she bolted up the stairs.

FORTY-NINE

Callie tore down the hall, the house around her reduced to a blur of colors. Outside, she had noticed a balcony off a room near the left side of the house. If she could make it there, she might be able to climb down the side and run for it. It was her only hope.

"Callie, come on!" Penelope called after her as thunder rattled the windowpanes. "Do you really think you can get away from me? We're in the middle of nowhere."

Callie slammed a door and dove into a small alcove that held a tiny built-in bookshelf and a little window seat for reading. She glimpsed down the hall and saw Penelope take the bait, opening the first door and walking slowly inside. The second Pen was out of sight, Callie raced for the end of the hall, her breath rasping and shallow.

She found herself in a big white master bedroom with the balcony off the side. Sitting on the bedside table was a cordless phone. She grabbed it in her sweaty hands and made for the glass door, dialing 911 with shaking fingers. At least Pen hadn't figured out how to cut the phone lines.

"911, what's your emergency?"

"Someone's shooting at me," Callie rasped into the phone, cupping her hand around the mouthpiece. "My friend. My friend Penelope is shooting at me. She killed my friends and now she's coming after me."

Callie had to choke back a sob. Lissa. Zach. Ted. All of them so full of life, with families and friends and so much ahead of them. And now they were gone. Why? How did this make any sense?

"What's your location, miss?"

Callie slipped out the door and onto the balcony. The rain instantly soaked her all over again as the sky flashed white with lightning. The question sank her heart into her toes as she gazed out at the endless trees, as if there would be a street sign or a billboard flashing her exact coordinates.

"I don't know," she breathed.

The crack of thunder was deafening. The storm had moved in fast and was now right overhead.

"I'm sorry?"

"I don't know where I am," Callie whined, casting around for a weapon. There were two lounge chairs and a table. Nothing else. Callie staggered to the guardrail and looked down. The ground seemed miles away. Callie began to shiver uncontrollably.

"I've been hiking with friends. I'm at a cabin in the woods, but I don't know where. We passed Mercer Pond at some point, but it was a few days ago. And there was a mudslide. We hiked north of an old mudslide," she added, recalling Ted's comments.

Ted. Poor Ted. And what about Jeremy? *Jeremy.* Was he really alive?

Callie heard the bedroom door open. She raced to the wall and pressed back against it, shaking from head to toe.

"I can try to triangulate your location. Can you keep the line open?" the woman on the phone said.

"I'll try," Callie whispered, tears springing to her eyes. "Please help me. Please come find me."

"What's your name, miss?"

"Callie," she whispered. "Callie Valasquez."

"You're one of the missing hikers. The rangers are out looking for you."

Callie felt a burst of hope. Then, ever so slowly, the glass door opened and that hope was gone. Callie bit her lip and tossed the phone over the guardrail into the underbrush below, knowing that if Penelope saw her with it, she'd cut the call short. She could only pray that the phone wouldn't shut itself off when it hit the ground—that the rain wouldn't short it out somehow.

By some insane stroke of luck, Penelope was looking the other way as she stepped out onto the balcony. Callie held her breath, grabbed the door, and yanked it toward her. As Penelope turned around, Callie let out a guttural cry and slammed the door as hard as she could into her friend's skull. It made a sickening but satisfying *crack*. Penelope reeled back, stunned, and dropped the gun. For a second, Callie was so shocked by her own bravery, her own strength, that she couldn't move. Then she snapped to and dove for the weapon, but it slid across the wet wood planks, out of her grasp.

As Callie pushed herself up to her hands and knees, Penelope shook her head and focused her eyes. Callie crawled for the gun, tears coursing down her face, but Penelope lunged for it. Callie saw that she'd never get there first, but then a plan quickly formed in her mind, playing out in slow motion like some sort of primal instinct kicking in. She swung her leg around and kicked Penelope's hand as hard as she could. Her foot hit the barrel of the gun, and the weapon spun on its side over the slick water-dotted wooden slats, heading for the edge of the balcony.

"No!" Penelope shouted, struggling to her feet.

But she was too late. The gun perfectly threaded the needle between two guardrail posts, teetered for a second, and then fell.

The second it was out of sight, Callie felt some of the pressure in her chest release. It had worked! Now it was just her and Penelope. Not that the odds were all that comforting. Lissa had been far stronger than Pen, after all.

Penelope ran to look over the side. When she turned around again, her face was a grotesque mask of fury. Tangles of rain-matted hair hung over her eyes and her nostrils flared. Slowly, she brought her hand to her forehead and touched the gash the door had left there. When she saw the blood on her fingertips, her lips flattened into a thin, straight, trembling line.

"I am so going to kill you."

Callie sprinted back through the door to the hallway. Penelope raced after her and Callie suddenly realized what had been off about her before, when she'd led Callie upstairs for a supposed shower. Her ankle. Her ankle was fine. She wasn't hurt at all. For a whole day, Callie had supported and half dragged the girl through the woods, and Penelope had been faking her injury the entire time. Had she been planning this all along? Had she known that when they finally got here, she was going to kill Callie—the very person who'd just done everything in her power to help her?

She's crazy, Callie realized fleetingly as she ran for her life. *Penelope is out of her mind.*

She whipped open door after door behind her, trying to stop Penelope's progress. As she reached the top of the main staircase, she heard Penelope finally catch her toe on one of the corners and fall down. Callie sprinted down the stairs, stumbling once and almost knocking her head against the hardwood, but she found her feet and careered toward the door. She toppled every piece of furniture behind her on her way out the front, hoping against hope that the police had figured out where she was—that they would be here soon.

Outside, the rain came down in sheets. Thunder rumbled, a long, sustained growl. Callie stumbled past Lissa's body to the muddy muck of the driveway. There was no place to go. No place to hide.

Callie trembled as she realized she had to do the unthinkable. She had to go back into the woods.

She could hear Penelope stumbling after her inside. It was now or never. Callie took off for the trees, branches and acorns and rocks stabbing at the bare soles of her feet. There was a small shed in the distance and she sprinted for it, thinking there might be some sort of tool inside that she could use as a weapon. She was halfway there—could see the intricate carving of a tree on the shed door—when she tripped. Her face hit the ground first and she saw actual stars float across her vision. For a second she couldn't breathe, and it was a second too long. Suddenly, a pair of hands came down on her shoulders. Her scream was drowned out by a burst of violent thunder.

FIFTY

"Callie! It's me!" Jeremy hissed. "Can you move?"

Callie coughed, her lungs expanding with oxygen and relief all at once. She nodded, and Jeremy pulled her to her feet, helping her around the side of the shed. Spent, Callie sank down with her back up against the wall. Jeremy peeked around the corner, then sat next to her.

"I don't see her," he said. He had a nasty bump on his forehead from where he'd landed face-first on the kitchen floor. And Callie imagined he had another bump on the back of his head where Penelope had struck him. But otherwise he was in one piece.

Callie clung to him. "You're okay. Thank God you're okay!"

"I'm so sorry," Jeremy said, hugging her close. His T-shirt was so wet she could see his skin right through it. "I'm so sorry. I thought she was better. I thought . . . I never thought this could happen."

Callie pulled back, looking Jeremy in the eye. Drops of rain clung to his lashes. "What do you mean? Better from what?"

Jeremy swallowed hard and peeked out from their hiding spot again. He settled back, looking up at the sky for a moment, blinking against the rain.

"After Penelope and I broke up last year, she was . . . institutionalized for a month," he said breathlessly.

"*What?* No. She went to France with her parents."

"Not true." Jeremy shook his head. His lips were bright red, his skin white. He was shivering, his teeth beginning to chatter.

"That's just what she told everyone. Everyone but me. My family knew because my mom is such good friends with her mom. Pen just kind of snapped. They diagnosed her with a whole list of mental illnesses. Apparently this stuff runs in her family. She can be really paranoid. That's why she was so freaked out about her phone. When she said it was her security blanket, she meant it. They took it away from her in the hospital and it freaked her out to be so cut off. Ever since then, if she feels too separated from the outside world, it really gets to her."

"Omigod," Callie said, pressing her hand over her mouth. Suddenly Penelope's ramblings about doctors made perfect sense. "How did I not know this? She always seemed so sweet."

"She is sweet. Most of the time. But then she goes into these rages . . ." Jeremy trailed off. "As long as she's on her meds, she's fine. But if she goes off them . . ." He shook his head. "I never thought she could be violent, though. I never thought she could *kill* someone."

Callie couldn't believe this was happening. She'd known a couple kids back in Chicago who were taking medication for anxiety or depression. But it was clear that whatever Penelope was dealing with was *much* more severe and complicated.

Suddenly a flood of realization hit Callie so hard she bent forward at the waist. "The stream! Remember how she flipped out after she emptied her backpack at the stream? Maybe her meds were in there and fell out when you guys hit the water!"

Jeremy's eyes widened. "Then she's been off them for five days." He kicked at the ground and cursed under his breath. "It makes sense now. The headaches, the staring into the distance, her random paranoia. They're side effects of coming off the drugs."

Callie was in shock. "She killed Lissa, Jeremy. Penelope murdered her best friend. And then she shot Ted and Zach like it was nothing."

"I know. I saw her do it right before she knocked me out." Jeremy squeezed his eyes closed and pinched his nose between his thumb and forefinger.

"How could you not tell me about her psychological issues?" Callie demanded, feeling a flash of anger.

"I tried to. I was going to. That first night under the stars, and then the other day when Lissa interrupted us," he said. "But before that I thought . . . I mean, I didn't want to gossip about her. She's sick, Callie. I wanted to respect her privacy."

Callie closed her eyes and banged her head back against the shed. She understood. She even thought his silence was kind of admirable. But she still wished he hadn't kept Penelope's secret.

"I'm so sorry, Callie. I should've told you not to come on this trip. But I figured if her parents were letting her go, then she must be all right."

"It's not your fault," Callie said finally, reaching for his free hand. "She should have known better than to come out here where anything could happen. She should have realized."

"Callie! Jeremy!" Penelope's voice was reed thin in the rain. "Where are you two lovebirds?"

Callie's fingers gripped Jeremy's arm as lightning flashed again. "She's going to kill us. She's going to kill us both."

"I have a plan," Jeremy whispered, sitting up straighter. "I'll go out there and let her see me—"

"Jeremy, no—" Callie's protest was drowned by the thunder.

"Just hear me out," he said. "I'll let her see me and then take off into the woods. I might not be as crazy as her, but I'm a lot faster.

Once we're gone, you go back inside and find something you can use as a weapon. Something to knock her out like a wine bottle or something. I'll lead her back to the living room. When we get there, you jump out and whack her over the back of the head. The closer you get to the base of her skull, the better it'll work."

"How do you *know* that?" Callie asked.

"I might not have gone to survival camp, but taking AP bio and criminology as a sophomore has its pluses."

"Jeremy! Callie!"

Callie's heart hit her throat. "She's getting closer."

"I'm gonna go," Jeremy said, holding on to her hands.

"Are you sure about this?" Callie whispered. "That we should split up?"

"We can do this. Just give me three minutes." Jeremy leaned in to kiss her, his lips cold. Even in all the insanity, Callie's breath caught in her throat. "Callie? I'm so sorry for everything. I love you."

It was the first time he'd said it to her, and she hated Penelope even more for making it happen this way.

Callie squeezed his hands, looking into his eyes. "I love you, too."

Then he stood up, ripping his hands out of hers, and stepped into the open. He didn't call out to Penelope. He was smart. Calling out to her would have been too obvious. He simply waited until she spotted him, then took off into the trees.

Just like that, Callie was totally alone.

FIFTY-ONE

Callie closed her eyes, gritted her teeth, and counted to ten Mississippis before pushing herself up and cautiously stepping out into the open. She glanced once in the direction where Jeremy had disappeared. Everything was still.

What if she catches up with him? What if she found the gun? Or grabbed another weapon from the house? What if she—

Thunder cracked overhead.

Go.

Callie finally ran.

Her breath was loud and broken in her ears, her lungs burning as she sprinted for the house. She caught her foot on the lip of a step on her way up the porch and went sprawling, scraping her knee on the wood and coming to rest right next to Lissa's stretcher.

I'm so sorry, Lissa, Callie thought, jumping up again and ignoring the dart of pain in her kneecap.

If only someone had told them about Penelope. If only they'd known.

Callie ran inside and over to the kitchen, avoiding Ted's and Zach's bodies. She searched the cabinets and found a heavy silver pot, but it had two handles and wasn't good for swinging. Her eyes fell on the knife set atop the butcher block. She yanked out the knife with the biggest handle, and it let out a *kling* as the blade glinted in the overhead light.

Her stomach turned. She couldn't drive a knife into someone. Not even to save her own life. The very thought made her feel faint.

From the corner of her eye, Callie saw a flash of white. Jeremy's shirt. He raced past the window, headed for the front of the house. Were three minutes up already?

Callie's pulse pounded in her ears. If she was going to save Jeremy, if she was going to save herself, she had to find something and she had to do it now. Her eyes fell on her backpack, which she'd tossed on the floor near the island. Still clutching the knife in one hand, she ripped the zipper open and yanked out her copy of *Jensen's Revenge*.

This thing weighs, like, ten pounds, she heard Lissa chide in her head.

Shaking from head to toe, Callie ran back to the front door. She dropped the knife on the bench where she'd removed her shoes earlier, and pressed her back against the wall next to the entry. Her sweaty hands clutched the book for dear life.

Please just let this work, Callie thought. *Let this work and I swear I'll never complain about anything again. Not my frizzy hair, not school, not my parents, not anything.*

She heard footfalls pound on the stairs and across the porch. The door ripped open and Jeremy stumbled inside. He kept running straight across the room. Callie hoisted the book above her head. She held her breath. Slowly, Penelope walked inside. She didn't glance left or right. Her gaze was focused on Jeremy. Swinging casually at her side was a heavy wooden baseball bat. Callie's gaze darted to the crate full of sports equipment. Sure enough, the bat was gone.

She felt so stupid. She hadn't even thought to look there for a potential weapon.

Then a sound came from the kitchen. Someone was moaning.

Jeremy's jaw dropped. Penelope's eyes widened.

"It's Zach!" Jeremy gasped, looking over his shoulder. "He's still alive!"

Callie felt shocked, and nearly sick with relief. Somehow Zach had survived. Could she and Jeremy?

Penelope clenched her teeth. "You've got to be *kidding* me."

Carefully, Callie stepped back behind a puffy jacket that hung from a rack near the door. She needed a second. Just a second to catch her breath. Pen hesitated, and Callie's throat prickled with terror. Her movement had caught Penelope's eye, or maybe she'd heard a board creak. But Pen didn't turn around. Her focus was on Jeremy as he whipped his shirt off and knelt next to Zach, who was coughing and sputtering.

"Jeremy! What do you think you're doing?" Penelope demanded.

Jeremy held the shirt to Zach's chest while Zach whimpered, and Jeremy took the phone from Zach with his other hand.

"What does it look like I'm doing? I'm calling the cops!"

"Come on, Jer. You're smarter than that," Penelope said, giving the bat one twirl and starting across the room. "Even if you get through to 911 now, it's going to take them twenty minutes at least to get here. By then it'll be too late. For you and your precious girlfriend."

Something inside Callie snapped. She wasn't going to hide and cower anymore. With an adrenaline-fueled cry, she stepped up behind Penelope and brought the book down as hard as she could on the base of her skull.

Penelope stopped, wavered a moment, then fell. The bat clattered to the floor and rolled, while the side of Penelope's head smacked against the coffee table and she bent sideways, crumbling awkwardly. Her arms went limp.

"Is she out?" Callie cried. "Did I do it?"

Jeremy blinked, looking stunned. "You did it."

"How's that for my big stupid book?" Callie spit at Penelope's back.

Then she sank to her knees, hugging the book to her chest as tightly as she could. She felt like she couldn't let go. Like if she did, she'd start shaking and never stop.

"It's over?" Callie heard herself say, her voice a nearly unrecognizable wail. "It's over? It's really over?"

Jeremy didn't answer. He helped Zach prop himself up against the door, where Zach held Jeremy's blood-soaked shirt to his upper chest, heaving for air. Then Jeremy unhooked the bungee cords that held his sleeping bag to his backpack and brought them over. Suddenly Callie remembered what Penelope had said on the trail about Ted's cords being missing. She'd probably used them on Lissa, and probably tossed her cell phone deep into the woods, trying to make Callie suspect him. Then she'd spouted all that garbage during their hike just to drive the point home. Callie felt so stupid. So gullible. She felt like she would never trust anyone again. A sob broke from her throat and suddenly, she couldn't stop crying.

"Hey, it's okay." Jeremy finished binding Penelope's hands and feet, and crouched in front of Callie. "It's over. Everything's okay."

And then they were wrapped in each other's arms. He held her close as they both sobbed. Jeremy could say what he wanted, but nothing was ever going to be okay ever again. Lissa was dead. Ted was dead. Zach, from the look of his wound, might not make it. And Penelope, the girl she'd come to think of as her best friend, was responsible for all of it.

How was Callie ever going to live with that? How was she ever going to feel safe again?

"Shh," Jeremy said. "It's over. It's over."

Slowly, Callie and Jeremy stood and made their way over to Zach. They sat down beside him, Callie keeping her hand on Zach's arm and her ear pressed against Jeremy's heart, until she heard the faint whoop of a police siren in the distance.

FIFTY-TWO

Half an hour later, Callie and Jeremy sat across from each other in the back of an ambulance, the rain battering the roof like ceaseless gunfire. Lissa's body was loaded into another ambulance, and the police had been forced to call for two more once they'd surveyed the scene. EMTs were tending to Zach while Ted still lay inside the house, his body covered by a black tarp.

Callie shuddered inside her warm cotton blanket. Penelope was now in handcuffs on the porch with a crowd of officers around her, but still, Callie didn't feel entirely safe. Every time she let her brain wander, she saw Lissa's dead eyes or Ted's oozing wound—heard Zach's plea for his life—and the dread and nausea would crash over her, fresh and violent.

At least Pen's aim hadn't been true when it came to Zach. According to the EMTs, she'd just missed his right lung. The bullet was lodged in his shoulder.

"Cal? Are you okay?" Jeremy asked softly.

The cop who'd been interviewing them, Officer Short, shot her a concerned look. He was crouched in the tiny space between their two benches.

Callie simply shook her head, not trusting herself to speak. Someone had taped up her feet, which were now wearing a pair of white fluffy socks. She had no idea where they had come from.

"We've talked to the owners of the house," Officer Short told them, looking down at his notepad. "Ted Miller was a friend of their son's at Syracuse, but they had no idea he was using their home."

Callie met Jeremy's eyes. So they'd been half right. There *was* a cabin, clearly, but it wasn't Ted's after all. Not that Ted had deserved to die for that.

The officer stood up and ran his hand over his military-cut blond hair. "The girl . . . Penelope . . . her parents corroborated your story. They had some reservations about her coming on this trip but thought she'd be okay for the five days, as long as she had her medication. I guess that's a decision they'll be regretting for a long time to come."

"Is Pen gonna be okay?" Callie asked.

The officer seemed surprised she'd posed that question. "I hope so."

Jeremy leaned his head back against the wall. His eyes were heavy with sorrow and exhaustion. Callie couldn't help thinking that if they'd never come on this trip, then everything would be fine. Lissa and Ted would be alive. Zach would be playing Xbox in his basement. Penelope would be on her medication and well. But now everything had changed. For all of them.

"I'm very sorry about your loss," the officer went on. "Your parents are on their way. Is there anything else I can do for you right now?"

Jeremy stared at some random point above Callie's head.

Callie sighed. "I don't think so. Thank you."

Once the officer was gone, Callie and Jeremy were completely alone in the little cave of the ambulance. Callie's heart felt tight, crammed full of sorrow over what had happened, and hope for her and Jeremy. She felt sympathy for Zach and the pain he was enduring, dread for Lissa's and Ted's parents, relief that she would see her own mom and dad soon, hatred for Penelope, but also pity. She clutched the blanket close to her torso and wished Jeremy would look at her. They had said "I love you" out there. But did it mean anything? Was it just something you said under extreme circumstances when you thought you were about to die? Technically, they were still broken up. Could they ever go back? Or was their relationship another casualty of this "vacation"?

And how could she even be thinking about this right now, when so much death surrounded her?

"Callie?"

The sound of a familiar voice made Callie sit up straight. "Mom?"

She turned just as her mother and father appeared at the back door of the ambulance. Her mother's face went slack with relief at the sight of her.

"Mom!"

Tears leaked down Callie's face as her mother climbed into the ambulance and wrapped Callie up in her arms. Jeremy got up from his seat and stepped out into the rain to give Callie's father room to get in. Callie pressed her face into her mother's shoulder and sobbed and sobbed and sobbed.

"Are you okay?" her mother asked when Callie finally lifted her head.

Callie's throat was so tight she couldn't speak. Her mother was so beautiful. Her black hair was pulled back from her face in a ponytail and her skin was even tanner than usual. Her face was lined with worry. But for the first time in days, Callie felt safe. She felt like she might actually survive this.

"Callie, answer me! Are you all right?"

Finally, Callie managed to nod. She reached past her mom's shoulder and grabbed her dad's hand. He held on to her tightly, tears shimmering in his eyes.

Behind him, she saw Jeremy hovering, still in his blanket, letting himself get soaked by the rain, and she smiled gratefully at him. Jeremy managed the slightest of smiles in return.

Then, Penelope appeared. She was being led past Jeremy, head bowed, her hands cuffed behind her, one cop on either side. Callie's insides froze as Penelope looked up and met her eye. There was nothing there other than a blank, evil stare. Then, just before she passed out of view, Penelope suddenly laughed. She kept laughing, cackling really, until Callie heard the pop of a car door closing. Then there was nothing but the rain.

FIFTY-THREE

Callie had just changed out of her T-shirt and jeans and into her brand-new tae kwon do *dobok* when the doorbell rang. She flinched. Ever since the woods, sudden noises sent her heart racing. She looked herself up and down in the full-length mirror on her closet door and shook her head. How was she supposed to handle martial arts classes if she couldn't handle a doorbell?

But she was going to do it. She had to do it. Helplessness was not something she ever wanted to feel again. From here on out, Callie was going to take care of herself.

A light rap sounded on her door and it pushed open. Instinctively, Callie closed her journal, which had been open on her desk to the story she was now working on every day. A story about a girl and a boy who break up in the woods, and the two friends who manage to bring them together again. No blood, no death. Just relationship conflicts and a happy ending. She was going to finish this one. She knew it. She was almost there.

Jeremy stood in the hallway with a fresh new haircut—no more bangs in front of his eyes—wearing crisp-looking jeans and a light blue polo shirt. Her heart caught at the sight of him. They hadn't spoken since that awful night. It had been five days.

"Hey," he said, giving her a tentative smile. "That's a good look for you."

She snorted a laugh and looked down at what were basically

blindingly white pajamas. She hadn't put the belt on yet because she had no clue how to tie it.

"Thanks." She blushed, feeling awkward with him hovering out there, even though he'd been to her house a dozen times. "Your hair looks nice like that."

He touched it self-consciously. "Yeah. Mom made me get it cut for school tomorrow." He cleared his throat and looked around. "Hey! You finished painting your room. I like the color."

The walls of Callie's space were now a bright, happy aqua, like the color of the ocean off the coast of Brazil. Every morning when she woke up, she saw the walls and smiled. Until the memories of the camping trip came crashing back.

"Thanks."

"So . . ." Jeremy shoved his hands into his pockets. "I just got back from visiting Zach. He's doing pretty well. But football's not happening this year."

Callie nodded. "I heard. I'm glad he's okay, though. And my mom says Penelope's getting the help she needs."

Jeremy nodded, too, his eyes momentarily unfocused. "Did you go to Lissa's funeral?"

Callie sighed and sat down on the edge of her bed. "No. I wanted to, but her parents decided to keep it small. Just family. My mom was worried about me dealing with all the questions, anyway. She thought it would be better for me if I stayed home."

Over the last week Callie had gotten about a million texts and emails asking how she was and expressing sympathy. Some of them were from people she didn't know and had never spoken to. Callie was sure that some of the sentiments were genuine, but she knew that a lot of the people just wanted to hear the story. There were probably a ton of rumors and untruths flying around, and it would be up to her and Jeremy to set the record straight.

Unfortunately, she had no desire to talk about it. Ever. In fact, for the past couple of nights she found herself identifying with that boy who had survived the Skinner. She now understood why it had taken him a year to find his voice.

"Mine too," Jeremy said. "But we're going to have to deal with it anyway, right? At school?"

"Yeah," she said. "That's gonna be a nightmare."

Jeremy leaned against the doorway and looked at her with hopeful eyes. "Well, it might be better if we . . . face them together?"

Callie's heart flip-flopped. A smile twitched her lips. "You think?"

"Yeah, I mean . . . you can only say 'no comment' so many times before your voice gets hoarse. And when that happens, I could take over."

Jeremy took a tentative step into the room. Callie stood up.

"You'd do that for me?" she said lightly.

Jeremy looked into her eyes. "I'd do anything for you."

In a rush, Callie realized she felt exactly the same way. She would do anything for him, too. Hadn't they already proven that to each other in that moment behind the shed? The moment they'd split up hoping to save each other's skins?

Callie collapsed into Jeremy, wrapping her arms around his back and pressing her cheek to his chest. His skin was warm and he smelled so clean. For days she'd been obsessing about what they'd been through, the fact that Lissa and Ted were gone, that Penelope was locked up in some psychiatric ward somewhere. But now, suddenly, the reality of where they were crashed over her.

They had survived, she and Jeremy. They were going to be okay.

"Callie Valasquez, will you . . . be my girlfriend again?" Jeremy asked, running his hand over her hair.

She tilted her head back to look up at him. "Yes," she said.

His smile was huge. He leaned down and kissed her, lightly, on the lips.

"But you have to promise me one thing," she told him.

He tucked her hair behind her ear and touched the side of her face with his fingers. "Anything."

"No more outdoors," she said. "From here on out, we go to movies, we go bowling, we go to the mall . . . but I don't want to step foot in the woods. Not ever again."

"Sounds like a plan," Jeremy said.

And then he kissed her again, and for the first time in days, for the briefest of moments, there wasn't a thought in Callie's head of blood and death, of fear and paranoia, of trees and rain and screams and despair. For that brief moment, there was hope.

RECOVERY JOURNAL
ENTRY 10

I was wrong about Jeremy. He hasn't even been here to visit me once. Six months I've been locked up and not so much as a letter or a phone call. For a long time I'd get my hopes up whenever I saw my mother come through the security door, but then she'd give me that sad-eyed look, and I'd know. He wasn't with her. He hadn't sent a thing. He even missed my birthday.

I don't get it. I mean, I let him live. He was the only one I let live. Well, except for Callie, but that was not by choice. If it wasn't for that stupid, monstrous book, I would have had her. And I would have taken such pleasure in bashing in her skull over and over and over again with that bat. Sometimes, imagining the splattering blood and the shattered bone is the only way I can get to sleep at night.

But, no. Moving on. It's not healthy to dwell on the past. That's the one thing they've told me in here that I truly believe. When I think back, think about the girl I was on those meds, I want to scream. She was so pathetic, that girl. Following Lissa around as if every move she made was perfection. Acting like it was totally fine for Callie to steal the love of my life out from under me. I actually thought—it's hilarious to me now—but I actually thought that if I could get through that camping trip with Jeremy and Callie, that would prove that I was fine. That I was over him. That I was strong and could move on.

What a loser I was. Moving on is not being strong. No. Taking what you want. Demanding what's yours. That's what strong is. I'm glad my meds fell out of my backpack that day at the river. I'm glad the world got to see who I really am. Sure, it was painful at first, what with the withdrawal headaches and the sweats. I tried to keep my temper in check, but toward the end, when everyone was snapping, that made it a lot easier. It was as if we were all in it together. Even Callie went over the edge a little. Perfect, sweet Callie. Ugh. The thought of her makes me sick.

But, no. There I go again, dwelling on the past. I will not think about how satisfying it was to pull those bungee cords taut around Lissa's neck. To tighten and tighten and tighten the coil until her tongue lolled out of her mouth and her beautiful eyes rolled back in her beautiful head. I showed her who was in control, didn't I? I showed her in the end.

And I won't think about the look on Ted's face when I shot him. Like he simply couldn't believe that I could actually pull the trigger. The jerk. I won't think about how satisfying it was to hurt Zach, either, the guy who had taken such pleasure in taunting us for days, who thought nothing in the world could touch him. Especially not a loser hanger-on like me.

No. I have other, more important things to focus on. Like keeping my shakes in check so the stupid medics won't realize I haven't been taking their ridiculous pills. They force me to open my mouth every time, but the little ones are easy to hide between my back teeth and my cheek, and the big ones . . . well, they're harder, but if I park them just so on the back of my tongue, just far enough down my throat, I can choke them out once I'm alone again. They don't understand that I can't go back to being that girl—that zombie. I can't and I won't. I can see everything clearly now. I know who I am, and I like me.

And besides, the thing is . . . I'm falling in love again. There's this girl down the hall, Marjorie, whose brother, Mitchell, comes to visit *her three times a week. I've seen him looking at me. We've exchanged a few smiles. And last week, when Marjorie didn't want the new socks he'd brought for her, he gave them to me.*

Clearly he cares about me. We haven't spoken yet. Not really. But I know he thinks about me the same way I think about him. And when we finally do get to know each other, I want him to know the real me. I want him to love me for who I am.

That was the problem between me and Jeremy. He could never truly love me, because thanks to the doctors and the therapists and my parents and the meds, he could never see the true me.

But Mitchell will see. He'll see me and he'll love me.

And if he doesn't? Well, I happen to know a few things I can do with his sister, make it look like an accident or self-inflicted. There are ways, even inside here.

And now, sadly, it's time to tear these pages out and flush them, so that Doctor Pea Brain will never see them. The new ones I write will be all tales of sorrow and regret, of repentance and disbelief. How could I have done such things? I wish I could take them back! Because, well, I'm not stupid. I realize I'll never get out of here unless the doctors think I've recovered, that I'm sorry, that I'm reformed. So on these pages, I need to lie. Because if Mitchell and I are going to be together and be happy, I need to be free. I'll do anything to be free.

And if you don't understand that, you don't understand anything.

ACKNOWLEDGMENTS

First and foremost I want to thank Aimee Friedman, who always believed we would work together one day and then did everything in her power to make that belief a reality. It's been a pleasure and I hope the partnership continues for many moons to come.

I'd also like to thank Abby McAden for similarly championing my work, and the rest of the Scholastic team, too, especially David Levithan and Jen Ung.

Thank you, as always, to my fantastic agent, Sarah Burnes, and her equally fantastic assistant, Logan Garrison, and to the lovely authors who agreed to give this an early read, Margaret Stohl, Melissa de la Cruz, and Micol Ostow. I am not worthy. Finally great big hugs and kisses to my cheerleaders, Jen Calonita, Elizabeth Eulberg, Jennifer E. Smith, Wendy Schwartz, Shira Citron, and the entire Scott-Viola clan, especially Matt, Brady, and Will. One day, I might even let you boys read this one.

ACKNOWLEDGMENTS

ABOUT THE AUTHOR

Kieran Scott is the author of several acclaimed young adult novels, including the He's So/She's So trilogy, the True Love trilogy, and *Geek Magnet*. She also wrote the *New York Times* bestselling Private series as well as the Shadowlands trilogy under the pen name Kate Brian for Alloy Entertainment. She lives with her husband and children in New Jersey and enjoys working out, baking, and—until writing this book—camping. Visit her online at www.kieranscott.net.